Elf Sight

Elf Sight

Avril Sabine

Cracked Acorn Productions
Australia

Elf Sight

Published by

Cracked Acorn Productions

PO Box 1365

Gympie, Queensland 4570

Australia

email: office@crackedacornproductions.com

978-1-925131-00-0 (Kindle)

978-1-925617-43-6 (EPUB)

978-1-925131-09-3 (Print)

978-1-925131-24-6 (Printed in Australia)

Genre: Young Adult Fantasy

Cover design by Caitlyn Petersen

*For my family, who have helped make me
who I am.*

Seventeen-year-old Shadow thinks their country is in bad shape if her Pa is considered one of their greatest heroes. To her he's the bitter man she has to escape before he learns the secret she's kept her entire life. Getting away, with the help of her brother Irlan, is meant to simplify things. Instead, they become involved in plots against the royal family, hidden identities and magic-wielding enemies.

*

This story was written by an Australian author using Australian spelling.

Chapter One

Careful not to smudge the glass, Shadow Morgan peered out the window near the tavern door, knowing she'd be safely hidden behind the door when her Pa came inside. She pushed her long, dark brown plait out of the way, jumping when a hand dropped onto her shoulder.

"Irlan." She glared up at him. "Don't sneak up on me like that." At six foot her brother was five inches taller than her, but had the same dark brown hair and eyes that both her and their Pa had.

"What are you looking at?" Irlan held a straw broom loosely in one hand.

"I don't know. I missed the start of the conversation. Pa's out there arguing with General Farnell Serensten."

"Isn't Serensten–"

She made a sharp motion with her hand. "Quiet. I

don't want to miss what's happening." Behind Irlan she could see several long-term patrons had left their ales on the wooden tables to peer out windows. Her Ma would have her cleaning the smudges off those windows later.

"Make room." Irlan pushed her aside.

Shadow shouldered her way back to the window. "Find your own space."

Irlan shrugged and moved to the window on the other side of the door. Peering past the smudge her brother had left on the glass, Shadow gazed at the tavern yard. Afternoon shadows spread out behind her Pa and the soldiers.

"Come on Gil, what'll one more time hurt?" From anyone else the words might have come out as a plea, they didn't when spoken by Farnell.

He didn't look like a man accustomed to pleading. He was completely army, from his arrow straight stance, his immaculate uniform, close cropped salt and pepper hair and cold blue eyes that Shadow bet could have a soldier quivering in his boots within seconds. Her Pa wasn't in the least intimidated. This didn't surprise her as he was usually the one making others do the quivering.

"One more time?" Gil bellowed. "One more time?" He pointed to his empty sleeve. "Only got one more of these. What do you expect me to do? Drink my ale through a straw?"

One of the General's men who held the horses' reins snickered and Gil's face grew even redder, right through to his scalp beneath his thinning brown hair. Farnell shot a look towards the man who quickly turned away from the cold blue stare.

"Look, why don't we go into your tavern and I'll buy a round of drinks. Matters like this shouldn't be discussed in the open." Farnell kept his tone even and his expression neutral.

"Never! I've got nothing more to say to you. I don't want to hear another word." Gil turned to walk into his tavern.

Shadow tensed, ready to hurry back to the bar. If her Pa caught her spying on him she'd never hear the end of it.

"Your last job gave you the money to buy this tavern. What if I told you this job is worth twice as much?" Farnell asked.

Gil halted. Then shook his head. He half turned to Farnell. With his one arm he gestured towards the tavern. "Twice the price of this? Can't be done. The last job cost one arm. I don't have two left to lose." He stomped towards the tavern.

Farnell called out as Gil reached the door, "We're

staying in the clearing just down the road. We leave at first light. Remember. Twice the fee." Not getting any response, Farnell turned back to his men. "Mount up. Back to camp."

As the soldiers hurried to obey Farnell, Gil made his way inside. He cuffed Irlan who randomly moved the broom about not far from the window. While her Pa was distracted, Shadow took the opportunity to hurry behind the bar where she was supposed to be serving.

"What are you doing? Get back to work you lazy lump."

"I was sweeping." Irlan stared defiantly at Gil as he held up the broom. Angry brown eyes were the only similarity between them. While Gil was an average height with a broad chest and thick legs, Irlan was tall and wiry.

"Sweeping! You lying little–" Gil raised his fist and took a step towards Irlan.

"Gil." His wife, Gennie, hurried over to rest a hand on his arm. She shot one of her usual looks of mingled concern and warning towards her son before she turned to her husband. "Your supper's ready. You'll want it while it's nice and hot." She was short, slight of frame, with mousy brown hair, and a perpetual look of worry in her blue eyes.

Gil stared at her a moment before he pulled away

and strode towards his table. Plonking himself down he looked over to Shadow behind the bar. "Shadow! An ale girl. Look lively."

Shadow grabbed a mug, quickly filled it and hurried to her Pa's table. He grunted as she placed it in front of him and downed it in one go. She forced her face to remain expressionless. Why had Farnell brought up all the things they tried so hard to avoid? No one spoke of the days when Gil had been whole, or if they did it was in whispers. And no one ever mentioned his elf sight or asked him to use it.

Gil slammed the mug on the table. "Another girl. Don't waste time."

Lips thinning, Shadow grabbed the mug and headed for the bar. She passed close to her brother as she did. At seventeen Shadow was a year younger than Irlan, but half the time felt like she was the one who looked out for him. "Stay out of his way, Irlan. He still hasn't forgiven you for racing his stallion yesterday."

"The old bugger never forgives. You should know that by now," Irlan muttered as they reached the bar.

"Shh, he'll take his belt to you again." Shadow glanced towards Gil. "And at the rate he's downing ale he'll be looking for someone to use it on."

"Hush you two." Gennie pushed them both behind

the bar. "Give me that." She took the mug from her daughter. "Now make yourselves scarce. I've sent someone to fetch Molly. She'll serve tonight."

Shadow looked out over the rapidly filling tables. "Are you sure?" Gennie looked exhausted, like she should be the one taking the night off.

Gennie nodded, brushing strands of hair back from her face. "Go on."

Nodding, Shadow followed her brother through the door behind the bar. It led into their living quarters. Two rooms downstairs and a cramped loft upstairs that she and Irlan shared. They took fruit from the table and Shadow borrowed her Ma's cloak as they left by the back door.

Shadow paused before she entered the woods, which started not far from the rear of the tavern. Night had fallen and darkness filled the spaces under the tall trees. She took a bite from her apple as she hurried after Irlan, who had stopped to look back at her. Leaves crunched under her feet as she joined him.

"What are you doing? Come on."

"I wish things were different." Shadow sighed. "If he'd only stay away from the drink he wouldn't be half as bad."

"He's still a moody old bugger even sober," Irlan said.

"I wish we'd known him before he lost his arm. Some of the stories they tell when he's not about are–"

Irlan interrupted. "Who cares? He's no bloody hero now. He's a useless old drunk."

Shadow fell silent as she continued to walk beside her brother. There wasn't anything she could say to argue that point. She didn't even know why she wanted to. It felt disloyal to always complain about their Pa. Especially when she heard some of the stories whispered in the tavern when the men had been drinking heavily. No one spoke to Gil about the days before he lost his arm. That was a sure way to make him angry. But stories were still whispered in tones of awe. Particularly the battle of Wolf Ridge.

"It's not right. We shouldn't have to sleep outside because he's going to get roaring drunk," Irlan complained.

"Oh Irlan, how would you feel? Look what he came back to."

"At least he came back. How many died?"

"He probably felt guilty. He hadn't been there when Ma caught childbed fever. Or when she couldn't work, or when they threw us onto the streets because she couldn't pay the rent. He had promised to be back in time to help her choose a name for me. And he wasn't."

"If he was a real man he wouldn't have called his daughter a shadow on his life," Irlan reminded her.

She pushed aside the flare of anger his words caused. "There's nothing we can do about it." She paused. "Don't go on about it tomorrow and upset Ma."

"I'm not an idiot. You don't have to remind me."

She held back a smile. Yes, she did. But soon he'd have to look out for himself. She wouldn't be at the tavern forever. She had plans.

Silence again fell between them, eventually broken by Irlan. "What did the soldiers want?"

"They need someone to find something magic hid."

"If I had elf sight I'd go with them. Why couldn't I have it?" He swore. "It's not fair. It's meant to run in families. Grandpa Morgan had it and his aunt had it and who knows how many before them."

"You'll find a way out eventually," Shadow said softly.

"How?" Irlan snarled. "I've got no money, and food and board isn't a fair pay."

"You'll have to find a new hiding place for your tips. Somewhere he won't think to look this time." Shadow rested her hand on her brother's arm and wished there was something else she could say. Something she could do.

"Do you know how many years it took me to save that money?" Irlan shook her hand off. "Four years! And I still needed more before I could afford to get away from him. I'm eighteen. A man! I can't spend the rest of my life under his thumb. If he doesn't end up killing me in a drunken rage, I'll probably kill him fighting back."

"Oh Irlan." Shadow threw both her arms around her brother and rested her head on his chest. "Don't speak like that. Please. When I marry Elrick, I'm sure he'll find a place for you on his family farm." Shadow felt Irlan tense. She drew back. "What? What happened?"

Chapter Two

Irlan shook his head. He looked helplessly at his sister.

"You're scaring me, Irlan. What happened? Tell me." Alarm raced through her at Irlan's expression that she could barely make out in the tree filtered moonlight.

"He refused him."

"What do you mean?" Shadow grabbed the front of her brother's shirt. She held her breath and hoped the roaring sound that started to fill her ears would stop.

"Elrick came today while you were at the mill."

"And? Come on Irlan, spit it out." She shook her brother's shirt, which she clutched tightly.

"He refused him," Irlan said softly.

"What do you mean… refused him?" Shadow's voice became higher pitched with each spoken word. The roar in her ears grew, making her wonder if she'd heard her brother right.

"He told Elrick if he even sets eyes on you again he'd beat him senseless. That he wasn't good enough for you. That no man around here was. You know Elrick wouldn't have stood a chance against the old man. Even with one arm he can still beat most of the men around here. They're farmers. Not a single one of them have been trained in combat. Shadow, I wish I didn't have to tell you."

She let go of her brother's shirt and stared at him. His words didn't change. The roaring sound in her ears threatened to drown all other noises. Her mouth opened, but nothing came out. She took in a deep shuddering breath and tried again. "I hate him." The words burst from Shadow as she turned away from her brother. Words she'd fought against uttering for years. She might not have loved Elrick, but he was kind and she had cared about him. He'd been a way to escape the tavern and she had to leave. Desperately.

"I know."

Shadow turned back to Irlan. "There's got to be a way to get away from him. I thought Elrick was it. He said he loved me and wouldn't let anything come between us. He didn't even mind that I don't love him as much as he loves me." The roaring subsided to a dull noise. She felt light headed. The world seemed to be both right up close and far away. The anger burning through her was doused by disbelief. How could Elrick have failed her?

"He went white as a ghost and disappeared faster than one."

"It's not fair!" Shadow clenched her hands. She didn't know whether to scream or cry. She turned away from her brother, lowering her voice. "I hate him so much. We'd have been better off if he hadn't come back."

"We'd have died of starvation."

She spun towards him, yelling, "Don't stick up for him."

"I'm not."

Shadow looked around frantically. "We've got to get out of here, away from the tavern." No escape appeared before her. It seemed like the night closed in on her instead. Eerie shapes reached out to her as the moonlight made patterns through the gently swaying branches.

"If I had elf sight I'd have taken the job he was offered today. I'd have used the money to buy you a house in some town far from here and me a merchant ship. But I don't. Why couldn't I have elf sight? Why did that old bugger deserve it and I didn't?" Irlan demanded.

Shadow stared up at her brother. Confusion, anger,

frustration, disbelief, desperation. She didn't know what she felt. Her head was a swirl of emotions and she could no longer think clearly. "I've got it."

"Got what?"

"Elf sight." She heard herself speak the words. The words she'd held in for what seemed like forever. The words she thought she'd never speak. It was still hard to believe she'd spoken them. Maybe she hadn't.

"What! Why didn't you ever tell me?"

Yes, she'd spoken them. She closed her eyes. How could she have told? "Because Pa threatened to beat either of us to death if we inherited it. He said it was a curse and he didn't want it in our family. He already saw me as a blight on his life, I didn't want to be a curse as well." She opened her eyes. "And he was sober when he said it."

"Shadow!" Irlan grabbed her by the waist and swung her around. "I've got the best of plans."

"Put me down before you drop me, oaf." Shadow laughed at her brother's excitement, a touch of hysteria echoing in the sound.

"We can do this, Shadow." Irlan lowered her to the ground.

"Do what?"

"Take the General's job."

"I can't. No females allowed in the army, remember?"

"So? You'll be my little brother. Come on Shadow, stop shaking your head like that. Didn't you hear what they offered? Twice the fee of his last job. His last job bought the tavern!"

"I know, but…" Visions of all that could be bought with that sort of money raced through her mind. Then she thought of what might happen if they were discovered. "No. You aren't going to convince me. You're crazy. We'd never pull it off."

"We can. Besides, they're not going to question us. They sounded desperate for someone with elf sight. And who cares why, as long as they pay."

"Some wizard made a mountain pass disappear and they need to find it so they can retrieve something that was stolen. They only wanted him to go as far as the hidden path. But we can't trust the General."

"Why not?"

"Because it was Farnell Serensten. He was a captain when the old man knew him."

"The man he blames for leaving him for dead when he lost his arm?"

"Yes."

"I thought it might have been."

"You can see why we can't go. We'd be mad to

trust him. Nothing about the mission seemed right. Farnell said it was straightforward. But if that was true, why would a general come begging for help? A general doesn't do the work of a lackey."

"There's probably a reasonable explanation for it. After all, the fellow knew Pa from years ago. Maybe he thought it was the polite thing to do."

Shadow shook her head. "You're not fooling me with that pathetic excuse. You're mad to even think about going."

"I'm not mad. I'm desperate. Please, Shadow. You heard what I said. He doesn't believe any man's good enough for you to marry. You're seventeen! Do you want to spend the rest of your life at his beck and call? Gran lived past eighty. He's likely to live another forty years at least."

"Oh god no," Shadow whispered. "Forty years." A chill shivered along her spine as she pictured herself at fifty-seven still being yelled at by her Pa and serving in the tavern.

"Or more," Irlan said quietly.

Shadow shook her head in horror. She stalked away from her brother and muttered under her breath. She reached out to touch a tree that stood near her, the bark rough against her hand. She couldn't get the image from her mind. "Older!" She pictured her Pa at one hundred years and herself with a walking stick as he still ruled her life. She pushed away from the tree, wanting to run as fast and as far as possible. Her feet stumbled forward. The roaring in her ears started again and she felt a wave of panic rush through her. "Never." She turned suddenly and Irlan, who'd followed, nearly stumbled over her.

"Hey, careful!"

Shadow stabbed him in the chest with her finger. "You've got to promise we stay away from any fighting. As soon as things get crazy we're out of there. And you make them give us some money up front. They also provide horses and supplies."

"You're the best." Irlan swung his sister around again.

"Put me down." Shadow tried to push away from him.

Irlan grinned down at her. "Let's get you ready little brother, before you change your mind."

Shadow groaned. Irlan grabbed her hand and half dragged her home, talking excitedly all the way. The moment they came near the tavern, they both fell silent. A quick peek inside showed the coast was clear and they hurried up to the loft.

They grabbed clothes, including some old ones of Irlan's for Shadow to wear. Using his Ma's shears,

Irlan hacked off his sister's hair and left it with a note for their Ma to find the next day.

Shadow stared at the hair lying on her bed, still plaited. "This is crazy."

"Get dressed. It'd be just like the old bugger to come out here and stop us." Irlan left her alone in the loft.

She stared at the boy's clothes she was to wear. Luckily she'd never gained those curves she'd always wanted. Reaching for the linen bandage, she bound her chest first, then dressed in Irlan's old clothes, which were slightly big. With one last glance at the hair on her bed, she joined Irlan downstairs. He held a pillowcase with some food and spare clothes. Her stomach lurched.

"Are you ready?"

She shook her head. "No." The motion felt strange and she reached up to touch her hair.

"You can't change your mind. Come on, Shadow. We have to leave. Now."

"This is crazy." She looked past her brother at the door that led to the bar. Movement felt impossible.

"So is staying."

Her gaze clashed with her brother's. The rolling in her stomach stopped and she slowly nodded. "I suppose it is."

Irlan grinned and reached out his hand to her. "Then let's get out of here."

Chapter Three

Shadow took hold of Irlan's hand and ran outside with him, grinning at the laughter that burst from him as they raced through the dark. "You're mad. We're going to run into something."

"After the amount of time we've spent out here at night, I could run through this place with my eyes closed." Irlan slowed and let go of her hand. He reached into the pillowcase. "Here." He handed Shadow an old felt hat of his as sounds from the camp reached them. "Keep it pulled low and hold your tongue."

Shadow nodded as she slipped the hat on. Her hand brushed against her hair and she touched the jagged strands, surprised at how light her head felt with her hair cut off. It wasn't all that was light. She alternated between fear of what was ahead and lightheaded joy at leaving the tavern. She only wished her Ma would go with them, but Gennie believed Gil would change. She'd pointed out each time he'd acted like the man he'd once been, telling Shadow that one day soon she'd know the man her Pa really was.

"Who's there? Show yourselves," a guard ordered.

Irlan stepped into the light cast from the torches. "We need to see General Serensten."

Shadow stayed close behind him, keeping her head tilted to hide her face with the hat's brim.

"Who are you and what makes you think the General wants to see two brats?" the guard demanded as they came into the circle of light thrown out by the burning torch, one end of which was pushed into the ground. The flame flickered in the soft breeze and the guard held his sword at the ready. "I'm waiting."

"I've got elf sight," Irlan said.

Shadow jabbed her brother in the back but he ignored her.

"Elf sight." The guard chuckled. "Hey Wardell, kid here reckons he's got elf sight."

Wardell came to join the guard. "What's that, Yarin? Bad sight?"

"That's about it," Yarin agreed. "Can't you see this is a soldier's camp? We don't have time for brats. Now take yourselves home and stop pestering us."

"What's going on here?" Another soldier stepped

out of the shadows to join them. He had black hair slightly longer than the two soldiers. His brown eyes looked between the two men and then over to Irlan and Shadow. He was broad shouldered, held himself straight compared to the slouched stance of the guards and a sword hung from his belt. He looked to be only a few years older than Irlan but acted like he'd seen more of life.

Shadow had never seen anyone like him before. She was glad Irlan didn't expect her to speak. She didn't think she'd be able to.

"Ah, nothing Captain Relth, ah Sir." Yarin stood to attention.

"Everything's under control, Captain Relth," Wardell said.

Shadow's gaze was drawn back to the captain as she wondered if having a surname so close to the name of their country, Relthon, had helped or hindered his career.

"I've got elf sight and I want to see the General," Irlan said.

Shadow's hands became fists and she wanted to hit her brother. What was he thinking? How was he going to get them to believe something that wasn't even close to the truth?

"Nothing, Wardell?" Carson asked quietly. Wardell took a step back under the hard look.

"They're just kids mucking around," Yarin said. "Ah, Sir."

"Let the General be the judge of that. What's your name boy?" Carson demanded.

"Irlan."

"And who's hiding behind you?"

"My brother Shadow."

Carson stared at them a moment and then chuckled. The tension left the soldiers and they relaxed again.

"How appropriately named. Follow me. We'll see what the General has to say." Carson strode away without looking to see if they followed.

Irlan and Shadow shared a quick look and hurried after Carson. They were led to a tent in the middle of the camp.

Carson halted at the entrance. "Wait here." He stared at each of them before he entered the tent.

"Why did you tell them you had elf sight?" Shadow hissed at her brother as soon as they were alone.

"We don't want them looking too closely at you."

Before Shadow could reply, Carson pulled the tent flap back and gestured them inside. The General sat at a collapsible table, with pen, ink and parchment in front of him. He stared at Irlan and glanced over at Shadow who stood close behind her brother.

"Are you telling the truth, lad?" Farnell asked.

Irlan nodded, pinned by the cold blue eyes of the General.

"There are four mugs in here. Magic hid. Find them for me," Farnell ordered.

Irlan glanced around. Shadow could see the panic rush in on her brother. She felt the same panic. She didn't know what the General would do if he found out Irlan had lied, but she didn't think it'd be good. Reaching out, she wrapped her hand around his right wrist and tugged slightly on it until he turned in that direction. He slowly turned until she stopped tugging. Taking a deep breath he moved forward until she dug her nails into his wrist. Guessing he'd have something to say about that later, she pulled on his arm. He stared at the ground for a moment then looked over at the General and Captain.

"Well lad, if you think it's there, bend down and pick it up," Farnell said impatiently.

Irlan looked at Shadow. She could see the question in his eyes. For a fleeting second she felt like reminding him it was his fault. Then she remembered the cold eyes of the General. He was too much like Gil. Irlan didn't stand a chance against him.

She moved forward and put her foot to a slight angle and hoped he understood what she was doing. Irlan crouched with his back to Farnell and Carson. He hesitatingly reached in front of him. Shadow saw the look of surprise as his fingers ran into the invisible cup near the toe of her boot. He picked it up, took it to the General and placed it on the table with a clunk.

"Hurry it up, lad. You've still got another three to find." Farnell drummed his fingers on the table.

Irlan swallowed visibly. Shadow tugged on his wrist and was relieved this time he was able to follow her directions quicker. Shortly, all four mugs were on the General's table, still invisible. Farnell pulled a bag of white powder from his belt pouch and sprinkled it over the mugs. It would have been a blend containing some of the same powder originally used to hide them.

Four ceramic mugs sat lined up along the table and Irlan sagged slightly. Shadow's hand circled his wrist again and she dug her nails in to make him stand straight.

"Looks like you weren't bragging, lad," Farnell said. "So what price are you looking for your services?"

"Same as you offered the tavern owner," Irlan said. "No."

Irlan shrugged and turned to walk out.

Shadow tugged on his arm but he dragged her along with him. She felt like hitting him over the head with something. Did he want to go back to the tavern?

"Half what I offered him," Farnell called out.

Irlan shook his head and turned to face the General. "I'll be doing the same job. Finding the path you're looking for. It was obviously important enough for you to offer that price this afternoon. I can't see why it should suddenly lose importance. Same price plus horses and supplies for me and my brother." Irlan met Farnell's eyes.

Shadow was surprised he could bring himself to, but she guessed it was no worse than all the times he'd stood up to their Pa. She shivered as she recalled how well those shows of bravado had turned out.

"You only." Farnell pointed at Irlan. "We're not nursemaids. You're brother won't be coming."

"I'm his only kin. There's nowhere to leave him," Irlan said.

"I'll pay the tavern owners to keep him while you're gone," Farnell suggested.

"No." The word burst from Irlan. "I've heard stories about that drunk. I wouldn't leave a dog in his keeping. The kid comes with me or I don't go. He won't be no trouble. He's a bit on the simple side. He gets upset if he's not near me. Ever since we lost our parents he hasn't been able to let me out of his sight."

Shadow dug her nails into her brother's wrist again. She wanted to kick him as well. Simple! He was the only simple one. This would've been straight forward if he'd let her admit she was the one with elf sight. There certainly wouldn't have been any reason for them to leave her behind then.

Farnell stared at Irlan, his chin resting on his linked fingers. "Eighty percent what I offered Gil, horses, supplies and the kid can come along. We ditch him the first time he gets in the way."

Irlan nodded. "I want some gold to show good faith."

"When we're riding out in the morning. One coin only."

"One each day," Irlan said.

"One each week," Farnell shot back.

"Done." Irlan stepped forward and held out his hand.

Shadow stayed back and dropped her head more so the hat shaded her face. She looked towards the brim and tilted her head slightly so she could watch Irlan shake Farnell's hand. Carson, who had stood behind

Farnell, stepped forward. Her breath caught in her throat as he smiled at her brother.

"Come on lad, I'll find somewhere for you and the kid to bed down for the night."

Chapter Four

"Roll out!" a soldier bellowed at daybreak. "Come on you mangy curs. Get moving. No breakfast for any slug-a-beds."

There were grumbles and groans as soldiers rolled out of swags and quickly readied themselves for the day. A man, who stood beside a large pot hanging over the fire, filled the bowls each soldier brought to him with the serving spoon he held.

"Hey lad," Carson called out to Irlan.

Irlan and Shadow looked over. Carson held up two bowls and then pointed towards the campfire. Irlan nodded and he and Shadow made their way over.

"Any second thoughts, yet?" Carson asked as they joined him.

Irlan shook his head, but Shadow was tempted to say she certainly had more than second thoughts.

"So, if you've got no kin, what have you been doing?" Carson asked as their bowls were filled.

Irlan looked over at Shadow and she saw the sudden look of panic cross his face.

"Peddler," she whispered, just loud enough for Irlan to hear.

"Speak up kid, I can't hear mumbles," Carson said.

"We travelled with a peddler. He dumped us in the last town," Irlan said.

Carson looked from one to the other. "He'll never learn to speak if you always answer for him." He gestured towards their bowls. "Better get that food in you. The General doesn't wait for anyone." With a last glance at them, he walked off.

Shadow and Irlan found a place by themselves to eat. "I keep thinking someone is going to see through me," Shadow whispered.

"Why would they? People only ever see what they expect." Irlan shovelled in another mouthful of food.

"I don't know. Every time the Captain looks at me I think he suspects something." Shadow's gaze strayed across the camp until they rested on Carson. He turned in her direction and she hurriedly stared at her bowl.

"Nah. Anyway, he's a dodgy character. He's far too young to be a captain. I was talking to one of the soldiers last night and they said he's twenty-one. And, considering he's only a captain he seems to get more respect than the General. Makes you wonder what he's planning. It might be rebellion."

"You wouldn't think the General would be that dense, would you?" Shadow glanced over to Carson. His back was to her again. She returned to staring at her food, not wanting to draw his attention.

Irlan shrugged. "Who knows?"

They fell silent for a while as they ate their food. Shadow scraped her spoon around the bowl. "I hope we don't take too long to get where we have to go. This not being able to speak when I want is frustrating."

Irlan laughed. "You manage to hold your tongue when the old bugger's in one of his rages. Just think of it being like that."

"Yes, but that's not all the time. Not every day, every minute. I'm going to go crazy with only you to talk to."

"Time to leave," a soldier standing beside the General's tent, which was being packed away, bellowed. "Saddle up."

"Come on. We don't want to get left behind." Irlan shoved the last spoonful of food in his mouth.

"That's what you think," Shadow muttered as she

rose to her feet. How was she to manage long hours of no talking, ducking her head in supposed shyness and fading into the background? None of it was her strong point. She could manage for short lengths of time, but hours? Days? Irlan expected the impossible.

The whole day was spent riding. Even the midday meal was broken on horseback with soldiers taking jerky, flatbread and fruit from their saddlebags. Shadow and Irlan had been given food to put in their saddlebags before they'd ridden out that morning. By the time the sun was setting and the light starting to fade, Shadow could no longer feel her legs. At some stage her backside and then her legs had grown numb. Now that they were stopping she wondered how she'd ever get off her horse. She watched as Irlan staggered to the ground, groaning. When some soldiers turned to watch him, he straightened and led his horse to where the others unsaddled. Shadow started to smile at her brother's behaviour then remembered she'd probably look worse. She didn't get to ride anywhere near as much as he did.

Taking a deep breath, Shadow dragged her leg forward over the saddle. There was no way she'd be able to dismount properly. She tensed, slid off the saddle and grabbed at the stirrup as her knees gave out. A hand grabbed her mid arm and hauled her up before she hit the ground. Looking up, Shadow saw it was Carson. She quickly looked away from his piercing brown eyes and tilted her head forward so the hat hid her face.

"I'm fine," she said in as deep a voice as possible, her words little more than a whisper.

"Thank you." Irlan appeared at her side. "I've got him now."

When Irlan took her other arm, Shadow gratefully pulled away from Carson who nodded sharply and then moved off. She watched him cross the clearing.

"Are you crazy?" Irlan hissed.

"You didn't stick around," Shadow hissed back. "And it wasn't like I asked for his help. You can let me go now."

"I'll unsaddle your horse," Irlan offered.

"I can do it." Shadow snatched the reins from Irlan.

"You're drawing attention. Let me deal with the horse. It's not like you ride every day like I do." Irlan tried to pull the reins from her.

She refused to let them go. "I know even you must feel sore after this amount of riding."

"Shut up Shadow, and quit drawing attention to yourself."

Shadow breathed out heavily and let go of the reins. Irlan led the horse away and she turned in the opposite direction. Seeing Carson under a tree watching her, she froze. She wondered what he had made of their whispered argument.

"Hey kid," a soldier said behind Shadow. She spun quickly and then had to stop a groan at the effort the movement took. "General wants you to collect firewood."

Irlan returned to her side the moment the soldier stopped near her. "I'll help him."

The soldier shook his head. "General wants you to groom horses. He said to tell you everyone pulls their weight."

When Irlan would have continued to argue, Shadow shook her head and moved away. Collecting firewood was a job even little children could do. The soldiers would wonder if she refused to collect it. Even though she would have preferred to collapse in a heap and not move she forced herself to search the densely treed area for deadfall. It didn't take her long to collect enough firewood and pile it beside the campfire before she found a quiet place to relax. The tree trunk she leaned against was hidden by bushes and felt as comfortable to her aching body as a feather mattress. Exhausted from the long hours of riding, she fell asleep.

Low voices woke her. She looked around, trying to

see where they came from in the last of the day's light. She couldn't see them for the trees, nor could she recognise the voices since she could barely hear them. About to rise to her feet, she froze as the occasional word became clear.

"No one yet... King... who'd suspect... anything... crown... mages... elf sight... careful."

"Dinner!" The word rang out through the camp and cut off the whispered conversation.

Shadow huddled against the base of the tree she leaned on and stayed deathly still. The words had made no sense, but alarm bells rang in her head at the snippets she had caught. Was Irlan right? Did Carson have a hidden agenda? She didn't want to know. She wanted to stay out of any possible trouble. Escaping the tavern was meant to save them, not put them in more danger. When she thought it was safe, she crept around the outside of the camp, staying in the trees. When she felt she was far enough away from where the conversation had been held, she walked into the camp and lined up for dinner.

"Where've you been?" Irlan demanded as they found a place to eat.

Shadow shook her head. She couldn't mention what she'd heard. That'd be completely insane. And what had she heard anyway? Nothing really.

"Don't give me the silent treatment. I was worried something had happened to you."

"I shouldn't talk. Who knows who's listening." Shadow couldn't stop thinking of the bits of conversation she'd heard. They made her food sit heavy in her stomach.

"No wandering off on your own again. Anything could happen."

Shadow nodded. She wasn't going to argue that order. She didn't want to put herself in the path of any more secret conversations. She didn't have a death wish.

Chapter Five

The following week passed in a blur. Shadow was too tired to even want to talk to her brother half the time. Although, towards the end of the week, she managed to last till after dinner before dropping off to sleep.

Each day they rose at dawn, packed, ate and moved out. The midday meal was eaten on horseback and they rode until the light started to fade from the sky. While the soldiers set up camp, Irlan brushed horses and Shadow collected firewood. On this particular evening, when Shadow dropped another bundle of wood by the fire, she glanced at the map the General and Captain pored over. As the General spoke, his finger traced a line on the map. Shadow stared at the map. When Carson looked up at her, she hurried away. She still didn't know if she should trust him. And why did they need a captain and a general for such a small group of soldiers?

"You've got to look at the map and tell them it's been changed by magic," Shadow told Irlan, who still brushed the horses.

"I can't do that. They'll want to know where the path is," Irlan argued.

Shadow squatted in the dirt and drew in the path they followed, then the path magic had made disappear. "Tell them if they let you have some parchment and ink you'll do an accurate copy."

"How am I meant to do that?"

"I'll do it if you can get them to leave you alone," Shadow said. "Oh hurry. It looks like they're finishing up."

Irlan leapt to his feet and hurried over to the fire. He reached them just before the last bit of map was rolled up. "Wait!" He reached out towards the map, but Carson was there between him and his goal.

"What do you think you're doing?" Carson demanded.

"I thought I saw something on the map. Magic," Irlan said. Carson stepped back and Farnell unrolled the map. "Yes! It's definitely been changed by magic. Look, here's the path you see. This is the path I see." He ran his finger across the map. He glanced up at Shadow who had come to stand with them and she gave the slightest of nods.

Farnell rose to his feet and ran his fingers through his close cropped hair. He spat out a few curse words before turning back to Irlan. "I want you to fix the map."

"I can draw you a new one," Irlan suggested.

Farnell shook his head. "Fix this one. Draw in the line where it should be."

Irlan glanced towards Shadow and this time she shook her head. "It can't be done. I'd have to start with fresh parchment. This one's been changed too much. The magic would interfere with the drawing."

Shadow almost grinned at her brother. She had to admire the way he could sometimes come up with excuses on the spur of the moment. She guessed it came from regularly trying to outwit their Pa and his many rules.

"How do we know you're not leading us off the path? It was convenient you turned up when you did. Are you certain this moment isn't what you've been waiting for the whole time? A way to throw us off course." Carson watched Irlan carefully.

Shadow held her breath.

Irlan shrugged. "I guess you don't. But I'd have to be mad to risk my brother and myself. Your problem, but I'd like to get to this pass you want me to find before winter. How long till we get near the mountains?"

"You've made your point," Farnell snapped. He turned to Carson. "Organise parchment and ink for him. He can do it in my tent. I don't want the whole company wondering what's going on."

Irlan and Shadow were left by the fire. "I wonder what that meant," Irlan whispered to his sister. "They changed their minds so suddenly."

Shadow grinned. "The path's meant to be climbing through mountains now. And you didn't show them the path quite right either. I hope they don't remember where your finger traced since you did it so quickly."

"This is tougher than I thought it'd be," Irlan said with a sigh.

Shadow was tempted to point out it was his own fault. She looked over towards the General's tent and saw Carson beckon them. "Come on, it looks like the Captain's trying to get our attention."

* * *

While Irlan stood watch at the tent flap, Shadow drew in the correct path. She put in some markers to be able to compare it to the true map and then she let her brother add the rest of the details. Several times she had to tell him that things were not there that he could see, but they managed to draw the map without problems.

"Do you think it was done by someone here or before they left the capital city?" Shadow asked.

Irlan shrugged. "I wouldn't think it was someone here. They're all great fellows." Irlan had taken to joining the games of chance played by the soldiers of an evening.

"That doesn't mean anything. A person can have two faces." Shadow couldn't help thinking about the whispered conversation she'd heard.

Irlan was about to argue when Carson came into the tent. "Is it ready?"

"Ready enough." Irlan moved back from the table so Carson could have a look at the two maps.

"Mmm, very close, but it slowly veers off, mostly at the end. I guess you're more useful to have around than we thought you'd be." Carson looked at Irlan thoughtfully before he rolled up the two maps. "Wait here." He strode out of the tent.

"What do you make of that?" Irlan asked.

Shadow shook her head. "I wouldn't have a clue. He was definitely thinking about something though."

"That's what I thought. Hope it was something good," Irlan said.

Shadow shrugged. "I don't know. You don't think they were planning on ditching us without pay, do you?"

"They better not. Elf sight's worth more than the two gold coins we've got so far."

A soldier stepped through the tent's entrance. "The General wants to see you. Immediately." He held the tent flap back for them.

Irlan and Shadow shared a quick look before they hurried outside. It was never good to keep the General waiting. Farnell and Carson were seated near the campfire. None of the other soldiers were near them.

"Sir?" Irlan asked.

"Sit down." Farnell gestured to the ground in front of him.

Irlan sat cross-legged in the dust, Shadow beside and slightly behind him. They waited as Farnell stared at them in a silence that dragged out. Irlan began to fidget and sensing he was about to speak Shadow nudged his thigh with her knee. His lips tightened. She didn't know what the General waited for, but she was sure there was a reason for his lengthy silence. Had he figured out their deception? Did he wait for them to confess? Several more minutes passed before the General chose to speak.

"We're willing to pay you the same fee as the tavern owner if you stay with us the entire journey."

"Would you pay us more of the fee each week?" Irlan asked.

"As soon as we're through the pass we'll increase it to five gold a week," Farnell said.

Shadow nudged Irlan. When he glanced at her she glared back. "The same price," he mouthed the words at her.

Her look was dagger sharp. Her eyes screamed no. Come on Irlan, say no, say no, she repeated the words over and over in her head, trying to get the message to him.

Irlan turned to the General. "How much further away is the end of the journey from the pass?"

"Not much further," Carson answered.

"My brother and I can't fight. If there's fighting and we got caught in it, we'd die," Irlan said.

Shadow sat angrily beside him. She wanted to hit him. She wanted to yell at him not to be a greedy fool. But she couldn't afford to draw attention to herself. Instead, she fumed, her head tilted forward so her hat shielded her expression.

"I'll see you're trained," Farnell said.

"How long is it to the pass?" Irlan asked.

"About another six weeks. Plenty of time to pick up some skills with a sword," Farnell said. "Come on, lad. We don't have all day. Make up your mind."

"We'll come with you to the end," Irlan said.

"Then we'd better find someone to train you and your brother." Farnell rose to his feet.

"I'm going to kill you before we get to the pass," Shadow hissed at Irlan as they followed Farnell.

Irlan's grin made Shadow grind her teeth in frustration. Her hands clenched into fists and she had to force herself not to hit her brother. It was close.

Chapter Six

The next day, instead of relaxing by the fire where the soldiers played games of chance after a long day in the saddle, Irlan and Shadow were shown the basics of sword fighting by Morell. He was a man of few words, broad shouldered and used his sword like he was in a dance.

Shadow watched the move Morell made and tried to mimic it. The sword was heavy and after half an hour of imperfect copying her arms were beginning to tremble. Someone kicked at the inside of her right foot and she spun to see Carson behind her.

"Widen your stance. You'll lose your balance and fall on your face."

"The weight of the sword will probably do that to me anyway," Shadow muttered, then held her breath as she recalled she wasn't meant to speak.

Carson laughed softly. "Maybe we should give you a dagger instead."

Or shoot me with a bow and put me out of my misery. She barely managed to keep the words to herself. She lowered her sword, resting the point in the ground. "This is ridiculous. I can't do it."

"You need to practice. Build up some muscle, kid." Carson took the sword from her and stepped back. He checked the balance and then waved Morell forward, the sword held up.

Shadow watched the two men attack each other. Their moves were lightning fast, the sound of their blades ringing in the clearing. She watched in fascination as they moved, an intricate dance. She had thought Morell surprisingly graceful. Beside Carson, he looked clumsy. She was mesmerised by his movements, her breath catching several times when it looked like Morell might get past his defences. Then Morell's sword lay in the dirt and behind her she heard men call out to Carson and coins change hands.

Carson clapped a hand on Morell's shoulder and turned towards Shadow. She watched him walk towards her, glad of her hat. She took the sword he held out and nearly dropped it.

"It might be best to build up your arm muscles

before we try and teach you how to use this. How old are you, kid?"

Shadow's heart stopped momentarily. How old? She wouldn't have a clue what age to tell him. She certainly couldn't say seventeen. "How do you build up arm muscles?"

Carson grinned and reached out to rest his hand on her shoulder. "I'll show you tomorrow. Better get some sleep, kid. We don't want you falling off your horse because you're too tired to stay awake tomorrow."

Shadow watched as he strode to the campfire. Just what she needed to hear. More work. First they expected her to collect firewood each day, then learn to use a sword and now Carson wanted her to build up her arm muscles. She was beginning to wish she'd lifted the kegs of ale at the tavern instead of rolling them, but she'd never imagined she'd end up in the army. She shot a daggered look towards her brother, even though she knew he couldn't see it in the flickering torchlight with her hat shading her eyes.

"Shadow! Get that sword out of the dirt. Hold it up now," Morell snapped.

Shadow lifted the blade and widened her stance as she gritted her teeth. Every muscle in her arm protested, but she wasn't about to argue. Carson might have told her it was time for bed, but Morell obviously had other plans.

By the time she was finally allowed to quit for the night, Shadow could barely put one foot in front of the other. She felt hot, sweaty and her arms ached worse than her legs had the first day of riding. Instead of heading to her bedroll, she decided a quick wash in the stream near the campsite might help. About to step out of the tree line, she stopped when she saw someone already crouched at the stream.

His head came up and he reached for the dagger on the ground beside him, spinning to face the trees. Carson stood shirtless, water droplets glinting in the moonlight. "Step out of the trees."

Shadow forced herself forward and watched as Carson relaxed and tucked his dagger into his boot. He beckoned her forward and she hesitantly walked across the rock strewn ground to stop in front of him. She flinched as his hand came up.

Carson knocked her hat to the ground. "The sun's down, kid."

"Shadow."

"Didn't I send you to bed already? Kid."

Shadow stared at Carson's boots, wishing she could pick up her hat and put it on. She felt exposed. What did he see when he looked at her? She glanced up quickly, his face patches of light and dark, then dropped her gaze again.

"Well?"

Head still bowed she said softly, "We practised some more."

"I didn't think you were that determined to learn how to use a sword."

She wasn't, but Morell had been. Why couldn't Carson leave her be? What did he want? Her arms ached, her back ached, even her legs ached. She wanted to go to bed.

"Kid." The silence stretched out. "Look at me when I speak to you."

Shadow slowly raised her gaze. She got as far as his chest, the water droplets nearly gone. She swallowed hard as the silence stretched out again. Her gaze reached his chin, then his lips. There was no smile, but they also weren't pressed together in a tight line like they were when he was angry. Her gaze finally met his gaze.

Carson reached out and pressed his hand against her shoulder. "Meet a man's eyes when you talk to him, and straighten up. We'll make a man of you yet."

Shadow's mouth went dry and all she could do was nod.

Carson stared at her a moment longer. "How old are you?"

Her mind went blank. She should have figured this out. She tried to remember how old Irlan had been when he'd been her height, but she couldn't think.

"Well?"

"I… I was wondering when you wanted to show me how to build up arm muscles tomorrow."

"Early." Carson grinned. "The sooner we start, the better."

"I guess."

Carson chuckled. "Don't be so worried, kid. You'll thank me for it one day. Now get to bed. You've got an early start tomorrow." He turned, gathered his shirt and headed back to the camp.

Shadow stood there a moment longer, her eyes closing as she tried to slow her heart rate. With shaking hands she crouched at the water's edge and quickly washed her face and arms. Once her hat was back on, she felt less exposed. She was going to kill her brother for agreeing to stay with the army to the end. It might be fun for him, but she was having a miserable time. Every second of the day she kept expecting someone to figure out she was female, and she dreaded to think what they'd do. Especially the

General. She didn't think he'd be impressed with being lied to.

She forced herself to her feet and hurried back to the camp. Her gaze scanned the area and her gaze stopped on her brother who was seated near the campfire. He laughed with the other four men there as he rolled dice onto the dirt. Anger filled Shadow. It was her elf sight that had got them away from the tavern. And yet, as always, she was the one left in the shadows, looking on.

Without thinking, head high, she strode across the camp to her bedroll and kicked off her boots. Until now, she'd moved through the camp like a ghost, trying to avoid attention. She sat on her bedroll and her gaze was caught by Carson, his back to the fire as he watched her. The anger evaporated and she cursed her momentary forgetfulness. Her shoulders slouched and she ducked her head, her gaze cut off by the brim of her hat. When she glanced up again, he was gone. With a sigh of relief, Shadow placed her hat beside her as she snuggled into her bedding, hidden away from prying eyes.

* * *

A boot nudged Shadow the next morning and she

peeked above her bedding to see Carson standing over her in the pre-dawn light.

"Come." His word was soft but the order was clear. He strode away, obviously expecting her to follow.

Shadow struggled out of her bedroll, automatically pulling on her hat. She watched to see where Carson went as she shook out her boots and slid them onto her feet. She hurried after Carson as he disappeared into the trees. He stopped in a small clearing of dew-dampened grass and she came to a halt in front of him, staring at the ground while she waited. A glance upwards showed Carson stood there, hands behind his back, feet spread like he had all the time in the world.

What did he want? Was he waiting for her to say something? Do something? She glanced up again and saw he still waited. She wanted to demand what his problem was. Why didn't he say something?

He reached out and tapped underneath the brim so her hat fell to the ground. Shadow fought the urge to bend down and pick it up. Instead she stared at where it lay on the grass. Her gaze flew up to meet his when he pressed against her shoulder and she recalled his words of last night. She held his gaze, expecting him to denounce her as the early morning light increased. Her stance straightened and she stared defiantly at him. She was tempted to tell him the truth, just to get it over and done with. The suspense was killing her.

Carson smiled. "Much better." He started to unbutton his shirt.

Shadow couldn't resist a glance at his chest, the broad expanse rippling with muscles as he moved. He hung it on a branch and she met his gaze again.

He gestured to the ground. "Lie face down." Carson dropped to the ground to show her what he wanted, his palms pressed against the ground. "I want you to do push ups every morning." His arms tensed and he pushed his body off the ground, only the toes of his boots and his hands in contact with the grass.

Shadow stared at him from where she lay prone on the damp grass. He expected her to be able to do that? She watched as he lowered himself and pushed away from the ground again. Her gaze was drawn to the muscles in his arms. She had seen plenty of men without shirts. Farmers. But this was different. Carson had no excess fat, especially around the middle from too much ale, and here and there were faint scars.

"I'm not doing this for the entertainment value, kid. And I'd be careful how you stare at a man. Some of them like pretty boys like you."

Her gaze flew to his face and saw the amusement there. "Your scars."

He pushed back to sit on his legs, a quick shrug. "Occupational hazard. Healers aren't always available when you're in the field." He reached out and took her hands, placing them the correct distance from her body and pressed the palms against the grass. "Your turn."

Shadow tried, she really did. And she wasn't without muscles, not completely. But she was unable to do the effortless push ups Carson had done. She glared at him when he chuckled and tried again. She managed to push her torso off the ground and then her legs. Another attempt was just as wobbly and her arms protested as she forced them to obey.

Carson shook his head as he rose smoothly to his feet. "Looks like you're going to be at this a while, kid." He walked over to his shirt and used it to wipe the dew and grass off his chest and arms.

Shadow watched him, her torso off the ground, her legs still against the damp grass. "I can't do this."

He walked towards her, pulling his shirt on, and crouched in front of her. "You will. Every morning. Twenty. Don't return to camp until you're done." He rose to his feet and strode away.

Shadow glared at his back and wished she was strong enough to use a sword. He'd be the first one she attacked with it, followed by her brother.

Muttering under her breath about overbearing captains and idiotic brothers she completed her twenty push ups. Wobbly, uncoordinated and nothing like the smooth ones Carson had done. But they were a start. She rolled onto her back, her arms aching and trembling. Six weeks to the pass and who knew how much longer after that. She wasn't going to survive. She dropped an arm over her eyes. If she was lucky, she might survive another day.

A shadow fell over her and she moved her arm slightly so she could peer up at whoever disturbed her well earned break. Carson stood there, his sword in his hand and pointed at her. She stared at him. Had he found out? Was this what lying to a captain got you?

Carson sheathed his sword and held out his hand. When Shadow hesitantly took it, he pulled her to her feet. "Anyone could have come along. We aren't the only ones to travel these roads. Stay alert or you could have a dagger at your throat and your blood spilled on the grass." He let her go and stepped back. "Do I need to stay and supervise you or did you actually do your push ups?"

She could only nod, her attention caught by his searching brown eyes.

"Come. Have breakfast before we saddle up." He strode back to camp.

Shadow stared after him. He was far more complicated then the men she knew back home. Farmers, craftsmen and merchants hadn't prepared her for life in the army. She picked up her hat, dusted it against her pants and pressed it down firmly. A quick brush at the dirt and grass on her shirt and she returned to camp.

"Where were you?" Irlan stood over her as she rolled up her bedding.

She ignored him. This was his fault anyway.

"Shadow!"

His voice was quiet but she could hear the anger in it. Good, let him feel how she felt. This was meant to be better than what they'd left behind. She didn't see much difference. Orders were thrown at them and they had no choice other than to obey, regardless of if they wanted to.

"Quit ignoring me, Shadow."

Rising to her feet she gave her brother a daggered look then took her bowl over to be filled.

Chapter Seven

After a week of trying to strengthen her arms and learn to wield a sword, Shadow could have quite happily pushed the sword between Carson's ribs, and Morell's too. She wasn't sure which one she'd kill first. Maybe her brother. Yes, he was the one who'd started it all.

She swung at Morell and landed in the dirt as he swept her foot out from under her. Her sword went in one direction, her hat the other.

Morell looked down at her with his usual expression of disgust, an expression he seemed to keep solely for her. He turned his gaze to a point behind Shadow. "I'm wasting my time, Captain. Maybe you should give him an eating knife and be done with it. Or better yet, a length of rope and tell him to go hang himself. It'd be less painful to die that way than being carved up on some battlefield."

Shadow glanced behind her to where Carson stood. She scrambled across the ground to grab her hat. Carson beat her to it, his foot on the brim. She looked up at him, slowly rising to her feet.

"Leave the hat off. Seeing what's coming at you might help." He turned to Morell. "Continue with Irlan." His gaze returned to Shadow. "Come." He strode away.

Shadow glared at his back, reached down to pick up her hat and jammed it on her head as she followed him. He stopped at the campfire and talked momentarily to Wardell. Taking the knife Wardell handed him, he continued to stride to the edges of the camp, grabbed one of the torches out of the ground and disappeared amongst the trees.

Shadow found him in a clearing that was longer than it was wide, the torch planted in the ground to cast flickering light. She flinched as Carson strode towards her and knocked her hat to the ground.

"If I didn't know better I'd think you slept with that damn thing on."

Shadow stared at the knife Carson held out to her hilt first. She reluctantly took it, Morell's words ringing in her mind. It might not be an eating knife, but it certainly wasn't a sword.

Carson made a noise of impatience and grabbed

her hand. "It'd help if you held it properly. I thought every boy knew how to hold a knife. I don't think you're even interested in trying. Irlan won't always be there to look out for you. Didn't you have a wooden sword, kid?"

Shadow started to shake her head, but recalled she was meant to be a boy. Irlan, like many other boys they knew, had owned a wooden sword as a child. She nodded instead.

"And fights? Didn't you get into fist fights?"

She shook her head. That wasn't something she could fake.

Carson sighed and ran his fingers through his hair. "Your brother hasn't done you any favours always standing up for you. A few fights when you were younger might have taught you how to avoid landing in the dirt so often."

She kept quiet, her gaze back on the ground. When Carson touched her chin and tilted her head up, her startled gaze met his.

"Stop staring at the ground like you expect someone to beat you. You're asking to be walked all over doing that. Show some confidence, kid." He kicked at the inside of her boot. "Widen your stance. Hold your knife like you mean business and come at me."

"I might hurt you."

Carson laughed. "Then I deserve it. Come. Make a move."

Shadow barely moved towards Carson before she ended in the dirt, a rock pressing into her hip as she stared up at him.

He held his hand out and pulled her to her feet. "Again."

More warily, Shadow attacked. It made no difference. Nor did the other numerous times. Again and again she landed in the dirt. She ignored the hand Carson held out to her and scrambled to her feet. "What am I doing wrong?" Anger and frustration filled her voice in equal measures.

Carson nodded and a smile slowly formed. "Finally."

She listened as Carson explained, watched as he demonstrated. She still landed in the dirt, but now she understood why. Four more times and the fifth, she stumbled, but spun and remained on her feet. Elation filled her as a grin formed. She was still standing.

"Not bad, but don't get too complacent. And don't stop."

Her grin vanished as she landed in the dirt again. She looked up when Carson threw a knife sheath at her.

"Put it in your boot and try with your fists. You're going to slit your throat with the way you fall."

She sheathed the knife and slid it into her boot. Now he told her. So good of him to finally decide to care. Pushing herself to her feet she dusted herself off again and reluctantly glanced at her hat.

"Fists up and try and hit me. Come on kid. I want to get some sleep tonight."

Shadow raised her fists like Carson did. She frowned. It didn't seem quite right. She guessed Carson didn't think so either because he reached out and altered the way she held her hands. He kicked at the inside of her boot again and she widened her stance. There were too many things to remember.

"Are you waiting for winter?"

She doubted he'd let her. With a deep breath, she swung. Carson moved quick and his foot connected with her leg as he tried to hook it out from under her. She threw her balance to the other leg and spun so she could see where Carson was. She was too slow. Her body met the dirt and she stared upwards. Just once she'd like to see him hit the ground. She knew where every rock was, and she was sure she'd have the bruises tomorrow to prove it.

Carson stared at her then held out his hand. "We'll

call it a night. Get some sleep, kid. You're going to be feeling this tomorrow."

Shadow let go of his hand the moment she was on her feet. "Good of you to tell me. Like I couldn't figure that out by myself." She wanted to clap her hand over her mouth the moment she saw the look of surprise on Carson's face.

He grinned. "Looks like you need a steady diet of dirt, kid. Makes you actually speak." He strode towards the camp, grabbing the torch on the way.

Shadow grabbed her hat and hurried after him, not wanting to be left alone in the dark. It had been pointed out to her very efficiently that she wasn't capable of taking care of herself.

* * *

Shadow groaned when she was nudged by Carson's boot the next morning. She peered blearily up at him. He gestured towards the left with his head and strode in that direction. Shadow forced her body to move, every bruise reminding her of the previous night. She shook out her boots, pulled them on and jammed her hat on her head. A glance at Irlan showed he was still asleep. It gave her a great deal of pleasure to nudge him not so gently.

She grinned at his growl and headed in the direction Carson had taken. It took her several minutes to find him because this time there was no clearing. He leaned against a tree with a low hanging branch that was almost horizontal. His shirt hung over the branch, close to the trunk.

Carson pushed himself away from the trunk and wrapped his hands around the horizontal branch. "Your new exercise. Chin ups." He pulled his weight off the ground and then lowered himself again. "Twenty chin ups, twenty push ups. Every morning."

Shadow stared at him. Maybe he did know and this was his way to punish her. He was going to kill her with an excess of exercises. She shook her head. "I can barely do twenty push ups." She was unable to do them really well, not like Carson did.

"Then maybe you should do them morning and night. You'll never be able to lift a sword if you don't work at it."

"What will it matter anyway? Even if I could lift it, I can't use it. You might as well give me that rope."

Carson strode towards her. "Are you giving up?" His voice was soft, his tone incredulous.

She couldn't meet his gaze. Sighing heavily she stepped around him to make her way to the tree. She had to reach up to the branch and annoyance went through her. He could have picked a lower one. She gripped the branch like Carson had and pulled herself up. Her arms protested and she couldn't get herself as far off the ground as Carson had. Teeth gritted, she lowered herself. One. That one made her feel like she already needed a rest, twenty was going to kill her. Carson still watched her so she pulled herself up again and felt sweat trickle down the side of her face. Two. By the fourth one, sweat ran down her back, soaking into the bindings that wrapped around her. She continued to watch Carson as she struggled on. He met her gaze, his expression neutral. On the eleventh chin up, her eyes closed as she lowered herself and she wanted to sit on the grass and cry.

Instead she continued. Her arms were on fire, her body soaked with sweat and she didn't even want to think about still needing to do twenty push ups. She was going to kill Irlan. Slowly. She was going to take the knife from her boot and carve him into little pieces while he slept. Maybe she should tie him up first. That way he couldn't escape. Her arms refused to do the fourteenth chin up. She stood there, holding onto the branch, arms trembling and eyes tightly closed.

"Let go."

Shadow opened her eyes and turned her head to look at Carson who stood at her left shoulder. She continued to hold on, her fingers seemed glued to the branch. "I'm nearly finished." She wasn't about to prove him right and quit.

Carson uncurled her fingers. "Take a rest. Then do your push ups." He grabbed his shirt and walked back to the camp.

Shadow dropped onto the grass. A rest! She wanted to curl up under the tree and stay there until the grass grew over her. She was never going to build up her arm strength. Maybe that was why women weren't allowed in the army.

"Shadow."

She scrambled to her feet to face her brother.

"You need to stop spending so much time with the Captain."

Her hands tightened into fists. Like she had asked for this morning torture. "It's not like I want to spend time with him. He's teaching me to fight."

"Because you didn't pay attention to Morell. If you did it right, he wouldn't have bothered. If you'd put some effort into it he-"

"I do put effort into it. I was doing mending and cooking while you got to fight with other boys and play with wooden swords. At least you have a clue what you're meant to do. I don't."

"You make it sound like you did all the work and I only played. I had chores too."

"Stop trying to ignore the point I'm making. You've had years of fighting and swordplay. It might only have been play, but it's more than I had."

"The soldiers say the Captain is observant. He's smart. You can't let him find out."

"Do you think I don't know? But what choice do I have? He gives an order, I have to follow."

"Maybe I should tell him you're too young to learn how to fight. Maybe–"

"Shut up, Irlan. You're being an idiot. And if you remember, this was all your idea. I didn't ask to learn how to fight." She jabbed a finger in his chest. "You did."

"I thought it might be useful."

"Thought? Really, Irlan? You actually tried to think for a change. I'd go back to your normal habit of jumping in without thinking. I believe it works better for you." She spun on her heel and strode further into the woods.

"Shadow! You'll get lost."

Ignoring him she kept walking. As if that'd be worse than things were now. She was tired, sore and worst of all scared. She was sick of being scared. First of her Pa, now of getting caught. Maybe they should go home. She recalled Carson's voice asking, 'Are you giving up?' She didn't want to, but maybe she wasn't suited to this. Maybe all she was good for was serving drinks to farmers and drunks. An image of herself pouring ale, grey haired and stooped, came to mind. No! That wasn't going to happen.

Her feet slowed and she stared at the grassed area in front of her. Twenty push ups Carson had said. She could do this. She wasn't going back to that life. If this was what it took to make her own life, then she'd get through it. Somehow. Her arms trembled as she did her first push up. Maybe she needed to do them each night too.

Chapter Eight

The next four days fell into a pattern. Shadow was woken in the predawn light by Carson and she headed off to do her exercises. After breakfast, they rode all day, making camp late in the afternoon. Once Carson had finished showing her how bad her ability to stay on her feet was, she disappeared to do her exercises again. She still couldn't do more than fifteen chin ups, but she was determined to eventually reach twenty. The fifth day Carson changed the routine.

"This is Iain. He'll teach you how to use a crossbow. Once he's done, come and find me and I'll continue to show you how to use a knife." Carson strode off.

Shadow stared at Iain, a man who looked close to fifty, grey in his beard and dark hair. Her gaze dropped to the crossbow he held out to her. She reluctantly took it and followed him as he led the way across the encampment carrying another crossbow. Iain pointed to a hessian bag that had been stuffed with grasses, which hung out the top. He handed her a bolt.

"Watch and then it's your turn, kid."

Shadow bit the words back that wanted to spill out. Why did they all have to keep calling her kid? What was wrong with her name? Instead she focused on Iain's hands as he loaded the weapon and fired. The bolt pierced the daub of mud on the front of the bag. When Shadow aimed for the same spot, her bolt went nowhere near the target. She felt like throwing the crossbow on the ground and finding Carson so she could tell him what he could do with his latest plan.

"Ya need to hold it steady. Try again." Iain held out another bolt.

Shadow tried. She really did. The bolt made a thunk as it hit the tree far to the left of the target. Without a word, she took the next bolt Iain held out. She didn't know how long Iain kept her practicing, but eventually she reached for a bolt and there was none held out for her.

"Collect ya ammunition kid. Put it near my bedroll when you're done. Keep the crossbow." Iain strode towards the campsite.

Shadow glared at his retreating back. How was she

meant to find them all? And what about the ones in the trees? Was she expected to pull them out too? She soon found it wasn't possible to pull most of them from the trees and some of them were broken. She left the bolts beside Iain's bedroll and the crossbow by hers, where she found a quiver of bolts, then went to find Carson. She wasn't looking forward to her next lesson. And she still had her exercises to get through. Maybe it was too much. Her steps slowed and she brought to mind the picture that kept her going. An image of herself old and decrepit and still serving at the tavern. That was not an option. This was the path she needed to take to stop that from happening.

* * *

It took Shadow two weeks before she hit the daub of mud on the hessian bag. Her mouth dropped open and she stared in disbelief. She looked over to share her excitement with Iain only to see he held out another bolt for her. This one caught the edge of the sack and she frowned in concentration. She could do this. It had not been a fluke. She took the next bolt and focused. She grinned when she hit the mud. Iain had his usual sober expression as he handed her another bolt. Shadow didn't care. She had done it.

Not once, but twice. And she managed to hit the bullseye another six times before Iain told her to collect the bolts.

Her step was light when she approached Carson who sat with the General by the fire. "I'm finished."

Carson nodded and turned back to the General. "I'll send twice as many out for game tomorrow. The closer we get to the pass, the scarcer it's become. We do need fresh meat."

"I don't like the men going off alone in this area."

"They can go in groups of three, but starving ourselves won't help either. There could even be snow up ahead and then it'll be harder to find game."

The General nodded. "Send them early then. Before we break camp. I want them to stay together while we're travelling."

Carson rose to his feet with a nod and turned to Shadow. "Come."

She obediently followed and wished she could tell him a please wouldn't go astray. Or even a few extra words. Her annoyance was soon forgotten as she worked on her stance and Carson surprised her with a longer knife that was to hang in a sheath on her belt. He showed her how to hold and wield the new knife then left her to do practice drills.

Once she'd finished, she did her twenty push ups

and then searched for a likely branch to do her chin ups. By nineteen, her arms trembled and twenty seemed impossible. She pictured the bolts that had hit the bullseye and forced herself on. Twenty. Her feet touched the ground and with arms stretched out, head flung back, she spun in circles, a grin on her face. Twenty. She'd finally done twenty chin ups. Laughter rose up and filled the clearing and the sound seemed foreign to her ears. She couldn't recall the last time she'd heard her own laugh. A twig cracked and she stopped abruptly, her hand falling to the hilt of her dagger as she faced the noise.

Carson stepped away from a tree. "How old are you, kid?"

Her heart raced as Carson crossed the clearing, her mouth going dry, all laughter forgotten.

Carson took her chin and tilted her head up to catch the moonlight, a frown on his face. "Well?"

Shadow pulled away. "I can do twenty chin ups." She stared at him defiantly, daring him to ask the question again.

"And hit a bullseye too I hear."

She started to relax. "Yep."

"Get some sleep, kid. You need to aim for twenty five."

Shadow watched his retreating back. She was torn between throwing a rock at him or following.

Chapter Nine

Determined to meet Carson's next challenge, Shadow managed twenty five chin ups just under a fortnight later. Her excitement was overshadowed by learning they were nearly at the pass and would likely reach it today. She guessed that meant they were getting closer to their destination. And the end of the journey. Shadow felt a strange lack of enthusiasm at that thought. She glanced around at the soldiers who broke camp in a well organised fashion. Her gaze rested on Morell who nodded at something Irlan said. The General and Captain were in a quiet discussion together, well out of earshot of everyone else. Iain saddled his horse and hung his crossbow on his saddle. The cook packed his items into the baskets on the back of a horse he led. These were the baskets that also held the General's tent.

A deep voice interrupted her thoughts. "Hey, kid.

If you've got nothing better to do than stand around, come help me with this."

Shadow looked over to Wardell to find out that 'this' was the General's tent. She guessed that would teach her to stand around doing nothing when everyone else was busy. She bit back the scathing reply she was tempted to make and helped with the tent. In no time they were all mounted and back on the road.

Over the past couple of weeks the road had continued upwards so they now travelled in forested mountains. The air had a crisp clear feel to it and the dirt road was overgrown since people rarely travelled this far. It was also narrower in the mountains and the trees thicker, some ending right at the road edge, causing them to ride mostly single file.

Shadow was nearly at the back of the line, only the cook and two soldiers behind her. In front was Irlan. Her breath frosted the early morning air in front of her and her horse snorted. She stared at the rump of Irlan's horse and wished she could be at the head of the column for a change. You couldn't see much from way back here, but being the one of least importance she doubted she'd ever be at the front. No, she'd always be stuck watching horse rumps and sitting in dust.

"Come up to the front, lad," Farnell called back. When Shadow started to follow her brother forward, Farnell yelled. "Stay at the back, kid. There's no room here for you."

Shadow and Irlan shared a look. Irlan glanced towards the front and then back at her. She looked worriedly at him. As she had already known, they weren't going to let her up the front. She was too insignificant.

"Come on, lad. Hurry up. We don't want to miss the pass," Farnell called back.

Having no choice, Irlan rode forward and was told to keep a sharp eye out. Shadow did the same, but it was difficult from the back of the column. She had to find a way to move towards the front of the procession. Maybe not right at the front, but somewhere a lot closer. How were they meant to maintain the illusion it was Irlan with elf sight if she couldn't warn him when something was hidden?

Spying Iain ahead of her, she nudged her horse forward. When the soldier in front of her protested, she indicated she needed to speak to Iain. One by one, she slowly passed the other soldiers.

"Can a crossbow be used from horseback while it's moving?" Shadow softly asked the man.

"Ya really going to have to learn to speak up, kid," Iain complained.

Shadow moved up beside him and repeated her question. There was barely room for them to ride side by side.

"Of course they can. I know men who can hit the eye of a fly while galloping," Iain boasted.

The soldier in front of them laughed, turning to face them. "Sure you do."

Shadow moved closer to the soldier in front. "Have you seen someone shoot a crossbow from a moving horse?"

"We all have. It's not as accurate as a man on his own two feet though."

"Of course it is. Ya only say that because ya can't shoot as well on a horse. Not everyone's as hopeless as you," Iain said.

Shadow looked ahead and wondered how to move up the line. She nearly gasped at what she saw. Men, holding bows with arrows trained on them, sat in trees along the path. Magic hid. She was torn. If she rode forward to warn her brother, she'd be amongst the archers and she'd have no way to explain how she and not her brother knew, but their lives were at risk. How could she not warn everyone? Fear pooled in the pit of her stomach and she looked frantically around.

Seeing Carson only a couple of horses ahead, she made a decision. She pushed forward and ignored the complaints.

Carson turned to see what was happening. "Didn't the General say you were to stay towards the back, kid?"

Shadow nodded as she came alongside Carson. She leaned as close as she dared. "There are archers, magic hid, in the trees. Nine horses ahead."

"Then why hasn't your brother sounded the alarm? You can survive without him for a few hours. I've seen you do so. Go on. Get to the back of the line." Carson faced forward again.

Shadow kept glancing at the archers as they rode closer to them. "Please Captain–"

"Fall into place, kid," Carson said firmly, not even glancing at her.

Anger rushed through Shadow. She was sick of being called kid, sick of staying quiet and having to blend into the background. She wanted to kick her brother up the rear for the stupid disguise he'd given her and she was terrified of what the archers in the trees would do. She had another tough decision to make and her stomach did somersaults as she steeled herself.

"Move back, kid," Carson said, this time more harshly.

Shadow nodded once and reined in her horse until Iain came alongside her. She asked him, probably the loudest she had spoken since starting the journey, "Can you shoot from horseback?"

The soldier in front of them laughed. "What a joke. Even I can shoot a crossbow better from horseback than he can. He needs his feet planted firmly on the ground for a perfect shot."

Shadow unhooked her crossbow from her saddle and readied it. "It doesn't need to be perfect. I just want to see it done. The tree, near the fifth horse ahead of us, shoot the knot in the wood near that straight branch that angles towards the road." She handed the crossbow to the soldier in front.

"I can make that shot too." Iain readied his own crossbow.

Both men fired at once and the archer in the tree was struck, becoming visible. He screamed. The bow and arrow fell from his fingers towards the ground only moments before he did. Sound erupted all around them. Arrows flew from the trees. Horses and soldiers went down. Carson wheeled his horse and raced back to Shadow.

"Where are they?" He demanded harshly.

"Every second tree on the left." She swayed on top of her horse. She'd never seen someone die before. She hadn't expected it to be like that.

Carson turned his horse again and shouted as he moved forward, "Every second tree on the left!" He repeated the cry as he moved along the line.

Shadow sat in the middle of the road on her horse, dazed.

"Kid! Kid! Snap out of it." Iain grabbed her by the arm.

Shadow blinked and looked over at him.

"Where are they, kid? Tell me so I can get 'em," Iain demanded.

Shadow nodded and looked ahead, trying to make sense of the nightmare scene around her. She described the position of the next archer. He quickly fell from the tree and Shadow had to cover her mouth at the way he landed. Bile tasted in the back of her throat and a horse in front of her reared as an arrow pierced it. The soldier fought to stay on.

"Kid! Come on. Keep up. We're fighting for our lives here. Don't go losing ya mind on us. And if it's ya stomach ya planning on losing, turn away from me. Where's the next one?"

Shadow tried to focus. The smell of blood and the sound of horses in pain filled the air. She quickly described the location of the next archer but looked away at the last minute so she didn't see the bolt find its mark.

"Don't go getting squeamish on us," Iain complained. "Come on, tell us the next one. It's them or us."

"And the one after that," another soldier with a crossbow said as he joined them. "But stick behind us. If they start ventilating you with their arrows we won't know where to find them."

Shadow quickly moved behind the men and started describing the positions of the archers. More soldiers joined them and Shadow was kept busy telling them where to shoot. Soon she had no time to focus on anything other than describing the position of the enemy. Her mind seemed to shut down, focusing on the job. Everything else seemed part of someone else's reality. The archers, realising they were being seen, began to retreat. Some of the soldiers started to give chase but Carson sounded a trumpet to bring them back.

Carson rode towards Shadow, his face harsh.

Shadow blinked rapidly, as if coming out of a long sleep. She looked around for Irlan and hoped her brother could help her out of her new predicament. Especially since he was the cause of it.

"You want to explain what that was all about?" Carson dismounted. When Shadow didn't answer and the soldiers stood around waiting to see what would happen, Carson snapped, "See to your animals." He handed the reins of his horse to one of the soldiers. "You and you stand guard. Check the wounded. Clean up this carnage." He turned back to Shadow. "Well?"

Shadow shook her head.

"You don't want to explain or you don't know. Which is it?"

"Have you seen my brother?"

"That doesn't have anything to do with the question. Dismount while I'm talking to you."

Shadow shakily slid off her horse, "Please, my brother-"

Relenting, Carson interrupted, "He's with the General and some of the other soldiers. They gave chase." He beckoned a soldier over to take Shadow's horse.

"No! Call them back." Shadow let go of the reins and forced herself not to step forward and grab

Carson's shirt to shake him. Panic hummed through her.

"They'll be fine. Your brother can watch out for archers," Carson said. "Now why didn't you tell us you had elf sight?"

Shadow closed her eyes for a second. She knew her brother was going to kill her, but she couldn't let him chase after invisible dangers. There'd been at least thirty archers who'd retreated.

"Kid, closing your eyes won't make me go away," Carson warned.

Shadow took a step closer. "He doesn't have elf sight."

"What?" Carson roared. "What were you two thinking?" He quickly picked up the horn hanging at his side and blew it three times to recall the General and the men with him. "Anything else you want to tell me while you're at it."

Shadow's eyes widened but she shook her head.

"Why don't I believe you? You, your brother, the General and I will be having a very detailed conversation when we set up camp tonight. I don't tolerate being lied to. I thought better of you than that, kid."

"Sorry." Shadow dropped her head so her hat shaded her face. Anger started to burn in her. She wanted to yell at him that none of this had been her idea. She reminded herself she had to fade into the background. She'd already drawn more than enough attention to herself for one day.

"Not good enough. You've put everyone in danger with this deception," Carson said harshly. "If you'd been at the front instead of your brother we wouldn't have been caught unprepared." Carson turned to the soldier who came over to him. "What?"

"We lost four men and three horses," the soldier said. The soldier named the men they'd lost. One of them was Morell.

"See they're buried." As soon as the man retreated, Carson turned to stare at Shadow. "Because of you and your brother four men lost their lives."

Shadow swallowed hard, unable to think of anything to say. Her anger instantly evaporated, replaced by guilt. She'd only known one of the men who'd died, but she still felt terrible. She hadn't thought their lie would end in deaths. A hidden pass. That was all they'd thought they'd needed to find. Hidden armies was something else altogether and the General hadn't warned them of that danger. Maybe her Pa had been right not to trust him.

"Well? Haven't you anything to say," Carson demanded.

Shadow shook her head. She had to force herself not to give into the tears that started to burn the back of her throat and make her eyes feel heavy. She couldn't believe how quickly everything had changed. She knew the journey was dangerous. All travel was dangerous with bandits found all over the country, but this was worse than bandits. Men were dead because she and her brother had tried to play at being soldiers. This morning she'd been excited by her progress. Now she felt like a kid playing make believe. She wasn't a soldier. She had no clue how to be one.

"You'd better have something to say for yourself when your brother gets back. I won't accept this silence then." Carson turned and rapidly strode to the camp the soldiers were setting up.

Chapter Ten

Shadow stood there, not knowing what to do. She didn't want to join the camp and have to answer questions, she wanted to go home. There'd been good times. Times when her Pa had actually treated them like he enjoyed having them around. Times when he hadn't needed a drink to face his demons. They might not have been often, but it hadn't been all bad. Not as bad as facing archers. Not as bad as watching men slaughtered and unable to do anything about it.

"Hey, lad."

Shadow spun as a hand landed on her shoulder. She saw Iain standing over her. Lad? Was that meant to be a promotion from kid?

"Come and have something to eat. You did good today. Real good directions an' all. We're proud of ya," Iain said.

"Four soldiers died." Shadow's words wavered.

"Soldiers always die. We live with that knowledge. Those archers could have wiped the lot of us out. They didn't. We sent them running. Come and eat," Iain said.

Shadow shook her head. "I don't think I can."

Iain laughed. "Well, if ya going to throw up, make sure ya use a bush away from camp." With a last clap on her shoulder, he returned to the camp.

Shadow winced. Her stomach churned and she breathed through her mouth trying not to think of what Iain had said. It hadn't been a problem until he'd reminded her of her urge to throw up earlier.

"Captain wants you." A soldier joined Shadow.

She looked up at the soldier. He pointed to where Carson was. Five men were mounted on horses, another man held two horses, one of them Shadow's.

"Hurry up. He's in a mood," the soldier warned.

Shadow nodded and hurried over to Carson who was giving orders to a soldier. She tried to ignore the rolling sensation in her stomach. She waited for him to finish speaking and turn to her. She stepped back at the look he gave her.

"Mount up. None of them have returned. We need to find the General," Carson said.

Shadow stood motionless, the words echoing in

her ears. She saw Carson's lips move, but couldn't hear his words over the roar in her ears. Irlan was missing. They had gone after archers and hadn't come back. Her brother! Missing!

Carson grabbed her by the shoulder and shook her hard. "Get on the horse. Now!"

Shadow blinked. Her body felt like it was miles away. She forced one foot in front of the other and took the reins from the soldier. As she swung into the saddle, she saw Carson mount. She couldn't lose her brother. They had to find him.

One of the other soldiers with them sounded the horn three times and then they moved out. Shadow was glad her horse followed the others with no encouragement. She wasn't certain she could remember what to do, her mind still spun with images from the earlier fight.

Oh Irlan, she thought, what have you got yourself into now? She should have known better than to agree to a plan her brother had come up with.

They rode through the trees and followed the signs the men had left.

"Any hidden archers?" Carson demanded of Shadow.

She snapped out of her thoughts and glanced around. Her brother was in danger. She had to focus.

Who was she kidding? They were all in danger. Seeing nothing, she shook her head.

"Speak up, damn it," Carson cursed. "And keep looking."

Shadow gathered her scattered thoughts. She tried to tell herself her brother would be fine, but there was a hollow feeling in the pit of her stomach that told her otherwise. She glanced around, certain she could feel someone watching them. No one was visible. The dark depths of the forest could have hidden an army, even without the use of magic.

"It's bloody creepy in here." One of the soldiers glanced around nervously.

"Sound the horn again," Carson ordered.

The soldier carrying it put it to his lips and sent out three loud calls. Only silence came back. They rode on, single file through the trees. Carson led, Shadow followed behind him and the other five soldiers followed Shadow.

"We're not going to find them alive," the soldier behind Shadow said.

"We are," Shadow snapped at him and turned on her horse to glare at him. He shrugged in answer.

"Keep moving," Carson ordered.

Shadow turned forward and gasped in surprise. She didn't have time to say anything, barely had time to think. Only react. The archer had already pulled the string back and soon the arrow would be released. While all these thoughts were going through her mind, she urged her horse forward enough to lunge at Carson. As she collided with him, she said, "Arrow."

They both tumbled to the ground. Carson let her slight weight throw him from the saddle at her warning. The soldiers following behind them jumped from their horses and hid behind trees for safety. The arrow that had been aimed at Carson hit a tree trunk with a loud thunk.

Carson pushed Shadow off him and jumped to his feet. He took the crossbow from his saddle. "Where?" He demanded of Shadow who stood beside him.

Seeing the man draw back his bow again, Shadow pulled Carson behind a tree. She quickly described the man's position, amending it as he moved slightly to the left and readied another arrow.

Carson let the bolt fly from his crossbow and the man called out in surprise as the bolt found its target. Shadow watched as the magic hiding him evaporated. He tried to pull back the string on his bow, his legs faltered under him. Five other bolts thudded into him now his magic was gone and the bow and arrow dropped uselessly from his fingers. He dropped first to his knees and then hit the ground face first.

Shadow stood there, stunned. She hadn't watched any of the archers die after the first couple in the earlier battle. It was too unsettling. Carson grabbed her roughly by the arm and shook her. Shadow looked at him, her hat having fallen off when they'd landed on the ground.

"Look around! Are there any more?" Carson demanded.

Shadow stared at him, his words not making sense.

Carson shook her again. "Archers? Are there any archers?"

Shadow glanced around then looked back at Carson. She shook her head.

"This is why they don't allow women in the army," Carson hissed under his breath. He bent and picked up Shadow's hat and shoved it at her. He turned to the men moving closer. "Keep behind us."

Shadow put her hat on and stared at Carson. She opened her mouth to speak to him, then closed it again. She stepped forward uncertainly. She began to doubt she'd heard the comment right. Surely he hadn't told her he knew her secret. A rush of anger filled her. She bet even the first time a man saw battle he felt the same.

Propelled by anger, she moved forward. There were no archers around, but neither was her brother. That thought started to weaken her and she pushed it from her mind. She made herself move to where the dead archer was, the grass around him turning red.

"Shadow! Stop!" Carson ordered.

She ignored him and kept moving through the thinning trees. She heard Carson curse and hurry after her. Trying not to look at the archer on the ground, Shadow stepped past him and stumbled into a clearing. A hand on her shoulder spun her around.

Carson stared down at her angrily. "Didn't you hear me? I gave you an order. Every soldier must follow them instantly."

Still angry, Shadow shrugged his hand off her shoulder. She was sick of taking orders, sick of being quiet and sick of fading into the background. She had pushed herself for weeks and all she'd got was more demands and being yelled at. She turned to look around the clearing. What she saw made her knees buckle. "No!" The word was wrenched from her and she ran forward. Dropping to the ground she pressed her hands against the soil. The anger that had driven her vanished and left her barely able to hold herself up. She wanted to throw herself onto the ground.

"What is it?" Carson demanded, having run across

the clearing with her. He looked down. There was nothing for him to see.

"Captain?" One of the soldiers said from the edge of the clearing.

"Keep out of the clearing. There's enough targets in here," Carson ordered.

Shadow swallowed the sob that tried to escape, unable to stop the tear that threaded it's way along one cheek. She felt Carson crouch beside her. A finger on her chin lifted her face so she looked at him.

"What can you see?" Carson asked softly.

"The marks of a magic portal," Shadow whispered.

"A magic portal? The kind you need two wizards to use?"

Shadow nodded. "My brother went through here. I can feel it."

"Where does it lead to?"

Shadow shook her head. "I don't know."

"Then mount up. We can't stay here," Carson ordered.

"My brother went through there." Shadow stared at him, wondering if she'd misheard.

Carson rose to his feet. "We can't help him. Nor can we help the General or the six soldiers that were with them." He started to turn away.

Shadow leapt to her feet and grabbed his arm. "My brother's missing!"

"I'm down to twenty men. I don't have time to look for him. There are more important things to do. Surely you didn't think you were going to a ball? There are no musicians here and I'm afraid ball gowns would be in the way. If you don't want to be left behind I suggest you find your horse and get moving. I won't wait for you. Kid."

Shadow watched as Carson strode back to his men. She was torn. The mark on the ground was all she had left to show where her brother had been. The army was her only way out of the mountains. She turned and dropped to the ground. Resting her hands on the mark left behind by the portal, she closed her eyes. Beneath her fingers she felt a strange hum and glimpsed a fortress high in the mountains. All around it lay snow. Archers manned the battlements and the ground leading to it was completely open. Eighty feet from the fortress a forest started, snow capped pines standing to attention.

"Shadow!"

Shadow's vision wavered and disappeared and she looked up to see one of the soldiers holding the reins of her horse. She rose shakily to her feet, uncertain of what had happened. Her Gran on her Ma's side used to have visions, but surely she couldn't be twice cursed. Elf sight was enough of a problem without that too.

"Are you coming? The Captain said if you don't hurry up we're to leave you," the soldier warned.

Shadow took the reins. "Thank you," she said softly.

The soldier nodded and mounted his own horse.

The return journey to the camp was made in silence. As soon as they reached camp, Carson stopped and looked around. Every man watched him.

"The General's been taken through a magic portal. There's no sign of the men who went with him. They may have been taken too. We break camp first light. We still have a mission to complete and anyone not ready gets left behind." His gaze fell on Shadow.

Her shoulders straightened and she glared back at him. When he turned his horse away, Shadow slumped in her saddle again. Oh Irlan, what am I going to do without you? She felt like screaming, or maybe crying, or throwing something. She didn't know how she felt, she was still half dazed by everything that had happened that day.

"Going to hop down? Or were ya planning on sleeping in the saddle so ya don't get left behind tomorrow?" Iain asked from beside the horse.

Shadow gave him a weak smile before she dismounted.

Iain took the reins of her horse. "There's stew if you're hungry. I'll take care of ya horse." Iain shook his head when Shadow opened her mouth to argue. "Do as ya told. Need ya wide awake tomorrow so ya can watch our backs. Ya look half beat."

Shadow nodded and took her bowl from her saddlebags before she made her way to the campfire. She watched as the cook ladled stew into the bowl and gave her some dry bread to sop it up with. She moved to a stump not far from the fire to enjoy its warmth, but it seemed wrong to sit and eat. Her brother was missing, she was stuck with an army and they'd been attacked by archers. Eating seemed too ordinary a task, but she automatically spooned up a mouthful.

"Captain wants to see you after you've eaten." A soldier came to stand beside her. "In the General's tent."

Chapter Eleven

The soldier was gone before Shadow could answer. The food she'd swallowed felt like rocks in her stomach. Shadow glared after the soldier. "Great," she muttered. She sighed, worried about why Carson might want to see her as she stared at her food. Eat with the worry of what Carson would say hanging over her? Not likely. She rose to her feet.

"Don't go wasting that," the cook snapped.

Shadow looked over at him. "I've got to see the Captain."

"Eat first," the cook ordered.

"I can't."

The cook scowled at her. "Bring it over here. I'll put your bowl near the fire to keep it warm. You might be hungry after you've seen him." When Shadow was about to head to the tent, he said, "His bark is far worse than his bite. He's a fair man."

"What if he has no reason to be fair?" Shadow asked.

The cook grinned. "Then I guess you'd better take cover."

Shadow gulped. "That's what I was afraid of." She walked slowly to the tent and stared at the flap she was meant to enter. What did he want? Was he going to tell her he didn't want her with the army anymore? How would she survive alone in the forest?

"Oh for crying out loud," Carson said a moment before he pulled the flap back. "Get inside and stop hovering."

Shadow stepped hesitantly into the tent. She glanced around and saw it was set up the same way it had been the first night she'd been inside. It was hard to believe that was nearly two months ago.

"Anything you want to tell me?" Carson demanded.

Shadow looked up at him. He was taller than her brother and more solidly built. The anger almost poured off him in waves. She couldn't have spoken if her life depended on it. Well, maybe my life does, or Irlan's, she thought as she recalled the fortress she'd seen that afternoon.

"I'm waiting!" Carson said impatiently.

"Where's the fortress?" Shadow blurted out, then cringed at the expression on Carson's face.

"The what? What are you talking about? I want to know about the deception you and your brother pulled. If he is your brother."

Shadow nodded. "He's my brother."

"Why? Why tell us he had elf sight? Why dress you up as a boy?" Carson demanded quietly.

Shadow swallowed hard. He definitely knew. "How'd you know?"

Carson smiled slightly. "I know what a woman feels like when she's lying all over me."

Shadow went bright red and looked away from him, ignoring his chuckle. "Our Pa is Gil Morgan."

"What! Are you mad? Do you think he's going to be pleased his kids ran off with us?" Carson demanded.

"He doesn't exactly know where we went," Shadow said. "We asked Ma to keep it from him as long as possible."

"He's one of the best trackers there is. Do you think a little problem like not knowing where you're planning to go would stop him?" Carson demanded.

"He won't follow us," Shadow protested.

Carson gave her a look of disbelief. "How well do you know your father."

A look of shock crossed Shadow's face and she groaned. "Oh no. He'll follow us. We're his and we left without his say so." Her hands covered her face. "What a mess."

Carson pulled her hands from her face as he shook his head. "What's your name?"

"Shadow."

Carson looked surprised. "That's not a name to give a girl."

"My Pa was angry when he named me," Shadow muttered.

"How old are you, Shadow?"

She smiled slightly, finally able to answer. "Seventeen."

He nodded and stared at her quietly for a moment. "What are we going to do with you?"

"You're not going to leave me behind, are you?" Panic edged through Shadow.

"Do you want to be left behind? The journey's only going to get more dangerous. You didn't cope that well today."

"And being left behind will be safer?" Shadow asked dryly. She nearly cringed at the tone she used. Relief poured over her when Carson smiled. "Today was my first battle. It wasn't what I expected."

"So what do we do with you?"

"Are you still going to pay us?" Shadow demanded. The smile made Carson seem less intimidating. And now he knew she wasn't a boy there was no need to watch her words around him. The relief of that almost made her light headed.

"Us? In case you haven't noticed, we lost your brother today," Carson said.

"Yes, but I'm going to get him back."

"You don't know where he is," Carson pointed out.

"I do now."

"Where?"

"In a fortress." Shadow described her vision.

Carson stared at her.

"You know it."

Carson shook his head. "Not personally. But it's where we're headed. Or at least, we hope it's the place we're looking for."

"Then I'm definitely going."

"I'll expect you to follow orders. No more ignoring me like you did earlier today," Carson warned.

"Sorry."

"And you continue to play the part of a boy."

Shadow nodded.

"And you stay by my side." When Shadow opened her mouth to protest, Carson said firmly, "That's not negotiable."

Shadow sighed and nodded.

"How long do you think your mother will be able to keep your disappearance from your father?"

Shadow was startled by the sudden change of topic. "She probably kept it from him for two weeks, no more than three."

"It might be enough," Carson muttered. Then louder, "Fetch your blankets. You sleep in here from now on."

"What? No!"

"That doesn't sound in the least bit like following orders," Carson said.

"Why?" Shadow demanded.

"Because we can't afford to lose you. Whoever's out there has to get through the entire camp before they can enter this tent."

Shadow frowned before she nodded sharply. "You didn't really want to leave me behind. You still need me. This was all to make me agree to your terms." She headed for the exit.

"Shadow."

She stopped, her back still to him.

"I couldn't take you with us if you didn't agree to follow orders. It would've been too dangerous. For everyone."

She nodded and reached for the tent flap.

"I'll inform the men you're to be guarded as well as the king himself."

Shadow ignored his words and returned to the fire where the cook silently handed her bowl of food back to her. She was angry again. She'd spent her entire life being ordered around by her Pa. How did she always end up being stuck with tyrants? She'd much preferred it when she'd been someone not worth noticing in the army. While the thoughts flew through her mind, she automatically ate, fuming at the latest drama in her life.

I'm going to kill Irlan when I find him, Shadow thought angrily. And I will find him. She refused to believe otherwise. He's going to regret ever getting us into this mess. I'll make sure of it. As she finished her bowl of stew, Shadow heard a single horn call and rose to her feet to join the rest of the soldiers. They made their way to where the sound came from to find Carson standing there, waiting to address them.

As soon as there was silence, Carson said, "It was a tough day today, but you all did well. We lost four men during the battle and I know they'll be missed. We have another six men as well as the General and Irlan missing. We believe they've been taken to the fortress, we're headed to, by means of a magic portal."

There was grumbling in the crowd and threats of

what they'd do when they got to the fortress. Carson gave them a moment and then held up his hand for silence.

"Now to the main reason for this talk. Some of you may have noticed Shadow has elf sight." Several chuckles erupted from the soldiers she'd been with during the fight. "We certainly found out today that we need him around, which means we're going to have to guard him well. I don't want him wandering off anywhere on his own. Someone else will have to collect firewood. He'll sleep in my tent and we're doubling the night guard, but you have to remember you won't necessarily see them coming. You might only hear them. So be careful. We're getting close to the fortress. We should reach the pass tomorrow morning. They're going to be trying extremely hard to keep us out of their territory. So what'll it be men? Think we can take them on?"

There was a roar of agreement from the soldiers and as the sound subsided, one soldier called out, "They'd better look out," followed by another soldier, "We'll pull their fortress down one stone at a time if we have to." There was a shout of approval at this comment.

Carson continued to stand in front of his men and smiled slightly as the bragging continued. When his gaze fell on Shadow he beckoned her to join him. She sighed. She wanted to be left alone. She could have kicked herself for all the complaints she'd made about being ignored. She remembered her Gran once saying 'be careful what you wish for'. This would have to be a perfect example.

Chapter Twelve

"I want you to check the map again," Carson said as soon as she reached his side.

"Which one?"

"Don't be smart." Carson turned sharply on his heel and disappeared into the tent.

Shadow followed him. She wasn't being smart. She bit back her protest and took the map he held out to her. She unrolled the map and looked at the drawing she and her brother had made. "It's different." She looked up at Carson.

He nodded.

"How did you know?"

"I memorised it. It isn't a great deal different, just enough to make me question if I remembered it right."

"It's one of your men, isn't it?" Shadow asked

Carson shrugged. "Maybe."

"Who?"

Carson sighed wearily. He turned away and picked up one of the goblets that Shadow had found that long ago day when Carson and the General had tested Irlan for elf sight. "I don't know." He took a drink from the goblet before putting it down.

"I can't help you," Shadow said.

"What?" Carson looked over at her sharply.

"Find the man. I can't help you. Unless I see him doing magic, I won't know who it is."

"I hadn't planned to ask."

"What do you want to do about the map?" Shadow asked. "Why would they alter it after they knew I'd be able to see it?"

"It was done while we were out chasing your brother," Carson said.

"So they didn't know?" Shadow asked.

Carson shrugged. "Who knows? Get your gear. It's time to call it a night."

"Do you think they'll try and change it back?" Shadow asked.

"It might even have been one of the archers sneaking in while we were gone."

Shadow sighed. "How are you meant to know?" Frustration filled her voice.

Carson grinned. "The joy of being a Captain.

Everyone's life is in your hands and you don't know if all the swords you're guarding will be with you or against you."

Shadow smiled back at Carson. He looked so different when he smiled, younger and carefree, more like the age Irlan had told her he was. She regretted her earlier anger at him. She hadn't realised how difficult being a captain must be. Her smile faded. "I'm with you," she said softly.

Carson stared at her solemnly. Silence filled the tent. "Thank you." The silence dragged out again. "Get your gear, Shadow."

"What about my training?"

"I won't hold you to that."

"Why? Because I'm not a boy?"

Carson shrugged.

"I want you and Iain to continue to train me." She met his gaze, determined not to give up when she'd come so far. So she'd been extremely squeamish in her first battle. She'd get better at this. Look how she'd improved with the crossbow. She could now hit the target more times than she missed.

"Tonight?"

"Yes."

Silence filled the tent again. Carson nodded. "I'll

have a soldier move your gear. As soon as you finish with Iain, I'll continue to teach you."

Shadow smiled, a sense of victory filled her. "Thank you." She hurried outside before Carson could change his mind and quickly found Iain. The older man was surprised she wanted to practice, but he patiently stood beside her and occasionally instructed her. Once she was finished, instead of joining the other soldiers seated quietly at the fire, Iain stayed with her while she gathered up the bolts. Handing the bolts back to Iain, she glanced around for Carson. He stood in front of his tent, his hands on his hips as he surveyed the camp. He looked towards Shadow as she continued to watch him and then strode towards her. He waved back the two men he'd set as guards on Shadow and led her into the trees.

Shadow widened her stance when Carson stopped in a clearing and turned to face her. He beckoned her forward and she attacked. She missed, spinning to face him, ducking as his fist came at her, landing on her forehead with little more than a tap. Five times she attacked him before she stopped, hands on her hips and glared at him.

"I know I haven't improved that much. By now I'd have landed on the ground at least twice."

"You improve a little every day."

"A little I'd believe. I must have improved way more than a little to still be standing. You're treating me like I'll break. If I haven't after the amount of times you've landed me in the dirt, I'm not likely to now."

"Fine." Carson beckoned her forward again.

Shadow attacked, she felt her foot go out from under her and the ground coming up to meet her. At the last second, Carson caught her. She stared at him, their faces inches apart. "Fine?"

"I can't do it. I've been trained from birth not to hit a lady. To protect them."

"I'm not a lady."

Carson straightened, pulling her with him, her body against his. He ran a hand down her side, slowing over the slight curve of her waist hidden by her shirt. "This tells me different."

"Captain–" she couldn't continue when she met his gaze. Words evaporated. She tried to think, but she'd never had someone look at her like that before, not even Elrick.

Carson closed his eyes and let her go. He turned his back on her. "I'm sorry."

She forced herself to focus. "You said you'd teach me. I'm still waiting."

Carson turned back to her. "Tenacious, aren't you?"

Shadow frowned. "That doesn't sound complimentary whatever it means."

Carson laughed. "Like a dog with a bone. Stubborn."

"Oh. Well, sure, if it's important."

"Why is it important for you to learn to fight?"

Shadow stared at him. Why? She didn't really know herself. But every time she got a little better at what she learned, it felt good. Like a spark igniting in her. As if for years she'd lived in a world of death, doing the same each day, dying a little more. As if everything she did had no worth. "So I can live."

"We'll protect you."

Shadow shook her head, trying to find the words. She reached out and touched his chest. "In here. Live. Everything else I've done has been waiting for death."

Carson placed his hand over hers when she started to draw it away. "I'll teach you. But maybe we should stick with drills for now."

Shadow nodded and when he let her hand go, pulled out her dagger. She moved into position and smiled when Carson glanced at her feet but didn't kick the inside of her boot. The smiled stayed in place even when he moved her hand slightly. She mimicked the movements Carson made, feeling like she was doing a type of dance. Deadly but graceful.

* * *

Shadow stared at the two men who'd followed her around since she'd stepped outside the tent the next morning. She growled in frustration before she turned and looked around the camp. Spotting Carson, she strode towards him, her gaze never leaving him once. As if he could feel her glare, he looked up. He stopped when he saw her coming. The two men he'd ordered to guard her continued to follow her.

"I need to talk to you," Shadow said through gritted teeth.

"I'm busy."

"Now. Alone," Shadow snapped, still keeping her voice low.

Carson sighed. "It better be important." He moved towards the fringes of the camp after telling the men who followed Shadow to wait. "Now what?" he demanded when they were out of earshot.

"I can't get a single moment to myself," Shadow complained.

"I warned you last night. We can't afford to lose

you. Now if you've finished complaining?" He started to move away.

"Don't you dare move from there. I need time without someone following me."

"Why?"

"Because!" Shadow looked away and felt her cheeks turn pink.

Carson chuckled as he realised what Shadow was getting at. "Fine. I'll take you to the bushes."

"I'm not going with an audience."

"I'll turn my back." Shadow opened her mouth to argue and Carson said firmly, "It's me or the two I set as your guard."

"Argh!" Shadow glared at him in frustration. "Fine!" She headed for the trees and when she found a sheltered enough place, she stood, hands on her hips. "Turn around."

Carson smiled before he did.

Shadow grumbled under her breath as she squatted behind a bush. "I'm going to kill Irlan myself when I get a hold of him," she muttered as she pulled her trousers up. She strode past Carson without looking at him.

Carson walked beside her. "Let me know next time you need a private moment. We can't have anyone else guessing you're not what you pretend to be."

"Hmph," was all the answer Shadow gave him before she strode to her horse and started to saddle up. Anger felt much better than the fear that coursed through her every time she let it evaporate. Her emotions were still raw from yesterday. The anger was a good way of keeping herself together. Especially after the dreams she'd suffered last night.

Carson motioned to the two men to continue to watch her and returned to his own tasks. Shadow watched him move away. She sighed. She should have thanked him. Life was far too complicated. It had been much easier to remain silent.

The soldiers had their horses saddled quickly and were back on the trail leading through the mountains. Shadow rode behind Carson and watched everything. After yesterday, the slightest sound drew her attention, and whenever the forest grew quiet, that made her more nervous. Her horse skittered as if her emotions put her mount on edge.

Carson glanced back at her. "Loosen the reins a little."

Shadow glared at his back for a moment, but did as he ordered. Then she returned to scanning the area.

The trees on their right soon gave way to a sheer cliff face and the trees on the left started to trickle away to a few as the trail narrowed and the left became a steep drop. Every minute they travelled the drop became steeper. Shadow looked above her nervously, unable to clearly see the top of the cliff wall. She couldn't see any of the slight glittery glow that meant magic so she turned her attention ahead of them. And there it was, the shine of magic she searched for.

Chapter Thirteen

"There's magic ahead," Shadow warned Carson.

"Might be the tunnel through the mountains," Carson said.

"From back here I can't tell. It might be an army waiting for us," Shadow said gloomily.

"That wouldn't be much good to them. They'd be in the same position as us. Single file on a path with a long drop on one side," Carson said.

"And that makes me feel so much better," Shadow muttered.

The soldier behind her heard and said, "At least we'd take them with us as we went over."

"Great," Shadow muttered.

"Are we there yet?" Carson asked Shadow.

She looked back up the path. "Nearly."

"An army?" The soldier behind her asked.

"No, Roper," Shadow answered him.

"Pity."

Shadow ignored Roper's comment, glad there wasn't an army ahead of them. "Stop," she told Carson as the glow of magic came up beside her.

Carson held up his hand and bellowed out, "Halt!" His order travelled down the line. "What is it?" he asked Shadow.

"The pass."

"Where?"

Shadow urged her horse forward.

"Shadow?" Carson stared.

"What?"

"I can't see you. Only your horse's rump, which is sticking out of rock." He dismounted and patted the cliff beside her horse. "It's solid rock."

"No it's not." She reached back outside.

"Your hand looks like it's poking out of solid rock." Carson took a hold of her hand and touched the wall again, this time plunging through. "Bad news. I can only get through when I'm holding your hand."

"And that's bad because?"

"You can't hold everyone's hand," Carson said.

"Maybe I won't have to. What if everyone along the way holds hands? Maybe that'd work," Shadow said.

Carson nodded and let go of Shadow's hand. He

mounted his horse, wrapped the reins around the saddle horn and reached out to take Roper's hand. "Let your neighbour know. This is how we have to enter the pass. We can't get through otherwise." Carson turned back to the wall. "Shadow?"

"Yes."

"Take hold of my hand so you can lead us all through," Carson said.

Shadow's hand came through the wall and she clasped Carson's hand.

"We're ready," Roper said.

Carson nodded and turned back towards Shadow.

She nodded and then remembered he couldn't see her. "Let's go." She moved forward, holding tight to Carson, her arm stretched out.

"At least I can see the entrance once we're inside the tunnel. It should make returning easier," Carson said.

"The magic is only to stop people entering, not exiting," Shadow said. The tunnel grew darker as horses and men filled the entrance. Her horse stumbled over some loose rock but she still managed to hold onto Carson.

"We'll light a lantern as soon as everyone's in," Carson said.

"Providing we don't all fall down a hole before then," Shadow muttered.

Carson chuckled. "You're full of gloomy predictions today."

"All in," Roper said behind Carson.

"Good." Shadow let Carson's hand go.

Carson rummaged in his saddlebags and pulled out a lantern, which he quickly lit using the tinderbox kept in his belt pouch. Along the line several other men also lit lanterns.

The soldiers travelled silently. They were too nervous at being underground to say much. Even the horses seemed quieter than usual. The tunnel ran on a slight upward slope.

Shadow breathed a sigh of relief when she saw the light from the end of the tunnel. It grew larger and brighter the closer they came to it and then she was out of the tunnel and breathing in the cold, crisp air. The area near the exit was clear of trees but not far from there was a pine forest. A thin layer of snow coated everything and the sky looked like there was more snow to come. Shadow looked over her shoulder, to ask Carson what the plan was, and noticed a glow at the top of the cliff.

Looking up Shadow saw men push at a pile of

boulders. "Away from the tunnel mouth! Trap!" Shadow screamed as she kneed her horse forward.

Two soldiers came out of the tunnel as the ones near the opening moved out of the way. Boulders poured over the cliff top, which was about twenty feet above them. Even before those boulders had time to settle more were pushed over.

"Where are they?" Carson demanded of Shadow as he came to a stop beside her amongst the trees. They all dismounted.

"Cowards!" Roper yelled.

"A bit to the left of where the last lot of boulders came down," Shadow said.

The five men who had made it through the pass with them readied their crossbows while Carson aimed at the area Shadow pointed at.

"You just missed him. A bit to the right and slightly lower," Shadow said.

Six bolts flew towards the place Shadow mentioned and the man yelled in pain. As soon as the magic on him evaporated another six bolts impaled him, making him sink to the ground before another heap of boulders barrelled down the cliff face.

"They've moved over to the right," Shadow said.

"Roper, only you," Carson said.

Roper aimed in the general direction.

"More right than that. Good height," Shadow said.

"Perrun, your shot," Carson ordered.

Perrun took the next shot while Roper readied his crossbow. The bolt caught the man in his shoulder and the magic on him instantly evaporated. Five more bolts followed. The man had no chance.

"They're running! To the left." Shadow watched the bolts miss the men fleeing. "More to the left. The ground! Watch the ground. Every now and then they kick pebbles that go over the edge. Aim a bit in front of that."

Roper hit a man and the other soldiers quickly fired at him.

"How many?" Carson demanded.

"Two more." Shadow looked at Carson. "More left than that," she said when she saw where he aimed.

"Damn it! You do it," Carson snapped.

Shadow shook her head. "I can't even hit a still target all the time."

"You don't have to get them between the eyes. Just wing them and the magic goes. Here." Carson handed her his crossbow. "I'll get yours. We have to stop them from warning anyone we're here."

He turned away before she could argue and she was left looking at the crossbow.

"Where now?" Perrun asked.

"Come on, boy. Don't have all day," Wardell, who had also managed to get through the tunnel, growled.

Shadow aimed at one of the men moving more cautiously along the cliff top. Not far from them the trees started. She closed her eyes for a second.

"You need to be able to see to aim," Wardell grumbled.

"Leave him be," Roper said. "Lad's tryin."

"In more ways than one," Wardell muttered.

Shadow opened her eyes.

"Remember lad. It's them or us. Them or us," Roper said.

Them or us, Shadow thought before she aimed again. She aimed for just in front of the man and by the time the bolt reached him, it was behind him. "That fell to the right of one." She readied the crossbow again and this time aimed further in front. "I hit him," she yelped in surprise.

"Get the other one." Carson took his crossbow from her hands and placed her own there instead.

She looked back up to the cliff top and saw the man she had hit fall to the ground. Bolts from the soldiers with her forced him off his feet. Them or us, she reminded herself before she aimed at the last man.

"I missed!" Shadow exclaimed.

"Where did it go? Left or right?" Carson demanded.

"Between his legs. He's just starting to move again," Shadow said.

Carson quickly aimed. The man grabbed at the bolt that pierced his hip. Five other bolts followed and he seemed to waver for a second before toppling over the edge of the cliff.

"Shadow, a shot like that would have been enough to freeze any man. Good job." Perrun clapped her on the back and caused her to stagger slightly.

"Beginner's luck," Wardell muttered.

"Who cares? At least we got them," Roper said.

"All right. Wardell find a way up there and check all the men are dead. Roper, gather the horses together. We can't afford to lose them. Perrun, Clem, see if anyone else can get out of the tunnel. Gwyn, don't let Shadow out of your sight," Carson ordered. "Shadow, have a look around for any more surprises."

Chapter Fourteen

Shadow moved away, Gwyn following. When she stood in the middle of the clearing she slowly turned and looked for the glow of magic. Nothing. She faced Gwyn. He was a bulky man with sandy brown hair, a scruffy beard and pale blue eyes. He carried no sword, only his crossbow and a dagger at his waist.

"It's all clear," Shadow said.

"We'd better tell the Captain," Gwyn said gruffly.

Shadow nodded and looked around for Carson. She found him near the tunnel exit. When she reached his side, he turned to see who it was.

"Well?" Carson asked.

"All clear."

Carson nodded and turned back to the tunnel exit. It was blocked. He looked at the boulders thoughtfully.

"If we stick around and clear the pass they'll notice the men are missing," Clem said.

Carson nodded, still staring at the boulders.

"We'll make camp in the foothills and wait for you," one of the soldiers called from behind the boulders.

"Come on, Captain, we can't stick around here forever," Clem argued.

"He's right, Captain," Gwyn said. "We'll find another way out on the way back. We don't have time now."

"But there's only seven of us," Shadow exclaimed.

Carson looked over at her. "Can you move these boulders?" Shadow shook her head. "Then we have to leave them there." He spoke louder. "If we don't meet up with you in four weeks, make your way to the castle and let them know."

"Yes, Captain," came a chorus of voices.

Carson turned away. "Let's move!"

"What about food?" Perrun asked.

"Keep an eye out for game. The man that makes the kill gets the biggest portion," Carson promised.

"Great. Now I'm going to starve," Shadow muttered.

Carson grinned at her when the soldiers had gone

on ahead of them. "I didn't mention anything about what portion is due a woman."

"Hush." Shadow glanced over at the soldiers who had reached their horses. "I thought you didn't want them to know."

Carson's grin widened in answer as he picked up his pace and caught up with his men.

Once mounted, they rode through the forest, the snow becoming thicker the further they went. Between the men they caught three hares that were on the thin side, and when they finally stopped for the night, Wardell was sent grumbling for firewood.

Shadow cleaned the hares while the rest of the men set up camp. With no packhorse, they only had what they carried on their horses. Saddlebags with some food and personal gear and their bedding rolled up and tied behind their saddle.

After the hares had been cooked and shared out, Shadow inched closer to the fire. Now the sun had gone, the clothes she wore weren't warm enough, even with the thicker tunic she'd brought with her.

"Here."

Shadow looked up from the bone she gnawed on to find Carson standing beside her holding out a cloak. She frowned.

"Can't have you freezing to death on us. No one

else can see through magic." Carson dropped the cloak around her shoulders.

"Thank you." The heavy woollen cloak enveloped her and she touched the soft material with her clean hand. The material was unlike any she had ever felt before. Never had she worn such a fine garment. It seemed more expensive than what a simple army captain could afford. Shadow looked up to ask Carson about it, but he'd already walked away. She remembered her and Irlan's earlier suspicions about Carson, but they didn't seem right. There was something he was hiding and she wished she could figure it out.

Shadow turned back to her food, but looked up when she felt a gaze on her. Wardell glared at her. Shadow hurriedly lowered her gaze. She wished anyone other than Wardell had come through the pass. He had never been friendly to her and Irlan, ever since he'd been reprimanded for not bringing them to the general. Her dinner finished, Shadow threw the bone into the fire and moved away to wipe her hands clean in the snow. Rubbing her chilled hands against her clothes, she buried them in the cloak as she pulled it close. About to go back to the fire, she noticed Carson.

No one stood with the same proud stance. He

looked out among the trees, his back to Shadow and the fire. Shadow moved towards him and she saw him tense and then relax.

"Go back to the fire, Shadow." Carson didn't even turn around.

"How did you know it was me?" Shadow stood beside him.

"Your walk."

"My walk?"

"The rhythm and lightness of your step." Carson looked down at her.

Shadow couldn't make out his features in the darkness, but she was certain he was grinning at her. "Why are you a captain?" she asked abruptly.

Carson turned away again. "Are you trying to insinuate something?"

"What do you mean?" Shadow asked.

"I didn't inherit the position or buy it," Carson said.

"I didn't say you did."

"Then what did you mean?"

Shadow sighed. "Exactly what I asked. How did you come to be a captain when you're so young? Did you save the King or something?"

Carson chuckled softly. "Or something."

"Can't you answer a simple question?" Shadow asked in frustration.

"All right. I've been a part of the army since I was five."

"Five! That's terrible."

"Not really, and I didn't say that was all to my life. It was only a part of it. Until I was fifteen. Then it was most of my life."

"Didn't your family want you?" Shadow asked. At Carson's chuckle, Shadow grumbled, "That was a serious question."

"I know. And yes, my family do want me. I see a great deal of them. It was my choice. Let's just say I'm a second son and the eldest inherits nearly everything. I chose to find my own path, to make my own way."

"Why can't you inherit anything?"

"I won't be left with nothing. The bulk of the estate goes to the eldest. I've known it since birth. It's the way it is."

"It seems unfair," Shadow said.

"It's always been that way in our family. There's a good reason for it."

"What?"

"That's a story far too complicated for a freezing cold night like this," Carson said lightly.

"It's not like there's anything else to do."

"You're a plucky thing. You've surprised me. Most

of the women I know would be in tears long before now," Carson said.

"I'm not much for tears. They don't help."

Carson chuckled.

"Do you think they're fine?" Shadow asked wistfully, thinking of Irlan.

"Your brother?"

"All of them. The General, the soldiers, my brother."

"I don't know, Shadow. I guess we'll find out soon enough," Carson said.

Silence fell. "What are we looking for?"

More silence.

"Does anyone other than you know what we're looking for?" Shadow looked up at Carson and wished there was more light so she could see him better.

"The General."

"Well, that doesn't help. What happens if you get taken too? Or killed? Who else will be able to lead?"

"A man." Carson bent towards her so his mouth was near her ear.

"What?"

"Shh. We're going after a man."

"What man?" Shadow lowered her voice. She wanted to step closer to Carson, but held herself still.

"The prince."

"The what?" Shadow shrieked as she pulled back to look at Carson. She still couldn't see his expression in the dark. She opened her mouth again but felt Carson clamp his hand over it, his other pressed against her back so she couldn't move away.

"Quiet!" He hissed in her ear. "Are you going to be quiet now?"

Shadow nodded. The hand remained on her mouth and she wondered if she could bite his hand to make him remove it. Before she could make the attempt, it fell away from her mouth, but the other hand stayed against her back, warmth seeping into her.

"No one's to know. The King's frantic. He's been given three months to sign away his kingdom in exchange for his first born. We're running out of time. The King can't give in and he knows this," Carson said.

"He's going to let his son die?" Shadow demanded.

"Yes. Why do you think we're trying to get him back? He sent out four companies to find him."

"He sent you?" Shadow asked.

"Not exactly. I volunteered."

"Why?"

"This is the sort of thing that turns Captains into Generals." Carson let her go.

Shadow frowned. She was beginning to know Carson. His tone of voice. The way he could reply to a question without really answering it. "What's the real reason?"

Carson stood quietly beside her. "He's been a brother to me."

"I can understand that reasoning."

"I know." Carson dropped his arm across her shoulder. "We'll do our best to find your brother too."

They stood there in silence until the next soldier came to take over guard duty. Shadow reluctantly returned to camp, wishing she could have stood there all night with Carson's arm around her shoulders, the warmth of him sinking into her as their breath frosted the air in front of them. She'd even ignored the urge to ask for another training lesson so she could remain at his side longer. It was too cold to train, anyway.

Chapter Fifteen

"Time to rise," Carson called out early the next morning.

Shadow poked her nose out of her bedding and quickly hid back under the covers. She shivered. It was barely light and flakes of snow had started to fall.

"You too." Carson gave Shadow a nudge with his boot.

Shadow groaned and quickly hopped out of her blankets before she changed her mind. She shook her boots then pulled them on, tugged the cloak close and rolled up her bedding. That done she looked around for Carson, urgently needing to relieve herself.

He was talking to Perrun, but when he saw her coming towards him, he moved away from Perrun with a last word and glanced towards the trees. At a nod from Shadow, he headed for them, Shadow close behind. Once she'd finished and began to head back to the camp, Carson took hold of her arm to halt her.

"What?" Shadow looked up into his serious expression. She hoped he wasn't going to tell her she needed to continue with her exercises. It was freezing.

Carson reached into his belt pouch and pulled out a bundle of material. He placed it in Shadow's hands. "Open it."

Shadow looked at him curiously for a minute. There were snowflakes in his black hair and his brown eyes held her gaze when she looked into them. He smiled slightly and glanced at her hands. Shadow dropped her gaze and unwrapped the bundle. It was a painting of a man. It was about three inches wide and six inches tall. The man was standing sideways, his black hair tied at the nape of his neck resting on his blue tunic, which looked like velvet. His eyes were brown, his nose was straight, his lips only a shade off being too thin and his jaw square. Shadow frowned at the image, trying to figure out why he seemed familiar. "Who is it?"

"The one we talked of last night," Carson said.

"Oh."

Carson took the painting from her and wrapped it

up again, slipping it into his belt pouch. "If I don't make it, the task is yours."

Shadow held up her hands and stepped from him. "Oh no!" She shook her head. "I can't be responsible for that. I'm a tavern keeper's daughter."

"No, you're the daughter of Gil Morgan, one of the most heroic men in the country."

"Our country must be in pretty bad shape then," Shadow muttered.

Carson smiled. "He endured a lot. Now don't change the subject. You will rescue the prince if something happens to me."

"I can't."

Carson grabbed a hold of her hands to stop her from retreating. "You have to."

"Why me?" Shadow asked in a small voice.

"Because you'll go after your brother. They're in the same fortress."

Shadow looked worried. "What if I can't do it?" What she really wanted to ask was what if she couldn't go on alone? What if she couldn't go on without him? The thought of something happening to him made fear race through her.

Carson pulled her close and stared down at her. "You're the one who stands the greatest chance of getting them out."

"Why?" Shadow asked softly.

"Because you have elf sight. The rest of us have about as much chance as a deer in an open paddock with a hundred hunters surrounding it."

"I'm scared."

Carson wrapped his arms around her and pulled her closer. He pushed her head against his chest and she heard his voice rumble from inside him as he spoke. "We'll look out for you as long as possible. If we're no longer there, you'll manage. You have plenty of courage, and you're tenacious."

"Even though I'm a woman who doesn't belong in the army?" Shadow couldn't help asking.

With a chuckle, he pulled back to look down at her. "You might make a soldier yet."

"I don't want to be a soldier. I want to get my brother back and find somewhere quiet where I can live my own life," Shadow protested half-heartedly. The words sounded false even to her. How could she return to a quiet life after all she'd seen? Would it bore her senseless?

"Really?" Carson ran his fingers along her cheekbone. "I saw you yesterday when you got over your initial shock. I actually think this life is starting to suit you."

Shadow stared up at him, her lips slightly parted.

She was torn between denying his words and rising onto her toes to press her lips against his, but she couldn't find the words for the first or the courage for the second. Instead she shook her head.

Carson's fingers trailed to her chin and tilted her head up slightly. His thumb ran across her lips, warm in the chill air. "You came alive. I watched you."

She felt alive now and wished she had the courage to do something about it. She rose slightly onto her toes.

Carson smiled down at her and pulled away. He steadied her with a hand, then let his arms fall to his side. "Come. We'd better start moving." He turned away.

Shadow felt cold and rejected. She glared at his back. If he wasn't interested, he shouldn't have stared at her like that. Or caressed her face. She watched him move away.

Carson glanced over his shoulder. "Come."

Grumbling, Shadow followed Carson back to camp and found Roper waiting with her horse saddled and ready to go. Shadow glanced around the camp and saw all the soldiers waited for them. Embarrassment flared.

"The area's clear," Carson said. "Mount up. If you

want anything to eat today you'd better look for game."

Relieved by Carson's comment, Shadow swung herself onto her horse. She fell in line behind him and quickly looked around to make sure his comment of the area being all clear was correct.

By midday, Shadow's stomach felt like it was plastered against her spine. It had long since stopped grumbling. All she had was melted snow to drink out of her leather canteen. Taking another swallow of water, she hung it back on her saddle and looked around again. Smiling, she moved her horse forward to come alongside Carson, all the time readying her crossbow.

Carson turned towards her, his hand going towards his own crossbow. He stopped as Shadow shook her head and took the crossbow she handed him.

"Food." Shadow pointed to a deer ahead and to the right.

Carson held up a hand to halt as he brought his horse to a stop. He quickly aimed and shot at the deer. While he was doing this, Shadow had readied his crossbow. The deer staggered and leapt forward. Shadow took her crossbow from Carson and handed him his own. He urged his horse forward.

"Follow!" Carson called.

All the men had their own crossbows ready and raced after the deer. They were hungry since the bit of dried food in their saddlebags was being saved for that night in case they didn't catch anything.

The deer was slowing and the soldiers gained on it. Roper shot at it, but missed. All of a sudden, the deer veered to the right and started to come back towards them.

Chapter Sixteen

Shadow looked ahead and screamed, "Stop! Ravine!"

"Shoot the deer!" Carson yelled at her.

Shadow had been well behind them and had stopped her horse the moment she'd seen the magic hid ravine. She fumbled for her crossbow. The deer came closer. She aimed. It was almost upon her.

"Shoot the damn thing!" Wardell bellowed. "Even a toddler could make that shot."

Shadow loosed the bolt and winced as it struck the deer. Her horse sidestepped as the deer fell towards it.

"Yes!" Perrun raced forward and leapt off his horse. "Food! Hey, it's got a rope around its neck."

"A tethered deer and a magic hid ravine. They knew we were coming," Carson said.

"They couldn't have known the deer wouldn't break the rope before we got there," Clem said.

Perrun looked up from the deer. "The rope was strong enough to hold unless the deer panicked."

"How could they know the deer would head for the ravine?" Wardell asked.

"The deer was on the correct side of the trail that if she was panicked she'd run in this direction," Carson said.

"Do you think we should eat it? It might be poisoned." Clem dismounted.

"No poison would have let it run that far," Perrun said. "Not without collapsing long ago."

"Might be magic poison." Clem nudged the deer with the toe of his boot.

Shadow shook her head when everyone turned to her. "I haven't seen any."

"Cut it open. Let's make sure the magic isn't on the inside," Carson said.

Perrun made quick work of the deer and then looked up at Shadow. She shook her head. Perrun grinned. "Guess we've got food after all. Someone want to get a fire started? I'll slice it thin so it cooks quickly. It should last long enough in this weather."

"Do it quick as possible. I want to cover more miles today." Carson looked to Shadow. "Come. Show me the ravine."

Shadow nodded and urged her horse forward,

taking the lead. The ravine was not far from them. Shadow dismounted and Carson followed.

"Here." Shadow knelt and put her hand over the edge of the ravine.

"It looks like you're pushing your hand into dirt." Carson knelt beside her.

"Try and touch it to see what happens."

Carson put his hand over the edge and then quickly drew it back. He frowned. "How can you hold your hand in there?"

"What do you mean?"

"That chill. Can't you feel it?"

Shadow shook her head. "It doesn't feel any different to me. Just like I can see straight through it."

"What does it look like?"

Shadow shrugged. "It's hard to explain. Sort of like looking through thin gauzy material. It has a slight glow or shine to it and like someone sprinkled shiny bits of gold flecks over it. When I was younger, I could only see the glow and glitter. As I got older, I could see the illusion as a sort of haze over the reality."

"I wish I could see as you do."

Shadow shook her head. "We had a travelling wizard come to the tavern one year. He created all sorts of illusions to entertain everyone. All I saw was the bits of gold flecks and I had to pretend the whole time I could see what everyone else saw. Their expressions as they watched him were amazing. I wanted to know what they saw, but I couldn't ask anyone. I was the only one who couldn't see it. Oh and Pa of course. He grumbled about what a waste of time it was."

"Why did you have to pretend you could see the illusions?" Carson asked.

"Because my Pa threatened to kill whichever of his children were born with elf sight."

"I'm sure he was joking."

Shadow shook her head. "When he was sober he never lied. If he said it, he meant it, and he'd do it too. He thinks it's a curse. One he never wanted to pass on."

Carson reached out and took Shadow's hand. He drew her away from the ravine he couldn't see. "I won't let him near you."

Shadow smiled slightly. "And what if you don't make it? Who's to stop him when he finds out?"

"I'll write a letter for you to give to the King and he'll protect you."

Shadow laughed. "What makes you think the King will listen to you?"

"He will. He always listens to me."

Shadow's laughter died and she pulled away from Carson. "You know the King?"

"Your father has met him too."

"Yes, but you know him. Don't you?"

Carson nodded.

Shadow stared at him. "Is your family very important?"

"They are to me."

Shadow frowned. "You know what I mean."

Carson smiled. "Come. Looks like that fire's going. I want the meat cooked quickly so we can keep moving."

Shadow slowly followed him. His lack of reply was an answer in itself. Once she reached the fire, she was ordered to help slice up the meat.

Several hours later, they were fed and the meat was cooked and cooled enough to pack into saddlebags. Once this was done, Carson led the way back to the trail they'd been following. By late afternoon it had started to snow again.

"Mad being out in this weather," Roper grumbled.

"Nice tavern, warm fire and a friendly wench," Wardell said.

"I'd be happy with the fire at the moment," Perrun said.

"I'd be happy to feel my toes again," Gwyn grumbled.

Carson glanced around. "Another hour and we should be able to set up camp."

"If we can see by then," Wardell complained as the snow began to fall heavier.

"If it gets much heavier we'll stop sooner," Carson said.

"Now I don't know whether to pray for heavier snow or be happy we'll have a fire in an hour," Perrun said.

Shadow was silent. It didn't feel right to join in the conversation. She never had before. The soldiers had never felt completely comfortable with her, probably because of her necessary silence. They had gambled and joked with her brother. The only one who'd befriended her was Iain and the taciturn man hadn't been much of a conversationalist. Thinking of him, she hoped he was safe. She hoped Iain and the other soldiers would find their way to the foothills. Shadow shivered as a snowflake landed on her face. At least they'd be warmer down there.

The next hour seemed to drag by and Shadow almost shouted in relief when Carson called out halt. He quickly assigned jobs to the men and took Shadow with him to scout the area.

"Can you see things that are magic hid in this weather?" Carson asked.

"They're easy to see because of the gold sparkly bits." She glanced around as they walked a large arc around the camp. "It shows up well against all the white."

"That's good," Carson said.

"You never answered if your family are important." Shadow was determined to get a proper answer to her question, even though she was certain she knew it.

"You're worse than a dog with a bone."

"And you're slipperier than a snake," Shadow retorted.

"I'm wounded by your comment." Carson pressed a hand to his heart and grinned.

Her own heart gave a leap, but she ignored it. "Are they important?"

"Why do you need to know?"

"I guess I don't really," Shadow said.

"Why?"

"Because you've already answered me." She turned away from him, unable to continue the conversation, disappointed he wouldn't answer her.

"No I haven't." Carson tugged on her hand so she spun to face him.

"You wouldn't have sidestepped the question so

much if they were unimportant. If you didn't want me to know, why didn't you lie to me?" When the silence dragged out, Shadow asked, "Well?"

"See, tenacious." Carson fell silent then smiled wryly. "I didn't think you deserved a lie."

"Even though I lied to you?" Shadow asked.

"Well, actually, I don't recall you lying to me. Your brother did. You remained silent."

"Isn't that as bad as a lie?" Shadow asked.

He stared at her silently for a moment. "Nearly. Come. We need to return to camp. You're getting a blue tinge to your face." He ran his thumb across her lips. "It's worst here."

Shadow's lips parted under the caress. Her gaze met his and the cold seemed to fade. Warmth filled her. She held herself still, not wanting to have him turn away from her like earlier, but it was inevitable.

His fingers trailed across her cheek until his hand cupped the side of her face. "We need to return to the fire. To get warm."

Shadow swallowed the words she nearly said. She was already warm.

"Come." Carson strode back to the camp. She hurried to keep up with him.

Chapter Seventeen

That night, they huddled in pairs when they went to sleep. Back to back to warm each other. It was too cold for only the blankets. One man had sentry duty and swapped throughout the night with the other four soldiers. Carson ordered Shadow to bed down next to him. She didn't argue, she didn't want to risk anyone finding out her secret in the night. She pressed her back against Carson's and was glad of his warmth.

The next morning, Shadow slowly woke. She felt surrounded by warmth and snuggled in, her eyes still tightly closed. The warmth around her tightened. Shadow's eyes flew open and she saw a chest in front of her, the top few buttons of the shirt that covered it were open. She tried to pull back in surprise, but it was impossible. She felt like she was held by iron. A surprisingly comfortable band of iron.

"Morning," Carson whispered near her ear.

Shadow relaxed as she recalled she'd gone to sleep next to Carson the night before. His warmth surrounded her and she snuggled in close. She felt Carson tense.

"We'd better get up. We're wasting daylight." Carson's breath tickled her cheek.

She was tempted to move her head slightly so his lips would be against hers rather than her cheek. "Oh. Yes. Of course." Shadow moved away from him. This time his arms relaxed and let her pull away.

"You'd better be careful, Captain," Perrun said from beside the fire when he saw them wake. "People'll be saying you like lads."

"Dolt." Wardell whacked Perrun on the head.

"What was that for?" Perrun jumped to his feet.

"Enough fooling around. We should make it to the fortress today," Carson said.

Shadow froze in the middle of sorting out her bedding. She looked up at Carson who still stood next to her. "Today?" Her voice came out as a squeak.

"Buck up, Shadow. Don't you want to find your brother?" Carson asked.

"Yes." Shadow's stomach flipped. I just don't want to go into the fortress to do it, she thought. She forced herself to return to sorting out her bedding. Anything to keep from dwelling on what would happen when they reached the fortress.

The camp was packed up in minutes and they were on the trail, chewing on venison for breakfast.

"Keep your eyes peeled, Shadow," Carson said from in front of her. "There are sure to be men guarding the trail closer to the fortress."

The venison Shadow swallowed sat heavy in her stomach. The rest of it was forgotten in her hand.

"Remember. Them or us, Shadow," Roper said from behind her.

Shadow nodded. She forced herself to keep eating, knowing she'd need the strength to get through the day. She looked around again. The snow lay thick all around them. The pine trees' branches were heavy with snow and the ground was like a white untouched blanket. Only where they had travelled was it marred. The forest was quiet. It seemed that even the birds and animals knew better than to come into this area.

"Anything out there?" Carson asked.

"All clear," Shadow answered.

"If you keep speaking like that everyone'll think you're a soldier," Roper teased.

Shadow turned towards him and smiled faintly before she faced the trail again and noticed a glow ahead as they crested a rise in the ground. "Magic," she hissed.

"How far?" Carson asked.

"About eighty feet away," Shadow said.

"Perrun, Roper, go through the forest on the left. Clem, Gwyn, to the right. Wardell, beside me. Shadow stay behind us." Carson snapped out the orders.

The men readied their crossbows and moved into position. They kept riding towards the magic hid army.

"What can you see?" Carson asked. "I only see an old man on a donkey being led by a scruffy kid."

"He's their captain. But the magic seems to come from a man behind him to the right. You can only see about half his body behind the image of the old man," Shadow said.

"I'll get him, Captain," Wardell offered.

"Hold off. I'll take first shot. You finish him if needed," Carson said.

"Yes, sir," Wardell said.

In one fluid movement, Carson raised his crossbow, aimed and fired. The magic hiding the army seemed to waver. Wardell shot at the wizard Carson's bolt had hit. The magic evaporated. The twenty men marching along the road pulled out swords and readied crossbows. Eight of the men braced their crossbows and aimed at Carson, Wardell and Shadow. The men wielding swords came bearing down on them.

"Take to the trees, Shadow," Carson ordered. "To the right." Then he bellowed, "Attack!"

Bolts flew from the trees and embedded in three of the men with crossbows. Carson hooked his crossbow on his saddle, drew his sword and kicked his horse forward. Shadow leapt off her horse once she'd gained the trees and readied her crossbow.

"Them or us," she muttered under her breath and aimed at one of the soldiers well away from Wardell and Carson. She caught him in the shoulder. He turned to see where the bolt had come from and changed the direction of his attack. Shadow fumbled for another bolt and quickly reloaded her crossbow. The next one hit him in the leg. The soldier staggered but kept coming.

A wave of panic washed over her and she dropped the next bolt she tried to load. "Them or us," she reminded herself. Taking a deep breath and holding it, she grabbed another bolt. She took aim and caught him in the throat this time. Shadow closed her eyes at the sight of the blood and let her breath out through her mouth. "Them or us. Them or us," she muttered.

Shadow opened her eyes again to see Roper and Perrun had joined Wardell and Carson on the trail their swords slashing at the soldiers. Shadow gasped as she saw a cut high on Carson's left arm. She aimed at another soldier. This one she caught high in the chest and he looked down at the bolt in shock, dropping the sword he swung. Hoping he was dealt with, Shadow readied her crossbow and looked for another soldier to aim at. A sound behind her made her turn and she saw a soldier with a long curved dagger trying to creep up on her.

Shadow screamed in surprise. The man rushed towards her. The crossbow Shadow had readied came up and she blindingly pointed it at him. She hit the man in the right shoulder. He barely paused in his rush towards her. Then somehow Wardell was in front of her. His sword sliced into the man. Blood sprayed everywhere and Shadow clapped her hand over her mouth.

Them or us, she silently reminded herself.

"Pull yourself together, girl," Wardell grumbled.

Shadow's gaze flew to Wardell. Her eyes widened in surprise.

"I'm not an idiot," Wardell muttered. "Now, stay out of trouble."

Then he was gone. Avoiding looking at the man

on the ground, Shadow readied her crossbow with trembling fingers and turned to face the fight on the trail. She saw Wardell move in near Carson. He spoke and then Carson nodded. Carson ran towards the tree where Shadow hid. Wardell blocked the soldier who would have followed.

Carson grabbed Shadow's arm as he burst into the forest. "Get on your horse," he ordered. A piercing whistle and his horse trotted towards him. Carson sheathed his sword and swung onto his horse. "Come!"

Shadow mounted her horse. Carson leaned over his and kicked it forward. She did the same, holding on tight as her horse followed Carson's. Branches whipped past her and snow fell on them in great lumps. Her surroundings blurred. They burst from the forest and onto the trail, the sound of fighting left behind, but still Carson urged his horse on. The sounds were muffled by the snow on the ground. Finally Carson slowed his horse to a walk and Shadow willingly did the same.

Carson looked over at her. "Whose blood?"

"Not mine."

Carson nodded.

"We left the men behind," Shadow accused.

"We have a mission to complete," Carson snapped. "They know what's expected of them."

Shadow followed him silently for a while. When the trail widened, she moved up beside him. Looking over, she was startled to see the cut on his arm was wet. "You're bleeding!"

Carson glanced down at it. Pulling his horse to a stop, he rummaged in his saddlebags and tore a strip off the tunic he found. He handed the strip to Shadow. "Bind it."

Shadow's lips thinned, but she did as she was ordered. Before she could lean away from him, Carson grabbed one of her hands. She looked up at him.

"I heard you scream earlier. Nothing happened?"

"What would it matter?" Shadow snapped.

"Wardell was closest. I sent him," Carson said.

Shadow sighed. "I want to go home." Sometimes.

"To your father?"

Shadow closed her eyes for a second and sighed. "Maybe not." But then where else could she go? Where would she fit in? The adrenaline that had coursed through her earlier had evaporated, leaving her slightly drained. Maybe Carson was right. Maybe the army was where she belonged. At least she had moments were she felt alive, where every action counted and every second was important.

Carson smiled. "Come. We've got a fortress to invade."

Shadow smiled at him and sat back in her saddle when Carson released her hand. And he called her tenacious.

Chapter Eighteen

They travelled less than an hour before reaching the edge of the forest. Shadow looked across the wide open area between them and the fortress. It was exactly as she had seen in her vision, even down to the archers on guard.

"Now what?" Shadow asked.

Carson shook his head. He looked around. "Anything magic hid?"

"No."

"At least that's a start," Carson said.

"How are we going to cross that?" Shadow pointed towards the open space still between them and their goal.

"Come." Carson turned his horse to follow the edge of the forest.

"Great." Shadow reluctantly followed. She was beginning to get sick of hearing that word.

When they were nearly half way around to the other side of the fortress, Carson stopped and dismounted. He cleared some snow from the ground near a tree so his horse could find the meagre frostbitten grass. Shadow did the same.

She watched as Carson pulled a white cloak from his saddlebags. This was much thinner than the one Carson had given her to wear.

"I don't suppose you've got a second one of those?" Shadow asked.

Carson shook his head and drew the cloak around him. It trailed on the ground. He pulled up the hood, took a few more items from his saddlebags and put them into his belt pouch. "Grab some food," Carson said, his back to her. "Leave your cloak with your horse."

Shadow frowned but did as she was ordered. "Now what?" Shivering, she crossed her arms over her chest to try and fight back the cold, but it didn't help.

Carson turned to look at her and grinned. "Now for some cuddling."

"What?" Shadow stomped after him as he made his way to the edge of the forest. Cuddling. Sure. Like that was going to happen. Or if it did, he'd soon pull away like every other time. "Be serious."

"I am." Carson lay in the snow on his stomach.

"Lay along my back under the cloak. Make sure the cloak completely covers us."

"No way!" Shadow backed away from him as she realised his plan. "It's too far."

"That was an order. You have two options. Follow orders or be left behind."

There was steel in his voice and Shadow knew he was serious. She looked across the open area they had to cover. It seemed an extremely long distance. She stared at Carson lying in the snow. Unless you were right on top of him, you couldn't tell he was there. She took a deep calming breath and slowly let it out. Them or us, she reminded herself, and they've got my brother. Shadow felt the anger build again. There was no room for fear when the anger was there.

Lowering herself to the ground Shadow shivered as the snow chilled her body. She lifted the cloak and wriggled under to lie along the length of Carson's back, rearranging the cloak to cover them. Her legs hung between his and she held onto his shoulders. She only hoped he had the strength to get them to the fortress. Chin ups and push ups had seemed effortless to him. She had no idea if this would be more difficult.

"Ready?" Carson asked.

"And if I'm not?" Shadow replied.

"Too bad. Hold on and stay still."

Carson started to manoeuvre forward, using his arms to pull them, pushing with his feet. It was slow going. Every inch seemed to take forever.

"We should have waited for dark." Shadow's cheek rested on Carson's back.

He didn't answer.

"Surely we could have waited until dark. It'll be nearly dark when we get there," Shadow tried again.

"Shut up," Carson muttered.

"Humph." Shadow hung on. The warmth of Carson's back seeped through her, finally warming her body. She watched his shoulder bunch and relax as he pulled them along. Then a bright patch on the snow caught her attention.

"Stop! You're bleeding on the snow," Shadow hissed.

"How bad?" Carson asked.

Shadow peered carefully behind them. There was no blood. She looked along the side of Carson. There was a bright red spot near his hip and one just past his shoulder. As she watched, another one fell onto the white snow.

"Well?" Carson asked impatiently.

"You've probably torn it open again or something," Shadow said.

"Have we left a trail?" Carson asked.

"Not yet. Just three places under the cloak," Shadow said.

"Cover them. Then bind my cut better," Carson said.

"With what?" Shadow asked as she covered two of the bloodstains with snow. There was no point in covering the third, as Carson's blood still dripped onto it.

"Be creative," Carson grumbled.

Shadow frowned. She thought of the binding she'd wrapped around her breasts before leaving home. Sighing, she started to wriggle so she could get to it.

"What are you doing?" Carson growled.

"Being creative," Shadow snapped.

"Be careful."

Shadow managed to pull the binding out from the neck of her tunic. She looked at the thin cloth and frowned again. The blood would soak through it too quickly.

"We haven't got all day," Carson complained.

Shadow's hand went to the worn felt hat she wore. Taking it off, she folded it twice. Happy with the thickness, she held it against Carson's arm. "Lift up a little," Shadow said as she tried to bind his arm. Carson shifted and she was able to wrap the wound.

"That should hold." Shadow covered the bloodstained snow with clean snow.

"Let's hope," Carson said. "Are you ready?"

Shadow wriggled into place and took hold of Carson's shoulders. When Carson breathed in sharply, Shadow asked, "Are you all right?"

"Stay still," he muttered before he moved again.

"Humph!" Shadow snorted irritably. She lay her head on his back and watched his shoulder as it bunched and relaxed. Her feet felt cold where they dragged through the snow, the leather of her boots not thick enough to keep them warm. Her legs were cold too, the rest of her warm. She snuggled in a little closer and her eyes closed as she got comfortable.

"Damn it! Stay still," Carson hissed.

"Fine," Shadow muttered.

They covered the rest of the ground in silence.

When they reached the wall of the fortress, Carson stopped. "Get off. Stay close to the wall."

Shadow wriggled off Carson's back and leaned up against the wall. The cold air made her shiver. Carson pulled off the white cloak and gave it to Shadow to wrap around her. It was too long for her to wear it properly.

"What now?" Shadow asked.

"Shh." Carson looked around. "See anything?"

Shadow glanced around. "Yes!" she exclaimed. "The snow there has a bit of glitter to it."

Carson quickly dug the snow away from the place Shadow pointed at.

"There's a door in the wall," Shadow said.

"Can you see the lock yet?" Carson asked.

Shadow shook her head. A moment later, she said, "Now I can."

"Good." Carson reached into his belt pouch and pulled out a small cloth bag. "Put a couple of pinches of this onto the lock."

"What is it?" Shadow asked.

"You're going to have to stop with all the questions if you want to make a career of the army."

Shadow opened the bag and pulled out a pinch of the powder that seemed to cling to her fingers and wiped it against the lock. "I don't want to make a career of the army. I'm going to live in a quiet little town where nothing ever happens," Shadow said automatically. She wiped another pinch against the lock. "It doesn't look sticky. It looks as dry as dirt until you try to pick it up." She peered into the bag.

Carson took the bag from her and tucked it into his belt pouch. "Clean your fingers off in the snow." As soon as Shadow had cleaned her fingers, Carson said, "Look away. Stand so your back's to the lock."

"Why?" Shadow asked as she stood in the place Carson wanted her in. He moved to stand beside her.

Putting an arm around her shoulders, Carson said, "Don't you dare look back." He muttered a couple of words under his breath. There was a pop behind them and Carson dropped his arm and turned around.

"What was that?" Shadow asked when she turned to see the magic spell had been broken and the lock was a streak of melted metal down the front of the door.

"Never mind." Carson swung the door open, his sword in his hand.

"Why couldn't I look?" Shadow asked.

"Because it'd temporarily blind you."

"What would happen if I hadn't cleaned it off my fingers?"

"Extreme pain. It wouldn't mark you. It only melts metal. Now shut up. How can I listen for guards if you don't shut up? And to think I encouraged you to talk."

Shadow stepped inside with Carson and glanced around in the completely black corridor. Very little light penetrated the darkness and what did, barely made it a foot inside.

Carson unwrapped the bulky bandage around his arm. He dropped the bloody felt hat onto the floor and held out the material to Shadow. "Rebind it for me." When Shadow took the material, Carson asked, "Where'd it come from?"

Shadow was glad it was dark enough Carson couldn't see the blush staining her cheeks. "From around my chest," she mumbled.

Carson chuckled. "You're nothing if not resourceful." As soon as Shadow finished, Carson shut the door behind them.

Shadow jumped slightly. "It's pitch black. I can't see anything."

"Any magic?"

"No."

"Good," Carson started to move forward.

"We'll trip over and break our necks."

"Shut. Up." Carson drew the words out through clenched teeth.

"I can't find you," Shadow whispered.

She felt a hand on her face and nearly screeched until she realised it must be Carson. His hand dropped to her shoulder and then travelled along her arm. Shadow shivered, and not from the cold.

"Hold onto my belt." Carson took her hand and placed it there.

Shadow's fingers tightened around the leather and she moved forward as Carson did. Shortly, they turned a corner. Shadow breathed a sigh of relief when she could see more clearly. Part way along the stone corridor magic glowed on the wall. This soft glow was enough to give Shadow some light to see by.

Chapter Nineteen

"There's magic ahead. I can see a bit better now," Shadow said. "Do you want me to go ahead?"

"Careful," Carson warned.

"There's nothing here."

"What's magic hid?"

"I don't know. I'm not close enough. I can't see how far this corridor goes. There doesn't seem to be any doors or passages leading off it," Shadow said as they walked towards the glow.

"Are we at it yet?" Carson asked.

"Nearly. It looks like a passageway." Shadow took a few more steps and stopped. She took a step into the corridor and yelped as Carson slammed her against the corridor wall. A sudden hiss passed by and several thuds sounded against the wall from the trap she'd set off. "That… I… arrows," Shadow stuttered.

"Don't you ever do that again," Carson growled

before his lips descended on hers. "I told you to be careful." The words were said against her lips before he pulled back slightly.

Shadow stared up at Carson. Dazed. "Why?"

Carson pushed away from the wall. "Enough questions."

Shadow grabbed his arm. "Why?"

Carson remained silent. He blindly reached out to her and his hand found her shoulder. His fingers lightly skimmed her skin until they reached the back of her head and he drew her close. "Twice in one day I've feared for your life. Do you know how much effort it took to send Wardell and not go myself when you screamed?"

Shadow shook her head, his fingers still threaded through her hair.

"I've been trained to put duty first. I've never before come so close to forgetting that training."

Shadow hesitantly reached out to press her hand against his chest, his heartbeat rapid under her palm. "Captain-" she broke off when he smiled.

"Captain? Really? Isn't that a bit formal for someone you've just kissed?"

Shadow grinned even though she knew he couldn't see it. "Carson-"

This time his lips interrupted her. Shadow's hand

was crushed between them, the other going around his waist. All sense of cold vanished as she lost herself in the kiss. She clung to him when he tried to pull away.

"You're a distraction. Even as a boy. I couldn't figure you out. Nothing added up. You couldn't completely hide yourself and flashes of you came through. Especially your tenacity. I've always admired that about you." Carson's arms tightened on her before he let her go. "We need to find everyone before the guards realise we're here." He looked back into the corridor they'd come from. "What's out there?"

"Nothing. I can't see anything from here. Just empty corridors." Shadow watched Carson, knowing he couldn't see her. In the dark his face was less guarded. He put out his hand before he stepped towards her, trying to find his way. Shadow took his hand.

Carson reached forward with his other hand, his sword having been sheathed not long after they'd entered the dark corridors. He ran his fingers through her jagged hair. "How long was it?"

"Why?"

Carson sighed. "Come. Back to the main corridor." He turned and moved cautiously forward, one hand still held Shadow's the other outstretched to prevent himself from running into a wall.

"To my waist," Shadow said softly.

Carson paused and looked back at her, a slight smile, his words soft. "Grow it again." He turned and moved along the corridor.

"Yes, sir," Shadow snapped.

Carson chuckled. "Please."

The light from the magic hid passage began to drop behind them and Shadow started to walk hesitantly, afraid she'd run into a wall. Another sharp corner and light shone from openings halfway along the passage. They hurried forward and peered cautiously down the left and right passages that intersected with the one they were on.

"Intruders!" A guard yelled to their right and ran towards them. They heard the sound of footsteps.

Carson pushed Shadow back into the main corridor. He fumbled in his belt pouch. "Your cloak. Quickly." He handed Shadow the small cloth bag and took the cloak she gave him. He spoke two strange words softly but clearly. "Activation words. Hide. Come back to this guarded door. I'll draw them away." He pressed a quick kiss against her lips and then turned her and pushed her back the way they'd come.

Shadow stumbled. Hearing a roar behind her, she turned to see Carson throw the cloak at a guard as he came into the corridor. He pulled his sword from his scabbard and thrust it into the guard in one smooth movement. The white cloak was instantly stained red, the patch growing larger.

"Go!" Carson ordered.

Shadow turned back the way they'd come. She ran down the corridor and stopped only when she reached the magic hid passage. Crouching, she ducked inside, not wanting to risk being impaled by an arrow. There was no sound. She hovered at the start of the passage, still hunched over. She wasn't taking a chance.

She could hear the sounds of swords clashing and guards yelling. She heard Carson as he tormented the guards attacking him and then heard the sound of running feet.

"Coward," a guard called out.

"Catch me if you can, clod," Carson mocked.

Shadow moved further along the passage, the sounds from the fight growing softer until she could no longer hear them. She came to a door. It was locked. Light from behind it shone around the edges.

"Who's there?" someone demanded from inside. "Answer me."

"Who are you?" Shadow risked standing up straight. Nothing happened.

"I believe I asked first," the voice answered.

"You're the one locked in," Shadow pointed out.

There was a chuckle from inside. "You win. Thornton."

"As if that helps any," Shadow complained.

"Thornton, Prince of Relthon."

"Typical. He tells me everything but a name," Shadow complained.

"Who tells you everything but a name?"

"The Captain." Shadow wasn't sure if she should give any more information than that. She didn't know if it was the prince locked up. It could be a trap.

"Captain? You don't mean Carson?"

"You know him?"

Thornton laughed. "Know him she asks! Of course I know him. I shared a womb with him. If only he could have done me the courtesy of being born first."

"What! Carson? Are we talking about the same Carson? Captain Carson Relth?" Shadow asked uncertainly.

"Let me out. And what's your name? I can't call you girl. My mother would be appalled at the rudeness of it. And what are you doing here? Where's the army? Surely my family didn't send a single female with my brother. Although I'm sure he wouldn't have complained."

Shadow stared at the door and worried at her lip with her teeth.

"Are you still there?" Thornton asked.

"Yes."

"Can you let me out?"

"How do I know you're the prince?"

"Guess you'll have to chance it. Come on. I don't have a single weapon in here. I'm sure you're armed to the teeth. You'd have to be to get this far."

Shadow frowned. She only had a knife in her boot and a dagger hanging from her belt.

"You still haven't told me your name."

"Shadow."

"Unusual."

"Isn't it just," Shadow said bitterly.

"Ah. Sounds like there could be a story there. But how about we wait till we're out of here to discuss it. Be a good girl Shadow and let me out."

Shadow gritted her teeth, annoyed by his condescending tone. "I don't think I like you."

"Fine! Just let me out," Thornton said impatiently.

"No."

"Oh for crying out loud. Shadow!"

Shadow started to laugh. "All right. Don't be so impatient."

"You've got to be kidding me. One minute you want me to spend the rest of my life in here and the next you're laughing at me and planning to open the door. What gives?"

Shadow started to smear the powder on the lock. "You sounded like Carson. The exact words and everything. Don't look for a minute."

"Ah, the metal melter?"

"Yes." Shadow turned her back. She remembered the smears on her fingers and opening the bag she tried to wipe them off against the material in the top. Hoping it was all off, she emptied her mind and tried to remember the words.

"Are you going to activate it?" Thornton asked.

"If you're so anxious to get out, why don't you?"

"I will," Thornton said before he spoke the activation words.

There was a pop behind Shadow and she turned to see the lock was a streak of melted metal marring the door. The door swung open and Shadow stared at Thornton.

"Anything you want, my lady, it's yours." Thornton made a flourishing bow.

Chapter Twenty

Shadow stared at Thornton in surprise. He was the same build as Carson, but his hair was longer, and not neat like it had been in the painting. Now she could see him face forward, he reminded her a lot of Carson. There were a few differences. Carson's lips were not as thin, and his nose was the slightest bit crooked where it had been broken before. Thornton's hair hung knotted down his back, his clothes were torn and dirty and hung loosely on him.

"If I'd known I was to have a visitor I'd have dressed accordingly," Thornton said dryly.

Shadow blushed. "Sorry. I was surprised at how much you look like each other."

"But I'm the more handsome one, right?" Thornton grinned.

Shadow smiled weakly. "We have to go." She turned and moved back along the passageway.

"Wait up. I've got to get my lantern," Thornton called.

Shadow waited impatiently as Thornton fetched the lantern and came into the corridor with it. "Ready now?"

"After you, my lady." Thornton gestured towards the corridor.

Shadow shook her head at his bantering and moved quietly towards the magic hid opening, Thornton following until they nearly reached the end.

"What are you doing?" Thornton asked.

"What do you mean?"

"A dead end." Thornton pointed towards the magic hid opening.

"Oh." Shadow laughed and grabbed his hand. Before he could protest, Shadow pulled him forward and into the main corridor.

"I'd have been stuck in there for decades." He glanced back. "I can still only see a solid wall."

"Come. Time's wasting," Shadow muttered.

"You've been hanging around my brother too long."

"Not for much longer." She was certainly going to have words with him about not telling her he was a prince. There'd been a few times when he could have easily told her, such as when he'd said the prince had been like a brother to him.

The corridors were empty, except for the two dead bodies they stepped around. Shadow hurried along to the door where the guard had been standing earlier. She smeared some of the powder on the lock and wiped her finger clean in the bag and turned her back on the door.

"When you're ready, say the words," Shadow said softly as she closed her eyes.

Thornton turned his back to the door and whispered the activation words. When the pop sounded, he turned to Shadow. "Do you know them?"

"Of course."

Thornton smiled. "Just not very well, huh?"

Ignoring him, Shadow flung the door open. The men inside leapt to their feet. "Irlan!" Shadow ran to her brother and threw her arms around him, holding him tightly.

"Uncle! Fancy meeting you here." Thornton smiled. "The people you meet when you're away from home."

"That's enough lip from you, boy." General Farnell strode forward to clap Thornton on the shoulder. He glanced around. "Where's Carson?"

"Uncle?" Shadow asked.

"Never mind that? Where's Carson? What about the rest of the men?" Farnell demanded.

"Carson led the guards away," Shadow said.

"Then we'd better find him." Farnell started for the door.

"Come, my lady. Show us which way he went," Thornton said.

Shadow groaned as Farnell turned and stared at her. He looked towards Irlan.

"I'll be talking to the pair of you later." Farnell glanced between Irlan and Shadow. "There's obviously a great deal more to discuss than I first thought."

"Come on, Uncle," Thornton said.

Shadow looked at the five soldiers with Irlan and Farnell. "Weren't there six?"

"We lost one. Now move!" Farnell strode into the corridor. He stopped at the two bodies and removed a sword from one and a long dagger from the other, handing the dagger to Thornton. "You'd better remember how to use this."

"After the amount of time you spent teaching us and hitting us with the broadside of your blade I doubt I'd ever forget," Thornton said.

"Good." Farnell turned to Shadow. "Which direction?"

Shadow pointed straight ahead and they moved along the corridor. Several more twists and turns later they came to another body. Farnell ordered one of his men to pick up the sword.

"Now where, girl?" Farnell demanded.

"It's Shadow." She stared him straight in the eyes.

Farnell glared back.

Shadow had put up with enough. Being female was not a bad thing and she refused to let Farnell act like it was. She raised her chin and continued to glare at him.

Finally Farnell said, "Which way, Shadow?" He stressed her name.

Shadow looked around. A fight won and no information to give him. She reached out and placed her hand on the stone of the corridor wall. The cold seeped into her and reminded her of the snow outside. She closed her eyes and wished she could find Carson.

She felt a vibration under her hand then she saw him, racing along corridors. He turned to attack a soldier who came close, leaping past him into an open room. The seven guards poured into the room after him. They circled him, swords drawn, all believing their rat cornered.

"No!" Shadow raced down corridors, following the maze she'd seen Carson take. Behind she could hear Farnell yelling at her to slow down. She didn't listen. Rounding a corner, she could hear the soldiers taunt Carson.

"No smart remarks?" one of the soldiers demanded.

"Cat got your tongue?" another tormented.

"No, but my sword will soon have it," another promised.

"No!" Shadow burst into the room, trying to come to a halt. She was moving too fast and collided with one of the soldiers. His arm went immediately around her waist and the other, which held his sword, went to her throat.

"Shadow!" Carson lunged forward. One of the soldiers barrelled into him and knocked him to the ground.

There was the sound of feet in the doorway behind them and the soldier holding Shadow turned and backed further into the room.

"Come any closer and I slit this one's throat," the soldier warned.

"Slit it." Farnell stepped into the room.

"No!" Carson and Irlan shouted together.

The soldier chuckled. "Sounds like insubordination to me. So what'll it be? Surrender?" The soldier turned slightly. "Or this one's throat slit and the one on the ground impaled."

Shadow saw Carson lying on the floor, a sword pressed against his back between his shoulder blades. She inhaled sharply.

"That bother's you, does it?" the soldier asked Shadow.

Shadow didn't answer. She frantically tried to think of something to do. Seconds counted. Something had to be done. Her mind raced. Her heart kept pace.

"We can afford a couple of casualties," Farnell said with a shrug.

"Not those two," Thornton argued as he reached his uncle's side.

"Make a decision. Drop your weapons and give up or I'll slit this one's throat and give the order to despatch that one." The soldier nodded towards Carson. "I'll give you to the count of ten."

"Can you count that high?" Carson asked.

"Right! You go first," the soldier promised Carson.

"No!" Shadow protested. Suddenly she knew what she could do. Her fingers groped for the bag she had hung at her belt.

"Oh how touching. What's he to you? Your lover?

Does he dress you as a boy so he can sneak you along with him on campaigns?" the soldier taunted.

"Leave her be," Thornton said.

At the same time, Carson demanded, "Let her go. She isn't part of this."

Shadow's fingers dipped into the bag. She felt the powder stick to her fingers. She didn't know if it was enough. She smeared more on them, spreading it to her palm.

"Her bad luck then, isn't it?" the soldier sneered. "One... two."

"How can we trust you to keep your word?" Thornton asked.

"Don't even think it," Farnell ordered.

Shadow pulled her fingers out of the bag, her gaze meeting Carson's.

"Three... four."

"I outrank you, Uncle." Thornton smiled.

"This is battle. I outrank you," Farnell argued.

"Five."

"Shadow! No!" Carson shouted as she raised her hand above her head, ignoring the blade that pressed harder against her throat.

"Six."

"Say it," Shadow ordered Carson.

"No," Carson said.

"Seven… eight."

"Do you want to die?" Shadow closed her eyes, but could still see what happened in the room, like she had in the corridor.

"Nine… t–"

Chapter Twenty-One

Carson closed his eyes and said the words to activate the powder. Thornton closed his own eyes, barely in time, as he turned and pushed his uncle towards the men in the doorway.

There was a pop. Light flared in the room and Shadow screamed. She dropped to her knees as the arm and sword imprisoning her let go. There was bedlam as soldiers called out, temporarily blinded. Carson staggered to Shadow who clutched her hand to her chest, tears streaming down her cheeks. She breathed shallowly as she tried to fight the waves of nausea that rushed in with the overwhelming pain.

"I tried to tell you." Carson cradled Shadow.

She barely heard him. All she could focus on was pain. Even the relief of escape did nothing to alleviate it.

Thornton, Farnell and two of the soldiers with

them rushed into the room, disarmed the guards and tied them up. There were cries of fright as the enemy stared blindly around.

"We've got to get out of here." Thornton crouched beside his brother.

Carson nodded.

"Do you need any help?" Thornton looked towards Shadow huddled in his brother's arms.

"I've got her." Carson lifted her. "Although you could get my sword for me." He smiled fleetingly. "I'd miss it."

All of them were armed again. As they made their way through the corridors, Farnell and Thornton led the way. The two soldiers who could see led their three companions and Irlan who had been blinded by the flash of light. They eventually came to the door that led into the snow. Farnell swung it open to show it was pitch black outside.

Carson looked at the felt hat that still lay on the floor and pushed it with the toe of his boot towards his brother. Thornton picked it up and glanced towards Carson who nodded. Thornton tucked the hat into the back of his belt and blew out the light of the lantern before they followed Farnell and the soldiers outside.

"Guess this is why you couldn't wait for night,"

Shadow murmured, the pain in her hand now bearable.

"So it was," Carson said.

Shadow heard the smile in his voice. "You can put me down."

"If I have to." Carson steadied Shadow when her feet touched the ground. "Are you all right?"

"Yes."

Carson's lips brushed across hers. "If you ever do anything so stupid again, I'll slit your throat," he growled.

"Sure." Shadow couldn't hold back the smile that formed.

"Can you two quit pawing each other so we can get out of here? Girls don't belong in the army for a reason," Farnell snapped.

"What!" Irlan demanded. "Get your hands off my sister. Who is it? Shadow?"

"How long until they can see again?" Shadow asked.

"You tell me. How long until you feel no pain?" Carson asked.

"I don't know. It feels like I shoved my hand in a fire."

"Shadow? Who is it?" Irlan demanded.

"Move it!" Farnell snapped, giving Irlan a push towards the trees.

They quietly walked across the open area to where the horses had been left. They whickered softly.

"Sorry old boy." Carson patted the neck of his horse. "Shadow, you and Irlan can ride on my horse. Two of the blinded soldiers can go on your horse."

"What about the other two?" Shadow asked.

"They'll have to stumble through the dark until we get back to the other men," Carson said.

"Will they have made it, do you think?" Shadow asked.

"We'll soon see," Carson said softly.

"How many did you lose?" Thornton asked.

"Quit gossiping. Move it!" Farnell snapped. "Now!" Farnell ordered when Thornton didn't move.

They stumbled through the dark until they were far enough from the fortress to be able to light the lantern. Carson put his tinderbox back in his belt pouch and handed the lantern to his brother.

Shadow gasped when she saw how exhausted Thornton was. She slipped off the horse. "You ride," she said to him.

"I will not ride while a woman is forced to walk," Thornton protested.

"Then I'll hit you over the head and have you

thrown over the horse like a sack of grain. Don't be stupid. You can barely stand up. I haven't spent the last few months in a cell," Shadow said.

Carson laughed at his brother's expression. "You'd better do it. It wouldn't surprise me if she did knock you out. And you don't look like you can defend yourself."

"Don't you know hitting the heir of the realm is a punishable offence? Look at how many witnesses I have." Thornton waved towards the men who turned their backs on him. "Fine," he grumbled and hauled himself into the saddle with Irlan. "Is your sister always like this?"

"Sometimes. She gets these notions occasionally," Irlan said. "Can be real stubborn."

Carson draped his arm around Shadow's shoulders. "Are you well enough to walk?"

"There's nothing wrong with my legs," Shadow said.

"That's not what I asked."

"I'll live. Hopefully. Oh no!"

"What?" Carson demanded.

"The boulders blocking the tunnel."

Hearing Shadow's words, Farnell demanded, "What's she talking about?"

Carson sighed and explained it to Farnell.

"Will we need to find another exit or can we move the boulders?" Farnell asked.

"I don't know. But I'm guessing we won't have the time to move the boulders. We'll have to get away as quickly as possible. We'll have soldiers following as soon as those guards are found," Carson said.

"Oh great," Shadow muttered.

"I knew that'd please you," Carson teased.

"Why are you so happy?" Shadow demanded.

"We're out of there. You're safe, the prince is safe and we found the General," Carson said.

"Your brother is safe," Shadow corrected.

"Ahh. What exactly did Thornton tell you?"

Shadow had never heard him so hesitant before. "Not much, Captain Relth, I mean Prince Carson of Relthon. I should have known something was odd that you're named after our country."

"Actually, the country's named after our family."

"Why didn't you tell me?"

"I did a bit," Carson said.

"Second son! Sure," Shadow muttered.

"I am."

"The second born twin of the King and Queen," Shadow corrected.

"Exactly. The second son."

"You're a prince?" Irlan demanded.

"Not exactly," Carson said.

"We've got to talk about that," Thornton said.

"No," Carson stated.

"You're more suited to all this," Thornton argued.

Carson shook his head. "I'm a soldier, not a statesman."

"I'm not interested in all the rubbish that goes with it. Or the headaches," Thornton said.

"Will someone tell me what's going on?" Shadow demanded.

"He wants to abdicate," Carson said.

"He what?" Shadow asked.

"I'm not king material," Thornton protested.

"He wants you to be the next king?" Shadow asked incredulously.

"If you'd waited a bit longer it wouldn't have been a problem," Thornton pointed out.

"You wanted to die?" Carson shouted.

"No, of course not. But if I had, you'd have been stuck with the job," Thornton said.

"We're not discussing this anymore." Carson looked away from his brother.

"Good." Farnell snapped. "I'm sick of hearing about it. Ever since you were children you've fought over who doesn't want to be king. Most people would kill to have the chance to be king. Hell! Are you both blind? What do you think all this has been about? Someone has been killing to get the throne."

"You don't want to be king?" Irlan said incredulously.

"I'd much rather have a nice estate, a pretty little wife and a quiet life," Thornton said. "What do you say, Shadow? Interested?"

"No," Carson answered for her.

Thornton chuckled. "I thought that."

"Shut up!" Farnell ordered.

"Yes, Uncle," Thornton said.

"General." Farnell quickened his pace.

Chapter Twenty-Two

The carnage on the trail brought them to a stop. Farnell, who held the lantern hissed, "Ambush places."

"What does that mean?" Shadow whispered as Carson led her and his horse into the bushes.

"That we don't make an easy target of ourselves," Carson said as soon as they were amongst the bushes. "Any magic?"

Shadow looked around. "No."

When Farnell was alone on the trail, he called out. "This is General Farnell Serensten. Any survivors?"

"General? It's Perrun." Perrun lifted his hand so Farnell could find him amongst the bodies.

"Perrun. How bad is it soldier?" Farnell knelt beside him.

"Can't feel my leg, sir. I must have blacked out at some point. Head feels like it's about to explode. Saw

Gwyn fall. And Roper. Don't know about Clem or Wardell," Perrun said.

"General!"

"Is that you Gwyn?"

"Yes, sir." He raised his arm for a second and then dropped it again.

"Saw you fall," Perrun said.

"Was Clem, sir," Gwyn said. "He turned on me. I ran out to warn you, but he hit me with something. Said money talks louder than loyalty." Gwyn struggled to sit up. Farnell helped him. Gwyn gingerly touched the back of his head. "Felt like a rock or something. Broke me head open good whatever it was."

Farnell stood up. "All out." The men came out of the forest.

Carson went first to Gwyn, checked his head wound and helped him to his feet. He knelt at Perrun's side and stared at his leg. "Probably a good thing you can't feel your leg, Perrun."

"Don't take it off, sir." Perrun clutched at Carson's sleeve.

"If we can't get you to a healer in a few days we might have to. You don't want to lose your life for the sake of a leg," Carson said.

"Check for horses," Farnell ordered the soldiers who could still see. "How's your hand, girl?"

"Still hurts," Shadow said.

"Girl!" Perrun glanced over to Shadow.

"Later," Carson said. "Let's get you out of this mess first."

"Did you find my sword?" Perrun asked.

"We'll find it," Carson promised.

"Only two horses, General," one of the soldiers reported.

"Check for weapons and gear we might find handy. See if you can find Roper or Wardell," Farnell ordered. "And if any of you find Clem still alive, try not to kill him. I need to have a little talk with him." His tone said the talk would be anything but pleasant.

Shadow knelt beside Perrun and looked at his leg. "Is there anything we can use to wrap it up? It's still bleeding."

"Starting to feel it now you've moved me," Perrun said. "Might have been better off staying put."

"Chin up, soldier," Farnell ordered.

When Shadow was about to snap at Farnell, Carson put his hand on her shoulder.

"I'll get something for binding. Wait here," Carson said.

"What's a woman doing traipsing around with soldiers?" Perrun asked.

"Escaping from other problems," Shadow said.

"Looks like you've stumbled into worse," Perrun said.

"Looks like it."

"General. We found Roper and Wardell. They didn't make it, sir," one of the soldiers said. "And there's no sign of Clem."

"Lay them to rest as best you can," Farnell ordered.

"Here," Carson shoved a torn and bloody tunic into her hands.

"This is the best you can do?" Shadow demanded.

"The laundress is nowhere to be found," Carson replied.

Perrun laughed.

Shadow glared at him. "It's your leg I've got to wrap this filthy thing about."

Perrun laughed again. "That's clean compared to some of the things I've had to use for bandages. Beggars can't be choosy."

As soon as Perrun and Gwyn had been doctored as well as could be expected, they were helped onto a horse each, along with a still blind soldier.

"We should make better time now," Farnell said as they set out.

By mid morning, the soldiers and Irlan could see again. They dismounted and let someone else have a turn riding. Irlan insisted Shadow take his place.

She eyed him up and down. His cheekbones were more prominent than usual. "Are you sure?"

Irlan nodded. "Yes."

"Good." She slapped him across the side of his head.

"What was that for?" Irlan rubbed the spot, glaring at her.

"Your stupid plan." She hopped on the horse in front of Thornton.

"Isn't this cosy." Thornton put his arms around Shadow's waist.

"Not for long." Carson pulled his brother off the horse. "Go find another horse to ride on." He swung up behind Shadow.

"That wasn't nice," Shadow said.

"He was asking for it," Carson said. "Besides, you got to hit your brother."

"That was different," Shadow muttered.

Still on the snowy ground, Thornton laughed. "Your expression was worth every bruise I'll have."

"Men!" Shadow rolled her eyes.

"Have a sleep. The General will push us hard," Carson warned.

"Why?" Shadow tilted her head so she could look back at him.

"We have to get out of here before we're trapped by the enemy," Carson said.

Carson was correct. The general pushed them hard. They alternated between walking and riding with riding the only rest allowed to any of them.

By the time they reached the clearing near the pass, the horses were being led, too exhausted to carry anyone other than Perrun. Farnell made his way immediately to the boulders.

He turned, issuing orders as he did so, "Thornton, Shadow. Stay here. Keep a look out. Gwyn, rub down the horses and see if you can find somewhere to tie them with a bit of grass, maybe under the trees. Carson, take two soldiers and head that way, Irlan, you go with the other three and scout the opposite direction. Look out for another way out of this valley. I prefer not to have to try and lower ourselves and the horses over that." He pointed towards the area where the guards who had pushed the boulders over had been. "I'm going hunting."

"Why do you get the fun job?" Thornton complained.

"Because I'm the general and you're the heir to the kingdom. The one others lose their lives for."

Thornton glared at Farnell. "You would have to remind me."

"You can find a shady spot for Perrun to lie in if you want something to do." Farnell strode into the forest, a crossbow ready.

"Anywhere in particular you want to lie?" Thornton asked Perrun as he helped him up off the ground where he'd been left.

Perrun grinned. "As close to home as I can get."

"Home it is." Thornton supported Perrun as he hobbled to a tree in the appropriate direction.

Shadow followed. "Thornton. Look. Oh, forget it. You won't see them. Wait here."

Thornton quickly left Perrun under the tree. "Wait up. We're not to leave the clearing. Orders you know."

"Stuff orders. There's four horses magic hid," Shadow said.

"It might be a trap." Thornton fell in beside her.

"There were four guards here and this is the direction they were headed when they tried to escape."

"Why didn't you see the horses when you came through here?" Thornton asked.

"Because there's a dip in the ground and I didn't come over this far. Look, can't you see the hay left on the ground for them under that tree?" Shadow pointed.

"I can, but I can't see any horses. How are we meant to ride them if we can't see them?" Thornton demanded.

Shadow shrugged. "Your problem. I'll give two of them to you." She grinned at him. "Wait here and I'll untie them from the tree."

Thornton watched as Shadow reached up and unwrapped something from one of the branches and then walked towards him, her hand held at the correct angle it would need to be to lead a horse.

"Here. Hold this," Shadow pushed the reins into Thornton's hand.

"Reins!"

"Of course. I did tell you."

Shadow soon collected all the horses and they took them to where Perrun lay under the tree.

"How're we meant to ride them if we can't see to get on them?" Perrun asked.

"See." Thornton grinned at Shadow.

"Oh, shut up." Shadow frowned at the horses.

"What've you got?" Gwyn joined them.

"Horses. Four of them. There's more hay over where we got them from." Shadow gestured in the direction.

"I'll get it for our horses," Gwyn said.

"I'll help you," Thornton offered.

"My lord, the General expects you to wait here," Gwyn said.

"Too bad, I've already left the area following her." Thornton gestured towards Shadow.

Gwyn shook his head. "I can't stop you, my lord, but…" He finished his sentence with a shrug.

When the two men left, Shadow continued to stare at the horses thoughtfully.

"What if you shot them with a crossbow? It worked with the men we killed," Perrun said.

Shadow's frown cleared. "That might work. Well, not shooting them with a crossbow, but making them bleed." Shadow took her knife from her belt and stood uncertainly near one of the horses. "I don't want to hurt him."

"Find a good vein and prick it with the point of the blade. Won't take much," Perrun assured her.

Shadow nodded. "I hope not." She closed her eyes briefly. You can do this, she told herself sternly. Come on. She opened her eyes, took a deep breath, held it and quickly did as Perrun suggested. Her breath whooshed out as she jumped away from the horse as it reared, whinnying in fright. "I'm sorry." Shadow soothed the animal.

"I can see it," Perrun exclaimed. "It worked. Quickly. Do the others."

"Great," Shadow muttered. "Three more to do." She got on with the task and all four horses were visible by the time Gwyn and Thornton returned with their arms full of hay. The horses followed along behind the men, wanting the hay they carried to their own horses.

"Not a bad effort." Thornton stood with hands on his hips as he looked over the eight horses. "We'll all be able to ride. Only half of us will have to double."

"If we can find a way out of here," Shadow said.

"You know, you should be the one doing the scouting. How will they find a way out of here? It's sure to be magic hid," Thornton said.

"I didn't think of that." Shadow glanced around. "What if they run into hidden guards? We have to go after them." Shadow looked first towards where Carson had gone and then in the direction her brother had taken. "I can only go in one direction."

"Settle down. There's nothing you can do about it," Thornton said.

"But-"

"Come on. Let's see what's with all those boulders." Thornton grabbed her by the hand and tugged her forward. "I'm not letting go so you might as well come quietly."

"I'll remember this," Shadow muttered.

Thornton grinned. "I hope so. Having a nice hand holding romantic walk in a snow capped pine forest with the heir to a country shouldn't be a forgettable moment."

Shadow laughed reluctantly.

"That's better. Come on. We might as well use the time rather than sit around wringing our hands and moaning."

"I never wring my hands," Shadow protested.

"What about moan?"

"What's going on?" Carson strode ahead of his men out of the forest.

"Carson. You're safe." Shadow dashed forward and threw her arms around him.

"Well, if that's the greeting I'm going to get every time I wander off it might pay to disappear more often." Carson's arms tightened around her as he bent his head to kiss her.

"What if there'd been magic hid guards? We have to go after Irlan. He can't see them either," Shadow said.

"I'm back." Irlan came out of the forest in time to

hear the last couple of sentences. "And what do you think you're doing? Get away from my sister."

"Enough," Shadow snapped. "How did either of you expect to find a way out of here when you can't find anything magic hid."

"What I want to know is how you all managed to get in here in the first place?"

They turned to see a man on horseback enter the clearing.

Chapter Twenty-Three

"Pa!" Shadow tried to step away from Carson. His arms tightened around her.

"And who do you think you are? Get your hands off my daughter before I remove them permanently." Gil wrapped his reins around his saddle horn and pulled his sword from his scabbard.

"That's not a very friendly greeting." Farnell held three hares by their ears. "And where did those extra horses come from?"

"This keeps getting better and better," Shadow muttered.

"I should have known you'd be behind this." Gil glared at Farnell. "And tell your soldier to unhand my daughter. And you," Gil pointed at Irlan, "Have a lot to answer for."

"Carson, let the girl go," Farnell ordered.

"No, sir," Carson said respectfully yet firmly.

"That's an order," Farnell said.

"Tell him where to go and I'll abdicate right this minute," Thornton said. "All I own will be yours. Only say the word and you'll outrank him."

"What's going on here?" Gil demanded. "Abdicate? These aren't the princes, are they?"

"I'm afraid so." Farnell looked from one prince to the other.

"Then why aren't they at the castle where they belong? And I'll be damned if I let some man paw my daughter. Prince or not," Gil stated.

Farnell gestured towards Gwyn. "Take these and clean them. You," he pointed at another soldier, "Get a fire started. I want these cooked so we can move as soon as possible." He turned back to Gil once Gwyn had taken the hares. "Your kids came to me offering their services when you turned down my offer."

"Elf sight!" Gil roared. "Which one of you has it?" He leapt from his stallion and glanced between his two children, his sword pointed first at one then the other. "Tell me and I'll put you out of your misery."

"Me," both Irlan and Shadow called out.

"Forget it Irlan. He'll have to accept it. I've got elf sight."

"Don't be a fool. It's me." Irlan glared at his sister.

"Answer me. Or do you both have it? I'm not

passing it along! Twice cursed trait." Gil's hand tightened on his sword.

"It saved our lives plenty of times," Shadow said quietly.

"You, girl?" Gil looked horrified.

"Me." Shadow pushed Carson's arms from her and stepped forward. "And I refuse to hide it any longer. I'm proud of what I've done. We found the heir," she gestured towards Thornton. "I found him. I found the path you didn't want to look for. I saw armies hidden. A ravine, the passage Thornton was hidden behind. It was better than spending my time growing old serving ale in a tavern."

Gil stared at her and his sword lowered. It was the first time his daughter had ever spoken back to him. "I'd expect this kind of talk from your brother. He's always had a smart mouth. But not you."

"And what has staying in the background got me?" Shadow demanded. "I've been the image of my name. Well, no more. Cut me down where I stand if you want. I'm not going back to the tavern. I've got to find a way out of this valley and get Thornton to the castle."

"It's always the bloody royals. See what they do to you?" Gil glanced at his empty sleeve.

"So what?" Shadow demanded. "They were willing to let their firstborn die for us."

"They wouldn't have," Gil snarled.

"Yes they would. And I finally figured out why. It's not because they want to rule the country. It's because they know what it would be like if there wasn't law and order. Even their sons fight over who'll escape the duty," Shadow said.

"They're stringing you along," Gil said.

Shadow turned to Thornton. "Do you want to be king?"

"Hell no!"

"Will you be?"

"Only if I can't talk Carson into the chore," Thornton said.

Shadow turned to Carson. "What about you?"

"Only if I have no other choice. I've seen what a nightmare it is. Give me a position in the army any day. Even if we were permanently at war. Much easier."

"So, what's an arm in the whole scheme of things?" Shadow demanded.

"Tell me that when you've lost one," Gil said bitterly.

"I will," Shadow answered softly.

"Crazy child. Must have got knocked around the head as a tot," Gil muttered.

"And I know who did the knocking." Irlan stared defiantly at Gil.

Gil took a step towards Irlan, his sword coming up. "You better watch that mouth of yours, boy."

Farnell stepped forward and pushed Irlan back a couple of steps, his gaze on Gil. "No more talk of killing your offspring. Put away your sword. We'll eat and be on our way. The enemy won't be far behind. How'd you get in here?"

Gil stared at him a moment. "I'll deal with this later." He glanced towards Carson. "Without interference." He sheathed his sword. "I got in up that way." Gil pointed behind him. "Found the tunnel blocked and went further along. There's another way in but not as easy as the first."

"Looks like you can get a horse through there though." Farnell eyed Gil's stallion that stood patiently beside him.

Gil nodded then rounded on Carson when he saw him put his arm around Shadow's shoulders. "Get your hands off my daughter!"

"Carson! One day of peace," Farnell demanded.

Carson stared at Gil. "No more threats about

killing her and I'll keep my hands to myself. For now."

"Permanently," Gil ordered.

"One day of peace I was ordered." Carson's lips twitched and a smile erupted for the barest instant.

"One day. Then the truce is over," Gil warned.

"Or renegotiated," Farnell said.

"One day," Gil and Carson both said.

Carson dropped his arm from around Shadow's shoulder but stayed near her.

Once the meal was eaten, the horses were collected and they mounted. Gil would only tolerate Irlan riding with Shadow, no one else was acceptable apart from himself. Carson wouldn't tolerate that plan.

"They're driving me crazy," Shadow said to Irlan as they followed their Pa through the forest.

Irlan grinned. "It's good to see men who don't fall at his feet in a quivering heap when he bellows."

Shadow sighed. "I guess. I just wish I didn't feel so much like the bone between two dogs."

"Your farmer wouldn't have made you happy. You need someone who'll stand up to Pa. You wouldn't respect anyone who couldn't," Irlan said.

"Maybe."

"You know I'm right," Irlan said.

"Oh no!" Shadow's hand covered her mouth as she stared ahead.

"What?" Carson rode closer to see what was wrong.

"We've got to go through there," she pointed to the stream ahead of them that appeared to go through an opening then drop over a cliff.

"Over a cliff?" Carson demanded.

"No. We've got to go through a horrible little tunnel the stream flows through. We'll have to walk the horses. The stream goes fairly fast and the rocks are slippery. You really need to be able to see to get through here," Shadow said.

"Their problem," Gil snarled.

"I'm not leaving them behind," Shadow protested.

"They'll see once they get past the first few feet," Gil said with an unconcerned shrug.

"We'll have to help them through," Shadow stated.

"I'll help Irlan. The rest can find their own way," Gil said.

Shadow slipped off her horse as they reached the edge of the stream. Her hands went to her hips and she glared at Gil, anger pooling in her. "What sort of man are you? I never realised how pathetic you are. You'd leave them here? The General? The princes?

These men who follow orders. Even the poorest soldier has a better character than you."

"Don't give me no lip, girl. See this?" He pointed to his empty sleeve, reins held in his hand. "No, you can't. That's because it isn't there. It's because of the likes of these that it's not there. What would you know about it all?"

"Perrun might lose his leg. Tell me Perrun? Are you going to hate the world if that happens?" Shadow demanded.

"Well… ah… I guess not," Perrun stammered, embarrassed to be put on the spot.

"No backbone. That's why it won't bother him," Gil said.

"No backbone! I think you're the one with no backbone!" Shadow shouted.

Gil raised his hand to strike his daughter. Carson was there first, grabbing his wrist and bending his hand back.

"Don't touch her." Carson's voice was deadly quiet.

Chapter Twenty-Four

"You think I should listen to that? A man's got a right to discipline his kids," Gil growled.

"She's no longer a kid. She's a woman who doesn't have to answer to you," Carson warned.

"Then if she wants to be treated as one, she should act like one. Not running around the countryside with shorn hair and wearing her brother's clothes." Gil pulled away from Carson.

"I don't care if she wants to run around the countryside naked. You'll treat her respectfully," Carson said.

Thornton grinned. "That's something I'd want to see."

Carson ignored his brother. "Do you understand, Gil?"

"Forget about him," Shadow said. "He's not worth the effort. He's whining about losing an arm. What about Roper and Wardell? And the other soldiers that started out with us, the ones who lost their lives. I bet they would have loved to have only lost an arm. Come on. I'll lead you through. Even if it takes the rest of the day." Shadow turned her back on her Pa.

"Do you want to go first, General?" Shadow asked.

Farnell nodded and dismounted. He led his horse over to Shadow. "The princes next," he ordered.

"Yes, sir," Shadow saluted.

"Don't get cocky," Farnell warned.

Shadow grinned. She felt extremely good after finally telling her Pa how she felt. Like a massive weight had been lifted. "Take my hand, sir. It might be easier if you close your eyes. That way what your eyes see and what your body feels doesn't confuse you."

Farnell took Shadow's hand and closed his eyes. He let Shadow lead him into the water, listening to her as she told him where to step and what to avoid.

Before they entered the tunnel, Gil called out, "Shadow!"

Shadow turned. "What?"

"Don't let them walk over the cliff at the other end. The illusion begins again out there," Gil said.

Shadow stared at her Pa for a moment. "Thank you." She turned back to Farnell and explained to him where he was to step next. Once they were past the illusion, Shadow said. "All right. Head towards the other end. Not too far though. You heard my Pa, you'll fall over the cliff. Just go far enough to give the rest of them room to get in."

As Shadow stepped outside, her Pa walked past her, leading Irlan. She looked towards Thornton. "You're next. Come to the edge of the stream and close your eyes."

Thornton willingly followed, teasing her the whole time. Laughing, Shadow finally told him he could open his eyes. Expecting to lead Carson through next, Shadow was surprised to see Perrun there with Gwyn supporting him. Not having time to argue, Shadow led them through. It was more difficult to direct two men.

She came back out to find another soldier ready to go in. She looked at Carson. "I was told to bring the princes through first."

Carson looked around. "Nope, no prince around here. You must have already taken him through. I'm a captain, remember?"

"The General didn't want you going through last," Shadow said.

"We're wasting time. My men go first," Carson said firmly.

"You won't change his mind, ma'am," the soldier waiting for her said. "He's always last out of any trouble."

"Fine." Shadow turned back to the waiting soldier. "Close your eyes." She took his hand and led him through the opening. When she had taken all the men through, she glared at Carson waiting there for her. "Close your eyes."

"Shadow."

"What?"

Carson stepped close. His lips curved momentarily before he dipped his head to press them against hers.

Shadow's hands went to his chest as the kiss deepened. When she finally pulled away, she said, "I thought you weren't going to lay a hand on me."

Carson held up his hands, the reins of his horse dangling from one of them. He grinned. "Nowhere near you."

"I don't think that's exactly what Pa meant." Shadow fought back her own smile.

"Shall we find out?" Carson put his hands behind his back. He leaned forward.

"What's taking so long?" Gil demanded from the mouth of the tunnel. "What do you think you're doing?" He strode forward. "I told you to keep your hands off her."

Carson pulled his hands from behind his back, still grinning. "Not a single hand on her, Gil."

"You think you're funny, don't you? Come on. I'll take you through and we'll see how funny you are," Gil said.

"No. I'll take him through. Close your eyes, Carson." Shadow took one of his hands. He closed his eyes. "There's a step down into the water."

"You're a fool, Shadow. He's playing with you," Gil warned.

Carson opened his eyes and looked at Gil. "I'm not."

"You mean you'd marry some tavern keeper's daughter?" Gil gestured towards Shadow. "You're second in line for the throne if anything happens to your brother. I'm not a fool."

"I'm not a liar. I'd marry your daughter tomorrow," Carson said.

"You barely know me. You can't talk about marriage after so little time," Shadow protested.

Carson smiled down at her, his hand tightening on hers. "I do know you. And I know my own mind."

"Well I'm not marrying anyone. I'm too young." Shadow ignored the fact she'd been willing to marry Elrick to escape the tavern and turned to her Pa.

"Now you get back to the rest of them." She turned to Carson, "And you close your eyes."

"Your Ma was only a year older than you when we married," Gil said.

"Go!" Shadow pointed towards the tunnel.

"This matter isn't over." Gil turned and headed into the tunnel.

At the other end Shadow found Gil had left Irlan near the edge of the cliff so he could prevent the men from falling over. Once Carson was through the tunnel, Farnell ordered them all to mount up and head down the narrow trail.

Shadow travelled alone on a horse towards the front of the column, directly behind Carson and the General. All down the narrow trail Shadow kept glancing over her shoulder. It wasn't until they'd left the narrow trail well behind she noticed a glow filled the sky behind them.

She slowed her mount and moved to the side of the track so she could ride beside her Pa. "It's an army, isn't it?" She nodded to the glow behind them.

Gil didn't answer. Instead he looked past her to where Carson dropped back to join them. "Looks like the wrong person was called Shadow."

"The glow?" Shadow persisted.

"An army. At least a couple of hundred hidden

men," Gil said. "I don't know why they've bothered to hide them so soon. That many will make plenty of noise and leave tracks a blind man could follow."

Carson didn't bother to look behind them. "How far back?"

"Half a day," Gil said.

"Two hundred! We can't fight that many." Shadow cast another glance behind, her gaze drawn to the glow of magic.

"A few miles ahead there's a shortcut," Gil said to Carson.

"How much of a shortcut?" Carson asked.

"You could be with your men that are camped in the foothills in a day," Gil said.

"How will an extra fifteen men help?" Shadow asked.

"What's to stop the army from following?" Carson asked.

"I'll lay a false trail after I show you where the shortcut starts," Gil said.

"Is anyone listening to me?" Shadow asked.

Carson turned to her and smiled. "Haven't you learned yet? A good soldier never questions their superior officers."

"Haven't you learned? I'm not a good soldier and never likely to be. What's the plan?" Shadow asked.

"I won't leave behind any men if I can help it. We'll collect the men from the foothills and take it from there," Carson said.

"So in other words, you don't have a plan," Shadow said.

Carson turned to Gil. "Can you let the General know?" He waited until Gil rode ahead with a curt nod then turned to Shadow. "I do have a plan. To get you and my brother back to the castle in one piece."

"That's not a plan, that's a wish."

"As far as I'm concerned it's a plan. I need to discuss this with the General. Don't stay at the back of the line."

Shadow glared after Carson, frustrated by their conversation.

Thornton rode over to her, Irlan on the horse with him. "He makes you want to throw something at him sometimes, doesn't he?"

"What are you thinking of, getting mixed up with him?" Irlan demanded.

"There's nothing wrong with him," Thornton said.

"Go away the both of you," Shadow said. "Or I'll be throwing something at you. Something sharp." Her hand momentarily rested on her dagger. When they had ridden ahead, Shadow looked towards the glow in the sky. She shuddered as she thought of what an army of two hundred men on horses would look like. An army of thirty archers had been frightening enough.

Chapter Twenty-Five

Shadow sat away from the fire and watched as Carson, Farnell and Gil discussed their plan. As Gil had promised, it had taken nearly a full day to make it to the camp the soldiers had made in the foothills. He'd joined them an hour ago, having spent the rest of his time laying a false trail for the army to follow. The sky was clear of the glow of magic, but Shadow couldn't resist checking regularly. They couldn't face an army that size. They'd be slaughtered.

A soldier brought mugs of ale over to the fire, gave one first to Farnell and then to Carson. Shadow held her breath as the soldier held out the last mug to Gil. He started to reach for it and then dropped his hand, shaking his head. The soldier moved away and Shadow began to breathe again. He still might be moody and short tempered, but Shadow was finally starting to like the man her Pa was when he wasn't drunk. It had been far too many years since she'd seen him sober. Shadow glanced up as a soldier came to stand beside her.

"Iain." Shadow nodded as he sat down.

"What are ya doing here? It was bad enough when we thought ya were a young lad. But a lass should be at home. Not risking her life."

"Not you too," Shadow complained.

Iain grinned at her. "It's only because we care, lass. If my girl wanted to join the army I'd drag her home and chain her up till she came to her senses."

"And if she never came to her senses?"

Iain looked startled.

"It's not the life I'd have willingly chosen. But at least there's meaning to it. More meaning than keeping some man's tankard filled."

"Then find yourself a young man and get married. Have a heap of kids and wait for the grandkids to come along to spoil," Iain said.

"Would you do that?"

"What?" Iain looked confused by her question.

"Sit around home waiting for grandkids after you've raised your kids."

"Well, no, but-" Iain started to say.

"Then why should I be expected to?"

"So you're saying you're never going to marry. That you're going to stick with the army," Iain said.

"No." Shadow glanced towards Carson. "Maybe one day I'll marry, but for now, I want to do something important. When I do have those children and grandchildren I want to be able to tell them tales of what I did when I was younger. Tales that'll make them sit mesmerised and half disbelieving as they listen."

"Well, I reckon you'll be able to do that. If we ever live long enough for ya to have those kids."

"I reckon I will too," Shadow said thoughtfully.

"Will what?" Carson joined them.

"Plans made yet?" Shadow asked.

Carson draped an arm around Shadow. "None that you'll like."

"I'll leave ya to it," Iain said hastily. They barely noticed him leave.

"What are they?" Shadow demanded.

"I need you to see Thornton safely back to the castle."

"No." Shadow pushed his arm away.

"Your father will stay and help us if we send you and Irlan to safety. Someone has to get Thornton back to the castle. Someone who can see magic. Your father won't do it and leave you here to face the army. So it'll have to be you."

"No." Shadow shook her head. "You have to come too."

"I can't desert my men. They're my men, not General Farnell's. Only a few of them were his. He came along because of the importance of the mission. You can take any two men with you, your choice, and Perrun too. He needs a healer. That leg of his is looking pretty bad. Thornton knows of a healer about half a day from here."

"Farnell can take care of your men," Shadow protested.

"Please, Shadow. Help me complete this mission."

"That's not fair," Shadow wailed.

"Come for a walk." Carson rose and held out his hand.

Shadow hesitated then took his hand and let him help her rise. She walked with him to the edge of the camp where they stood in the privacy created by the darkness. Carson wrapped his arms around her and his gaze met hers before he lowered his head. His lips were gentle on hers until Shadow's own arms wrapped around him and her body moulded to his.

Minutes passed before Carson reluctantly pulled

away slightly. "I need you to do this. Do you know what'll happen if there's no heir?"

Shadow sighed. "You could take him back."

"You know better than that."

Shadow rested her head against Carson's chest. His arms tightened. "Promise to be careful?"

Carson's hand stroked her short hair. "I promise."

"When do we have to leave?"

"Before daybreak. I don't want too many people to watch you go. Who do you want to take with you?"

"Iain and Gwyn. I know them," Shadow said.

"I hope we can trust them."

"So do I."

"You be careful and wait for me." He reached into his belt pouch and pulled out a folded parchment. "Here. Give this to my parents for me."

"Why can't Thornton take it?"

"He'll read it. I trust you not to."

"You didn't always trust me. I had to hear from your brother who you are. All you told me was the prince had been like a brother to you." Shadow took the parchment.

"You knew who I was without him telling you all that rot. That isn't me. I'm a captain. I've been part of the army since I was five, remember?"

"What as? The mascot?"

Carson grinned momentarily and his lips brushed against her forehead. "No. Learning how to look out for myself in case I was kidnapped. Thornton learned too."

"Were either of you ever kidnapped?"

"You mean besides this time with Thornton?"

Shadow nodded.

"There were a few attempts."

"Do they still try and kidnap you? Or just Thornton?"

"Let's talk about more pleasant things," Carson said.

"They do! And you want me to marry you. You've got to be kidding me," Shadow exclaimed.

"I thought you turned me down."

"I did."

Carson laughed. "I'll ask you again when I return to the castle."

"I might not be there."

"You will." Carson kissed her again. "I hate that I've had to ask this of you. That I'm putting you in danger."

"I could stay with you."

He shook his head. "I guess either way you'd be in danger. I'm sorry."

"I'm not. I've never felt more alive in my life as I have these past months."

Carson slowly smiled. "I knew we'd make a soldier of you eventually." He pressed his fingers to his chest. "When your heart is racing you know you can't be anything other than alive."

Shadow grinned. "Battle isn't all that makes my heart race." She moved his fingers to her heart before her lips met his again.

Carson held her close, eventually breaking off the kiss. "You'd better get some sleep. I'll wake you. I've got last watch."

"Who'll organise the soldiers going with us?"

"I'll take care of that. I'll leave it till the last minute. I don't want to risk too many people knowing." He stared down at her for long moments before he took her hand and led her back to the fire.

"Where've you been?" Gil demanded when he saw them come towards him, holding hands.

"Goodnight." Carson looked at Shadow, ignoring Gil. His fingers momentarily tightened on hers before he let go and strode away.

Shadow watched him leave before she turned to her Pa. "I'll see you in the morning?"

Gil looked like he was about to say something and then changed his mind. He nodded.

Shadow was tempted to let the moment go, but she'd come too far for that. "What?"

"What do you mean?"

"You were going to say something." The silence stretched out and Shadow began to think her Pa wasn't going to answer.

"I woke up one morning to see your Ma packing her bag. I hadn't even realised you two had left. She never told me."

"Don't you think it's something you should have noticed?"

Gil shrugged. "She told me that since I couldn't let go of the past she'd be the one doing the letting go. That the tavern wasn't a home without her children and only a bitter old man. I need you to come back so she will."

"I don't think that's what she meant. I think she was probably talking about the bitter old man part."

"Watch your mouth, girl."

"Why don't you let her go? You hate everything and everyone. Why hold onto her?"

"You have no idea what you're talking about."

"Then tell me. If I'm so clueless why don't you explain it?" She met her Pa's glare, refusing to lower her gaze as she had so many times before.

It was Gil who looked away. "Everyone said it was

a miracle I survived. They all believed me dead. It wasn't a miracle. It was the thought of Gennie. The promises I made her." He met Shadow's gaze again. "I never thought she'd leave me. She's always been there for me. Always."

"Maybe she was sick of waiting for you to be there for her too."

Gil pointed a finger at her. "You don't know nothin'. I've been there for her. Only one time I wasn't and it was his fault." His gaze was drawn to Farnell before it returned to Shadow. "They care nothing about us, only what we can do for them. You're a fool for being here."

"I'm not–"

Gil interrupted. "But it doesn't matter. You will come home with me. I won't lose Gennie over this. They're not taking any more from me than they already have."

Shadow shook her head. "I'm not the only one who knows nothing. Ma believed you'd change. That you'd be the man she kept telling me you were. She probably figured out she was wasting her time." She turned away from Gil, ignoring his growl and crawled into her bedding, which was not far from the fire. Her Pa's bedding was on one side of her, on the other side was her brother's. She leaned on one elbow and gestured towards the bedding. "You can't keep me from going my own way."

"You're still my girl," Gil said possessively.

"I know," Shadow said heavily. "But I'm also my own person. Just like Ma is." She rolled over and, laying her head down, stared at the flames until she fell asleep.

Chapter Twenty-Six

It seemed like minutes since she'd closed her eyes before Carson leaned over her and brushed her cheek with the back of his hand. Shadow opened her eyes and looked up at him. She smiled sleepily. He returned her smile. She reached up and cupped Carson's cheek with her hand, sliding it around to the back of his neck to pull him closer.

"Get up," Gil growled softly from beside them.

Carson grinned then brushed his lips across hers before he slowly pulled away from her and rose to his feet.

Shadow sat up and saw her brother drag himself from his bedding. As soon as she rose, Carson draped his cloak around her shoulders.

"Go eat. I'll pack your bedding," Carson said softly.

When they were ready to leave, Carson, Gil and Farnell walked with them as they moved away from the camp. They had a horse each except for Perrun who was too ill to ride alone. He rode in front of Gwyn.

Carson hugged Shadow close. "Take care," he whispered against her ear.

"You too." Shadow turned her head so their lips met. Carson's arms tightened around her.

"Hurry up," Irlan complained. "It's freezing standing around here."

Carson's arms dropped from her and he pulled a battered item from where it was tucked into his belt and handed it to Shadow. She smiled when she saw it was her felt hat. Looking the worse for wear, but no longer bloody. She pulled it on as she turned towards Farnell. "Sir," a sharp nod accompanying her word. Then she turned to her Pa. She hesitated then threw her arms around him. "Take care of him for me."

Gil didn't pretend ignorance. "You're wasting your time."

Shadow pulled back and looked her Pa in the eye. "But you will, won't you?"

"If you stay at the castle till I come for you. I don't want to have to track you halfway across the country again."

"Deal." Shadow mounted her horse and looked back at Carson. He smiled at her. Shadow smiled weakly before she turned away and urged her horse forward.

"He'll be fine," Thornton said when they were far enough away no one would hear them. He wore clothes that several soldiers had given him since his own had been unsalvageable. Even the clothes of a lowly soldier couldn't take away the air of authority that seemed to surround him.

"I hope so."

"He's faced worse odds and made it through. Why do you think he was made a captain so young?" Thornton asked.

"I don't know. He never told me."

"Don't look at me like that. You'll have to ask Carson. I'm not telling tales he might make me regret telling," Thornton protested.

They kept their horses at a fast pace most of the time, determined to get Perrun to a healer as soon as possible. Thornton took the lead, as he knew where they were headed. Just before midday, they entered a small town. They tied their horses up at the wooden hitching post in front of the tavern and Thornton and Gwyn carried Perrun to the healer's.

As soon as she saw him, she ushered them inside. She laid her hands on Perrun's leg. "I don't know if I can save it," she warned.

"Do the best you can." Thornton grabbed a handful of coins out of his belt pouch and placed them on a table. "If the treatment costs are higher than that, send to the castle. His name is Perrun and he's a soldier in Prince Carson's personal army. He'll be extremely grateful if you save the man."

"Of course. I'll do the best I can," the healer gushed, her gaze drawn to the coins on the table. "Now out. I can't treat him with you lot hovering."

Thornton nodded and made his way to the front door. He opened it and gestured towards Shadow. "My lady."

Shadow smiled and started to step through the door. She hurriedly stepped back inside and pushed the door shut. "Six soldiers. Magic hid. One of them's Clem."

"That lying, cheating–" Gwyn started for the door.

"Forget it." Thornton put a hand on his shoulder and pulled him back. "We've got to get away from here." He turned to the healer. "Is there a back door?"

She nodded and showed them into the narrow alley that ran behind her house.

They hurried along and paused at the corner. Shadow peered around the building, her gaze scanning the area. Anger and fear swirled through her. "It's safe. For now." They ran to the next building and made their way along until they were behind the tavern.

Thornton opened the door and a woman busy stirring a pot that bubbled over the fire looked up at them.

"Get out! What do you think you're doing bursting in here?" The woman came at them, flapping her tea towel.

"Good woman, we need your assistance." Coins appeared in Thornton's hand and instantly disappeared into the woman's.

"Well, why didn't you say?" The woman was suddenly all smiles and a friendly manner. "What do you need?"

"We're trying to avoid some men. Might we check to see if they're in your tavern before we proceed?" Thornton asked.

"My, aren't we a fancy one?" the woman asked. "Wouldn't be able to tell it by your clothes, but you sure do talk a treat."

Thornton nodded, his smile still in place.

"Well, go ahead." The woman waved towards the door that led into the main room of the tavern.

Thornton looked at Shadow who moved forward and peeked through the door. Not seeing the men, she opened the door further and had a better look.

Crowded tables, stained timber floors, a barman wiping up a spill on the long bar and several barmaids expertly avoiding the patrons. A wave of homesickness hit her, quickly followed by relief she no longer served in a tavern every day.

"All clear," Shadow said.

"Thank you, good woman," Thornton said before he followed Shadow and the other three men. Thornton turned to Shadow. "Check outside for me?"

Shadow nodded and made her way to one of the grimy windows. Gennie would never have tolerated that in her tavern. She ran a finger across the glass before she looked at the road that passed in front of the tavern. Their horses were still tied to the hitching post, cobblestones with struggling weeds ran down the main street and in clusters here and there people talked. Everything looked normal other than the glow of magic hid soldiers in several strategic places. Shadow turned to Thornton who came to stand beside her. "They're waiting. And they've got crossbows."

Thornton nodded. His attention was drawn to a large shout not far from them. One of the men seated at the table stood and raised a large tankard and downed it in a single gulp. A cheer went up from the rest of the table. Some coins were thrown on the table and the man gathered them up and pocketed them.

"I think I know what to do. Tell me exactly where the men are." Once Shadow had described their positions, Thornton said, "Let me know the moment one of them moves. All of you wait here."

Shadow watched as Thornton charmed the men at the table, several cheers erupting at the end of his tale.

"He's smooth," Gwyn said from beside her. "Too flighty to be king though."

Shadow looked at him. "He doesn't want to be king."

"Neither of them does. But Carson'd make the better king. And I'm not saying that because he's my captain. He's got what it takes to be king. He'll always put his people first."

Thornton strode over to them and rubbed his hands together with a grin. "All taken care of. Now it's time to watch the entertainment. Pick a window. This should be delightful."

Shadow turned back to the window and exclaimed, "There's a man stealing stuff from our saddlebags, even with all those people wandering around."

"Relax," Thornton said. "He's just making it look like that. He's checking our gear hasn't been tampered with."

"Oh. That's a good idea," Shadow said.

The man looked around before he tucked his hand inside his tunic and hurried inside the tavern. He made his way to Thornton and his empty hand came out of his tunic once he was inside. "Second horse from the entrance. Loose girth. Whoever rides that one'll be under it in no time."

"Thank you, good man." Thornton threw some coins towards the man. He caught them in mid air before he returned to his table, which was nearly empty of the men who'd sat there earlier. "Now for the second act."

"That's my horse," Shadow said.

Thornton nodded. "Yes. You'll have to ride with me until we get far enough away to tighten the girth. Keep your eyes open. When they're all occupied let me know. Tell us run."

Shadow nodded and turned back to her window in time to see a brawl break out in the street. Another three men joined the two who had started it and men went bouncing all over the street. Shadow watched as the magic hid men moved out of the way. Soon all of them had been disturbed. "Run."

The five of them sprinted for the door. They each headed for their own horse. Once Shadow had the reins of her horse, she allowed Thornton to swing her up behind him. They urged their horses into a gallop and quickly left the town behind. When Shadow said she couldn't see any soldiers behind them, they stopped long enough for her to tighten her girth and mount her own horse.

Chapter Twenty-Seven

By mid afternoon, and a whole day of riding, Gwyn demanded, "Where are we going? This isn't the way to the castle."

"How observant of you," Thornton said lightly.

"Thornton." There was both a warning and an order in Shadow's tone.

"To see a friend."

"What sort of friend?" Iain demanded suspiciously.

"Relax," Thornton said easily. "A wizard who has a portal tower that'll take us to the capital. We'll be across Relthon in an instant."

"To Crell?" Iain's voice still held a hint of suspicion.

"That's the only capital city Relthon has," Thornton said.

"Then why couldn't the captain use it?" Gwyn demanded.

"Because the wizard can only send eight at a time.

That means we'll have to leave most of the horses behind," Thornton said.

"No guess who'll be walking," Iain grumbled.

"We'll all walk," Shadow said firmly. "If there isn't enough horses for all of us, no one rides."

"So harsh." Thornton's voice remained light.

"It won't hurt you. How much further is your friend?" Shadow asked.

"We won't get there until late afternoon. We'll stop for something to eat soon, but not for too long. Not while those soldiers are on the loose," Thornton said.

"Did Carson know about this plan?" Shadow asked.

Thornton nodded.

"Then why didn't he tell me?" Shadow demanded.

"Because he knew you'd argue," Thornton said. When Shadow remained quiet, he asked. "Was he right?"

Shadow shrugged.

"Of course he was right," Irlan said.

"And so she should. It ain't right us getting back to the capital like that and the captain and the rest of the men stuck out there," Gwyn complained.

"He uses the portal towers too sometimes," Thornton said irritably. "No need to act like I'm the only one who does."

They all fell silent until Thornton called a halt for them to eat and rest. Tired, Shadow leaned up against a tree trunk as she nibbled on a handful of dried fruit and nuts. Her eyes closed and the sound of Irlan and Gwyn talking faded. She relaxed as she noticed the sounds of birds, wishing she could pull out her bedroll and stretch out for an hour. The food eaten, her hand dropped to her side and she sighed heavily, not wanting to move. An insect landed on her hand and she opened her eyes to see what it was. A glimmer from the corner of her eye caught her attention and she turned to see Clem sneaking up on Thornton, magic hid, sword drawn, still a good distance from him.

A glance around showed crossbows trained on them, the men remaining amongst the trees. Shadow's heart raced as she tried to think what to do. The insect crawled across her hand and with her eyes hidden by her hat Shadow glanced towards Clem. The distance between him and Thornton was slowly growing smaller.

Making sure her voice was high pitched and sounded panicked, Shadow called out loudly. "There's a snake slithering over my hand. Someone get it for me." She watched as Clem froze and looked towards her. She hoped her face was shaded enough from her hat that he couldn't tell she could see him.

Irlan rose to his feet. "What kind of snake?"

"I don't know. I can't bring myself to move. What if it bites me? I can't see anything past my hat." Shadow watched as Clem took a single step forward then stared at her again.

Irlan shook his head. "Baby." He started towards her.

"Thornton? Can you help me? I don't trust Irlan not to get me bitten."

Thornton laughed softly, but rose to his feet and strode towards her, Irlan at his side. He stood above her. "Shadow–"

"Don't tell me what type it is. I don't want to know. Just get rid of it." She motioned them closer with her hand that rested in the grass.

"Shadow I don't–" Irlan began.

"Shut up, Irlan. I don't want to hear it. Help me with this situation." Shadow could see Clem had changed direction and now headed towards them. He took a step at a time, pausing to check Shadow still hadn't seen him before he took another cautious step.

Thornton crouched beside her, tugging Irlan down to join him, before he whispered, "What's really the problem?"

Shadow spoke in barely a whisper. "Clem is sneaking up behind you and the rest are hidden in the trees with crossbows. I can see all of them so unless they've gathered more since we outran them, there's none behind me. Is there any cover there?"

Thornton glanced past Shadow. "Plenty of trees and bushes." He raised his voice. "The snake looks like it wants to strike. Gwyn, Iain, get behind and distract it." He lowered his voice again. "How close is Clem?"

Shadow's gaze slid past Thornton. "If they don't hurry, he'll soon be close enough to see there's no snake. I can't even get to my weapons without alerting him."

Thornton's hand closest to her slid inside his boot and withdrew a slim blade. He turned it so the fingers of her right hand could reach the handle. Her fingers tightened around it and she held it close to her leg to hide it.

"Don't do anything stupid, Shadow. Get to safety. Irlan, you get Gwyn, I'll take Iain. They're nearly in place."

"What about our gear. And horses?" Shadow glanced again towards Clem. Only another few steps and he'd be able to see her hand.

"We can walk." Thornton raised his head. "Don't

come any closer. You're upsetting the snake." He lowered his gaze to Shadow. "Count of three."

She nodded slightly.

"One, two, three." Thornton dived past her and Irlan did the same on the other side.

Instead of joining them, Shadow leapt forward, her knife aimed at Clem. She struck out at him, dodging as he recovered from his surprise and swung at her. As she dodged, she dropped to the ground to hear a thunk in the tree behind her.

"Shadow!"

Ignoring Thornton's bellow, she rolled as Clem attacked again, pushed herself from the ground and threw herself into the shrub in front of her. She eyed the distance between her and her crossbow. A check at where the magic hid men were showed it was impossible. Clem's sword slashed at the shrub hiding her and she darted from it, aiming for the next one. She couldn't keep dodging forever, and she noticed the men were starting to move towards her hidden companions.

When Clem attacked the shrub she hid in, instead of running, Shadow dodged to the side and struck out at him. She came in under his raised arm, slicing at it as she slid behind him. She felt exposed as she dashed for another shrub, holding her breath until she was amongst the leaves and twigs, cringing at the sound of bolts hitting trees. But one of them was no longer magic hid. Only five more to wound.

Clem came at her again. She grabbed a handful of dirt and threw it into his face. She ran as he cursed and rubbed at his eyes, stumbling in her direction. She had to do something. The other men were intent on quietly crossing the clearing to attack her companions. Their backs were to her. A quick, sharp intake of breath and she dashed into the clearing. One man turned as she grabbed her crossbow and bolts and continued for cover. She felt the rush of the bolt as it barely missed her face. Shadow slid to the ground and pressed her back against a tree as she tried to slow her breathing, her fingers trembling as she readied her crossbow.

The clearing was quiet. She'd have to look and see where they were. Her cheek could still feel the cold rush of metal and it took all her willpower to rise on one knee and turn towards the clearing. None of them looked towards her. They had nearly reached their destination.

Heart in her throat, Shadow took aim. She fired at one of the soldiers and ignored his cry of pain as she readied a bolt and wounded another. She was forced to turn away and shield herself with the tree as the first man she'd wounded shot at her. Another glance showed Gwyn dash behind a tree.

"Stay back. There's three more." Shadow called out. She heard footsteps run towards her tree and knew it was time to move. Without looking, she ran, dodging trees and shrubs. Behind her she could hear her pursuer. She angled her direction, not wanting to get too far from the clearing. Ahead of her, Gwyn rose from dense shrubs, a crossbow aimed behind her. Shadow dived towards the side, rolling as she landed in the rock strewn grass. A cry of pain sounded as she spun to face her pursuer and watched as he crashed forward, a bolt protruding from his chest. She darted forward and checked he was dead.

Gwyn ran to her side. "Where are the rest of them?"

Shadow turned towards the clearing. "I don't know." She ran, stopping only when she reached the edge. She quickly aimed at one of the magic hid men and shot him. Before he could turn, Gwyn finished him off. Not hesitating, Shadow shot at the next man, surprised when he crashed to the ground. The last magic hid man ran for cover. Shadow raced after him.

"Shadow!"

She didn't glance towards Thornton. "One left hidden. He's trying to get away." She didn't stop.

Ahead she could hear the man. If he got away he could easily circle back. And Clem was still out there somewhere. She tried to shoot the man with her crossbow, but she missed. Not even close. The man went to ground.

Shadow slid behind a tree, expecting him to fire. Nothing. Crouching low, she inched forward, listening for sound. All was quiet. Not even the birds were singing. Behind her she heard her name called by Irlan and Thornton. She hoped they didn't follow.

A noise ahead made her freeze. She turned slightly. There it was again. Like a branch cracking. She hurried forward. A glimpse of movement amongst the trees drew her attention. He crouched low like her. Hooking her crossbow over her shoulder, Shadow pulled out her dagger and ran towards the man who rose to meet her. He parried her attack with his crossbow, leapt back, dropped it and pulled out his own dagger. They circled each other. Shadow watched him warily, his bearded face expressionless.

The attack was swift when it came and Shadow barely managed to dodge. She had no chance against this man. He was far more experienced. Behind her she could still hear her name being called.

"Here!" She lunged at the man but he seemed to slide away from her effortlessly. She nearly stumbled over a berry bush as he attacked her. The thorns scraped her hand.

"Shadow!"

She didn't need to turn to know Thornton was nearly with them and he couldn't see the man who looked towards him. A trickle of blood ran down her hand and Shadow glanced at the berry bush again. She grabbed hold of a long thin stem, and slashed at it with her dagger. She struck out at the man and blood trickled down his face from the jagged scratches.

Thornton raced towards him, pulling his sword to attack. Shadow jumped back, barely missing the berry bush. She watched as the two men fought, Thornton far more skilled than his opponent. A sound drew her attention, and she turned to see Clem aim a crossbow at Thornton. She threw herself across the short distance, crashing into Clem, the dagger still clutched tightly in her hand. She pulled her hand back and plunged it into him, her mouth falling open at the ease with which it sunk into his stomach. Warm blood gushed over her hand as a startled gaze met hers.

This man had caused the death of those who had trusted him. Might cause Perrun to lose his leg. She pressed harder with her knife then pulled it out.

"Loyalty would have been cheaper. It wouldn't have cost you your life."

Clem's hand pressed against his stomach. "You don't understand."

Shadow pushed away from him. "I understand all I need to." She looked over her shoulder when she heard footsteps. It was Thornton.

He came to a stop beside her and stared down at Clem. "I hope you found the time to spend your blood money. You won't be able to take it where you're going."

Clem tried to speak, but doubled up in pain instead. More blood flowed from the wound. "End it. Please."

"You don't deserve it." Thornton stared at him a moment longer then swung his sword.

Shadow looked away at the last second, but she still heard the sound as the weapon was driven into Clem's body. She stood still, waiting for the usual rush of nausea to follow. It didn't. All she felt was a grim satisfaction that they'd caught the traitor.

Thornton's arm dropped on her shoulders. "Let's get cleaned up. We're going to arrive later than I expected."

Chapter Twenty-Eight

They reached the wizard's tower as day was fading into night. Shadow felt a sense of dread. With one step she would put even more distance between her and Carson. She'd thought he wouldn't be too far behind them as they travelled to the capital. She urged her horse forward and dismounted when he wouldn't budge.

"Shadow!" Irlan exclaimed. "Stop. There's a chasm in front of you."

"No there isn't. The path is safe enough, but only where I'm walking." Shadow walked across the chasm illusion, avoiding the real traps and grinning at the gasp behind her.

"Why? What's behind that illusion?" Irlan asked.

"A mixture of pits with spikes in them, sharp blades protruding from posts and a few other nasty surprises." Shadow stopped in front of a magic hid door.

"We'll wait here until he's ready to let us in," Thornton said.

Shadow rapped on the wood. Minutes later the door was flung open by a man who was almost bald. He was about as tall as Shadow, going to fat around the middle and had a permanent frown.

"What do you want? Hate elf sight. You think you're so clever to be able to get past it all, don't you? Who've you got with you?"

"Mayhew, my friend. Aren't you going to shine the path for us?" Thornton called out.

"You! If I have to." Mayhew muttered under his breath and a black path appeared, leading to his door.

The men followed the path and Irlan led Shadow's horse for her. Once they had dismounted, Mayhew stared at them.

"What do you want?" Mayhew demanded.

"A trip to the capital," Thornton said.

"Should have known. Where's your brother? Off playing soldier I guess. At least he makes himself useful sometimes," Mayhew muttered.

Gwyn snickered.

Thornton ignored them both. "We'll have to leave

some of the horses with you. Can you send them through when the energy builds up again?"

"You'll leave them all here. I'm not depleting the energy for frivolous requests when times are uncertain. I'll send one or two a day. Have someone ready at daybreak to fetch them," Mayhew said.

"That'll be fine," Thornton said.

"It'll have to be. Put them in the stable. Don't have anyone to do for me. I'm not some useless noble." Mayhew turned his back on them and the door slammed shut behind him.

"Friend?" Shadow asked. "So how do your enemies treat you?"

"Surely you recall. They offer me the finest of accommodations, serve the best of meals and make sure the laundress takes the utmost care of my garments," Thornton said lightly.

"I'm sorry." Shadow reached out to him and rested her hand on his forearm, guilt filling her.

Thornton smiled wryly. "Don't be. Come on. I'll show you to the stable."

Once their horses were stabled, they made their way back to the tower, their saddlebags slung over their shoulders. This time Thornton knocked on the door. No one was there to open it, but it swung open anyway.

Shadow saw the faint glimmer that showed magic had been used.

"Come on. We've got a million stairs to climb." Thornton led them to the stairs a few paces inside the door. As soon as all of them were inside, the door closed itself with another glimmer of magic.

They headed for the top of the tower, using the steps that travelled all around the inside, sandwiched between two rock walls. At each level, a closed door stood. At the top level, they walked straight into an open area. All that was in there was a circle painted on the floor, magical symbols around the outside.

"Stand on the circle," Mayhew snapped. "I haven't all night. Now, elf sight, close your eyes or you're likely to be sick. You'll see stuff, the others won't. It'll be black around them and they'll only see each other. About five minutes and you'll be there."

"My name's Shadow."

"What do I care? If I'm lucky I won't have to see you again. Everyone get ready or you'll miss out. I don't have time to waste." As soon as they all stood on the circle, Mayhew muttered the chant to activate the portal.

Shadow quickly closed her eyes. It seemed to take ages. Surely a quick peek wouldn't hurt. She opened her eyes to see grotesque creatures coming for her.

Her mouth opened to scream, but no sound came out. She staggered as she tried to avoid the creature coming for her and would have fallen if Thornton hadn't caught her arm. With his other hand, he covered her eyes.

"Don't you listen to anyone?" Thornton asked.

"Never," Irlan answered for his sister.

"Where are we?" Shadow asked shakily.

"I've been told it's better not to know," Thornton said.

"Does anyone get trapped here?" Shadow asked nervously.

"That's not a question to ask while we're in a portal," Thornton said.

"Do they?" Gwyn demanded.

"Ah, we've arrived." Thornton took his hand away from Shadow's eyes.

"Do they?" Shadow glanced around to see they were in a similar place to the one they had left. The only difference being the guards on duty who hastily bowed when they saw Thornton.

"Not often and not for very long. That's why it's good to let people know you're using them. In case the portal tower you're going to is destroyed. Then a wizard can use another portal tower to bring you back," Thornton said.

"If you're sane enough to be worth bringing back," Shadow muttered.

"Don't tell me what you saw. I don't want to think about it next time I've got to use a portal tower," Thornton said. "Now, let's go to the castle."

"I'm heading for the barracks," Gwyn said as they headed outside to see a city sprawled in front of them, numerous lights holding the night back.

"And me," Iain agreed.

"I'll let Carson know where you can be found when he returns," Thornton said.

"We don't need to go to the castle," Shadow protested when Thornton led them towards the imposing building that towered over the city.

A stone bridge spanned a moat that surrounded the castle and was the only entrance. Guards lined the bridge, lanterns hung at intervals. It was the largest building Shadow and Irlan had ever seen. It was even larger than the fortress.

"Surely an old building like that doesn't scare you," Thornton teased.

"Of course not." Looking up at the castle made Shadow feel insignificant. "I just don't think we need to go there."

"Come on. Procrastinating will only make it harder." Thornton strode ahead of them.

There was a murmur through the guards he passed as they realised who it was. "My lord," each guard said as he passed, bowing low. Thornton paid them no attention as he walked along the bridge. Shadow followed, Irlan by her side. They received shallower bows since they accompanied the prince.

At the massive front door, Thornton turned to grin at them. "Manage to live through that?" He turned back to the guards. "Open."

"Yes, my lord." The guards bowed low and then pushed hard on the massive doors, which swung slowly open.

Inside the door, a servant rushed forward and took the saddlebags Thornton carried. Shadow protested when he would have taken hers.

Thornton waved him away. "Fetch my parents and have a meal prepared. I'll be in the breakfast room. It'll be quieter there. Come," he threw over his shoulder to Shadow and Irlan as he moved across the room. They hurried to keep up.

"How do you remember your way around here?" Shadow asked once they were seated in the breakfast room at a polished timber table.

"You learn. I've had twenty-one years to learn the layout," Thornton said as servants entered the room. "Ah, food. Help yourselves, I've missed this service."

A petite blonde burst into the room, followed by a man who it was easy to see was Thornton's father. He carried a few extra pounds and had silver in amongst the black strands of his hair.

The woman threw herself at Thornton, weeping. The jewelled rings and diamond necklace at her throat caught the light as she pulled back from her son, still holding onto him. She looked around the room. "Where's your brother?" There was fear in her voice.

"Mother, please, Carson is fine." Thornton untangled his mother's arms from him. "Let me introduce you to our guests. Irlan, Shadow, these are my parents. Nickel and Brisa. Or should I say King Nickel and Queen Brisa of Relthon?"

"I have a letter from Carson." Shadow rose awkwardly to her feet and took the parchment from her belt pouch.

"That's his cloak." Brisa frowned at Shadow as she took the letter.

"He's very generous. I was cold." Shadow's words trailed off when Brisa read the letter, ignoring her.

"Well. I'll have a chamber prepared for each of you," Brisa said frostily when she had finished the letter.

"Mother! What has he written to have you act like

that? This woman saved my life. She has elf sight." Thornton strode forward and took the letter from his mother.

"That's none of your business." Brisa tried to snatch the letter back.

Thornton let her after he had briefly read what was written. Nickel then took the letter from his wife.

"Is nothing private around here?" Brisa demanded.

"She turned him down," Thornton said.

"And so she should," Brisa sniffed.

"He won't tolerate interference," Thornton warned.

"And I won't tolerate being discussed like I'm not here." Shadow still stood at the table. "I have better things to do than wait around here, freezing to death." She turned to go. She'd been through too much to ever stand by meekly and let someone walk all over her.

"Wait," Nickel ordered. "Carson requests we make you welcome." He shot a look at his wife. "It's the least we can do for our youngest son. He asks so little of us."

"Only until he returns. My Pa is expecting to find me here," Shadow said.

"And who is he?" Nickel asked.

"Gil Morgan."

"A fine man. Quite a hero," Nickel said.

"Really?" Shadow asked incredulously.

Nickel nodded. "I'll have to tell you all about it while you're here. Now, I'm sure you're famished and tired. We'll leave you to eat and then servants can show you to rooms we'll prepare for you." He and his wife left the room. Brisa went amidst protests she had barely seen her son.

"You do realise you're meant to bow to the king and queen, don't you?" Thornton asked.

Shadow shook her head. "Was I?"

Thornton laughed. "I'm going to enjoy having you here."

Chapter Twenty-Nine

Shadow slowly sat up, pushing the bedding aside as dread pooled in her. She wasn't looking forward to another day of boredom and being reminded how useless she was by the court ladies. She eyed the dress laid out on the wooden chest at the foot of her bed, wishing she could return to wearing Irlan's old clothes. Her eyes closed as she tried to force herself to feel some enthusiasm. There had to be something seriously wrong that a week of castle living made her yearn for the army. There were probably a million people who'd jump at the chance to change places with her.

She forced herself to her feet. They weren't going to have her hiding in her room. Brisa already thought little enough of her as it was. Yanking her soft linen nightgown off, Shadow slipped the dress on. The folds of the garment fell around her legs, hindering her movement when she tried to stride across the room. Taking smaller steps, she slid her feet into the black cloth shoes by her door and ran her fingers through her hair. As one of the court ladies had pointed out, it was a waste of time trying to do anything with hair as short as hers.

Reaching for the door, Shadow paused, trying to remind herself she'd promised to stay. Promised Gil she'd wait for him here if he looked out for Carson. She leaned forward, resting her forehead on the timber door. She couldn't do this, not anymore. She'd rather face down a hundred archers. A knock on her door caused her to jump away from it.

Another knock. "Shadow? You in there?"

Relief coursed through her and she opened the door to her brother. "Yes."

"You're not hiding are you? It's not like you to still be in bed at this hour, but no one had seen you, so…" he finished his sentence with a shrug.

Shadow's eyes narrowed. As always her brother seemed to be getting the better part of the bargain with his new clothes and the sword that hung at his side. "No." The word was sharp. "What do you want?"

"I'm going into the city. I'm meeting a merchant

for the midday meal at one of the taverns there. Do you want to join us?"

"No."

"What's wrong with you? Isn't this what you wanted?" He waved his hand around. "You're free. No more serving drunks, no more being dragged around the countryside with the army, no more orders. You've been sulking for days."

"Get out of my way. I've got things to do." She pushed past her brother and tried to stride down the hall. Instead her legs became tangled in her skirts and she landed on the thick carpet that did nothing to cushion her fall. The hard stone beneath caused her to curse. Laughter brought her head up and she caught sight of Lady Krisa on Thornton's arm.

"Breeding always tells." Krisa's lips twisted in a mocking smile.

Thornton dropped her arm and stepped forward. With a glance at Krisa, he said, "It certainly does." He held out a hand to Shadow at the same time as Irlan stepped forward to offer his hand.

"Leave me alone." She rose to her feet, sending a glare around the hallway before she retreated to her room, slamming the door closed. Anger, humiliation and tears vied for supremacy. She ripped the dress from her body and left it in a pool on the floor, ignoring the repeated knocks on her door. Flinging open the chest, she pulled out the worn clothes she'd lived in for months. This was her. Not the finery on the floor. The pale blue silk belonged to someone else. Some lady. As she'd told Carson, she wasn't a lady.

Sitting on the edge of the bed, she pulled on her boots and looked down at herself. Dressed in her brother's cast offs and boots, that were starting to wear through in several places, she felt more comfortable. But she still didn't know what she was. Not a lady, not a barmaid. Where did she belong?

Rising to her feet she knew one thing. It wasn't here. This castle wasn't her place. She pulled the door open and froze when she saw Thornton lounged against the wall opposite her. A glance in both directions showed Irlan and Krisa were gone. Shadow crossed her arms over her chest. "What do you want?"

Thornton pushed away from the wall with a smile, offering her his arm. "My lady?"

"I'm not your lady. I'm not anyone's lady."

His smile became a grin. "Then let's remedy that."

Shadow's eyes narrowed and she continued to stare at Thornton. "What are you planning?"

"A surprise. Do you trust me?"

She shook her head. "Not at all."

Thornton laughed. "Then how about you humour me. I am the prince."

"Only when it's convenient."

Thornton nodded. "I can't argue that. But sometimes I still happen to be one when it's inconvenient too." He reached out and tugged on her arm until she uncrossed them. He placed her hand on his forearm. "We have places to be."

"What places?" Shadow walked alongside him.

"Surprising places."

"You can be really annoying sometimes."

Thornton nodded. "I've heard that before. Never believed it though because it's always Carson who says it. I did say you've been hanging around him too much. See, you're even starting to think like him." He grinned. "Isn't that a terrifying thought?"

Shadow tried to hold onto her anger. "You're also an idiot," she muttered.

Thornton laughed. "Come. The horses should be ready."

"Horses?"

"You don't understand the meaning of surprises, do you?" He led her down the stairs at the end of the hallway. "Never mind. I shall endeavour to teach you."

"Why were you near my room? Your suite is

nowhere near our rooms. Nothing is near our rooms. Are you sure your mother didn't have some dark, distant attic she could have shoved us in?"

"I came to see you."

"Why?"

"That is something for later. For now," he gestured towards the horses at the front of the castle. "Your ride awaits."

With another suspicious look at Thornton, she mounted the horse. She guessed anything had to be better than spending another miserable day in the castle. Several hours later she began to rethink that thought. Thornton dragged her from tailors to cobblers and then made her wait at the front of an armoury while he collected a parcel. The one place she would have been interested in visiting he refused to let her enter. She was still glaring at him when they arrived at a tavern, after midday, for a meal.

"Maybe food will put you in a better mood," Thornton said as they were shown to a private parlour. "When did you eat?"

"Last night." She waved the waiter away when he tried to seat her.

"You should have said something."

"Would it have made a difference?"

Thornton grinned. "I would have grabbed an apple for you to eat on the way."

"Nothing could have improved all that poking and prodding. I've already been measured enough times. How many more dresses do you think I need?"

Thornton stared at her a moment. "Give it a few hours and I think you'll change your mind. Stop glaring at me and order something to eat." He beckoned the waiter forward who had retreated to the wall near the door. "Today's special for me." He turned to Shadow. "And you?"

Shadow shrugged. "That'll do." Anything to get this trip over and done with.

The moment the waiter had left the parlour Thornton lifted the parcel onto the table and slid it towards her. He then pulled a folded letter from his belt pouch and handed it over. "Read this first."

"What is it?" She stared at the letter.

"Read it and find out. You can read, can't you?"

A glance at Thornton and then her gaze was drawn to the folded parchment. She slowly opened it, to see bold handwriting filled part of the page.

Chapter Thirty

'Shadow, I have asked Thornton to arrange a present for you. We could not have completed the mission without you. I will see you as soon as loose ends are tied up. Your father is well and in good spirits if his constant threats to castrate me are any indication. My men miss you and there are times I wish you were still with us, but at other times I am glad you are not forced to play this cat and mouse game. I hope you enjoy my gift, it was once mine many years ago. Love Carson.'

Shadow folded the letter and tucked it into her belt pouch. "When did you get the letter?"

"It was with this morning's dispatch."

"And you waited this long to give it to me?"

"He wanted you to have the letter and the gift at the same time." Thornton gestured towards the parcel. "Are you going to open it?"

Shadow stared at the parcel a moment longer until, with a nod, she began to untie the string that held the wrappings closed. When the wrappings were spread across the table, a sword sat amongst them, a scabbard beside it. She reached out a finger and ran it down the middle of the blade, feeling carvings that were worn in some places. She rose to her feet and lifted the blade, checking the weight. "This was Carson's?"

"Yes. Back when he was a skinny little kid that would have been knocked over in a good breeze."

Shadow's daggered look did nothing to repress Thornton's grin. "Are you trying to tell me something?"

Thornton laughed. "That you had best sheath your sword, you're making my guards nervous."

Shadow glanced behind her and saw two men she had seen on and off during the day. Their hands were on their sword hilts and one of them strode towards the parlour. "We've had guards with us all day?"

"They've been trained to be discrete. I don't like having them under my feet."

Shadow reached for the scabbard. "That might be why you ended up kidnapped." She undid her belt and slid the sheathed sword onto it.

"Maybe." He waved the guard back. "But I have nothing to fear with you at my side."

Shadow snorted as she sat at the table. "Then you are in trouble. I'd probably end up in the dirt at their feet."

"That was only because you were wearing that ridiculous dress."

"See, you do know I'm not a lady."

"You are a lady, just not the sort that needs to primp and pose all day. And I shouldn't have needed Carson's letter this morning to point that out to me." He glanced behind her and pushed the wrappings onto the floor. "Finally. I don't know about you, but I could eat a pig."

Shadow breathed in the scents of the meal as it was placed in front of her. "A good thing the special is roast pig." Her eyes narrowed. "But you probably knew that before you ordered."

Thornton smiled in answer and gestured towards her meal with his fork. "Eat. We have places to be later."

Shadow groaned. "No more shopping. Please."

"Eat."

Knowing it would be impossible to get another word from him, she did as ordered. But only because she was starving and the food was making her mouth water.

Once the meal was ended, Thornton returned with

her to one of the tailors where an outfit of black trousers and a dark red shirt and black vest had been altered to fit her. At the cobbler dark brown leather boots waited and Shadow soon rode beside Thornton in her new finery with the promise of the rest to be delivered to the castle.

"Where to now?" Shadow glanced around when they stopped in front of a large guarded building.

"Here." He dismounted and waited for her to do the same. "Some friends of yours were wondering where we were keeping you." He nodded behind her.

Shadow turned to see Iain, Gwyn and Perrun in the doorway. She grinned when they waved at her in greeting. Shadow turned back to Thornton. "Thank you."

Thornton shook his head. "I am the one who can never thank you enough. Your gift saved my life. I am eternally in your debt. And Shadow, don't you ever forget that. The Lady Krisa and all her cronies together aren't worth one of you. Don't let them treat you like you're insignificant. Not a one of them could have done what you did, regardless of your gift." He glanced behind her. "I think your friends are getting impatient. When you've finished visiting the barracks see that someone rides back with you to the castle. Carson would never forgive me if something happened to you."

Shadow nodded.

Thornton smiled. "I'd never forgive me either." He beckoned a boy forward and gestured for him to take Shadow's horse. "Go have some fun. I've barely seen you smile since we arrived."

Shadow could only nod before she turned away and ran to Iain, throwing her arms around first him, then Gwyn and Perrun. She held Perrun at arms length. "You're well? When did you get back?" Her gaze dropped to his legs. "She was able to save it."

Perrun nodded, his face bright red. "My Lady-"

Shadow scowled at him. "Not you too. I'm Shadow. Can't anyone remember my name?"

Iain chuckled. "I don't know, kid. It's such a mouthful."

Shadow laughed. "Oh I wish I could stay at the barracks instead of the castle."

"That's no place for a lass." Iain shook his head.

"Why not?"

"It's full of men," Iain said.

Shadow shrugged and glanced behind them. "Do I get to see inside, or are we going to spend the afternoon on the doorstep?"

"Not much to see," Gwyn said. "Mess hall, training

grounds, dormitories and storage. The officers' quarters are at the castle along with the training grounds for the new recruits."

"Helps keep them in awe of their superiors starting them off at the castle." Iain grinned. "Maybe that was your problem."

"I want to see." Shadow peered behind them.

Iain shrugged. "Can't see why you'd find it interesting, but I guess no one will complain."

The mess hall, storage rooms, and dormitories where they left Perrun, who needed to rest, were uninteresting. Once they reached the training grounds, where Gwyn was called away to join a sword fighting session, Shadow stared around in fascination. Her hand dropped to her pommel as she watched two men fight with swords, light on their feet, weapons cutting through the air. She felt alive watching them. This is where she belonged. Not in some stupid dress at the castle, but here, in trousers, with a sword at her side.

She turned to Iain. "I want to learn how to use my sword properly."

"I don't know lass. The Captain'd want us to look out for ya, not encourage ya to risk getting hurt."

Shadow drew her sword and held it out to Iain, hilt

first. She watched him stare at it a moment before he took it from her. "I want to learn to use this."

Iain looked up from his examination of the sword. "Where'd ya get this?"

Shadow smiled. "Carson."

"The Captain's back?"

She shook her head. "He asked Thornton to give it to me."

"This was the Captain's first real sword. I was there when the king gave it to him." He handed it back to her. "Ya sure he gave it to ya?"

Shadow nodded. "He sent a letter."

Iain gestured behind him. "This isn't the place, lass. Ya need to be at the castle training grounds. Learn how to do it right. Train with lads at your level."

"How do I do that?" She sheathed her sword.

Iain shrugged. "Drill Sergeant Dore will be the problem. He's set in his ways. The best there is at training, but a look from him has some of them lads wetting their britches."

"So I need to get his permission?"

"That'd be the day." Iain snorted. "Ya can expect the sun to stop rising first. Might be best to talk to the prince. He'd probably help."

Impatience tugged at her as she turned to watch the soldiers. "Can you at least show me a few moves?" She brought her attention back to Iain. "Please? I only got it today."

Iain grinned. "We'll find a quiet corner, lass."

Shadow nodded eagerly and followed Iain across the training grounds. They found a place that started quiet, but they soon had several spectators. This didn't bother Shadow. After all the time she'd spent with the army she was accustomed to this type of attention and grinned when she heard several place bets on how long she'd last.

She knew Iain was going easy on her. Not like Morell had. A twinge of sorrow hit her and she attacked harder, determined to show everyone that Morell's student wasn't completely useless, and then her sword was on the ground and the point of Iain's blade at her chest. He held it there a moment before he sheathed it, holding out his hand to her.

Shadow shook the offered hand. "Thank you." She grinned. "For not making me eat dirt."

Iain chuckled. "And how'd I explain that to the Captain?"

She bent to pick up her sword, brushing it against her trousers before she sheathed it. "Training? I believe that's the excuse Carson used."

Iain clapped her on the back. "Come on, lass. Let's get ya back to the castle before the day's ended."

Shadow's gaze was drawn to the splash of red and orange in the sky from the setting sun. Her smile faded. "I guess."

"What's troubling ya, lass?" Iain walked to the front of the barracks with her where he called a boy to fetch their horses.

Shadow shrugged. What could she say? Her bed was too soft? Her dresses too pretty. There was only one complaint she could make. "I miss him."

"He'll be right. Back before ya know it."

"I know." The words were soft and lacked conviction. She took the reins of her horse from the boy who brought him to her. "You don't need to come with me."

Iain mounted his horse with a speaking look. He shook his head and urged his horse forward. Shadow fell into place beside him and they made the trip back to the castle silently. They halted at the stone bridge that led to the castle and Shadow tried to think what to say. The words 'don't go' didn't seem the best option, but they were all she could think of.

"Visit us whenever ya feel like it, lass," Iain said. "And don't ya let Dore scare ya witless."

"Let me guess, he's really sweet under all his bluster."

Iain laughed. "If ya believe that I've got a castle in the Northern lands ya might want to buy."

"Then why shouldn't I be scared?"

"Because he won't respect ya if ya show any fear." Iain gave her a nod, turned his horse and rode away.

Chapter Thirty-One

With a sigh Shadow urged her horse across the bridge. That's all she needed, another tyrant in her life. She seemed to collect them like some girls collected admirers. She dismounted and handed her horse over to the boy who waited. "Thanks." She ignored his startled expression and headed for her room where she found several parcels of clothes on her bed.

Her gaze flickered between the dress laid out on the chest and the unopened parcels. She strode across the room and lifted the dress, bunching it into a ball before she threw it in a corner. No more. Not even for the elaborate meals every evening. If the gentleman were allowed to wear trousers at the table, their swords at their sides, then she would too.

The whispers and catty remarks would be the same no matter what she wore. At least she'd be comfortable. She unwrapped the parcels, choosing an outfit suitable for dinner. Once she was dressed, she grinned. Now Brisa would have reason to give her one of her looks that made her think she was wondering who had forgotten to take the rubbish out.

Shadow's hand went to her pommel and she wished Carson was here with her. She dropped her hand, straightened her shoulders and lifted her chin. She could do this. Without help. She was Shadow Morgan, daughter of Gil Morgan, supposed hero of the realm. And she had elf sight and tenacity. She grinned, and she didn't care what anyone said. Tenacity was good.

She flung open her door and strode down the hallway. No turning back. She was ready to face the hordes. The entire jewelled horde. And then she was entering the dining room, conversations stopping as she strode to her seat. For a split second she began to wonder what she was doing, then she met Thornton's gaze. His eyes were so similar to Carson's. Even down to a touch of humour in the deep brown. He rose as she came closer and pulled her seat out for her.

"You look stunning." He sat beside her, letting her pull her own seat into the table.

Shadow grinned. If they were alone, she'd argue his comment. "I need to talk to you later."

"About?"

"Dore."

Thornton chuckled. "A good thing I didn't place a bet on that conversation. I was thinking it'd be tomorrow."

Around them the conversations that had restarted came to an abrupt halt. Shadow looked up to see her brother slide into his seat as the King and Queen entered the room. Brisa's gaze fell instantly on her and became frosty enough to make Shadow think winter would be early this year. Her winter anyway. Nickel seated his wife then gestured to the servants to begin filling plates.

Brisa's gaze remained on Shadow. "Did you perhaps need a maid, Shadow?" Brisa's voice was as frosty as her gaze.

"No thank you. I've been capable of dressing myself since I was a toddler." Then quickly added, "Your majesty."

Thornton eyed Shadow. "And here I was about to ask who her tailor is. She looks exquisite. I shall have to pay the man a visit."

Shadow lifted her goblet to her lips to hide her smile. Under control again, she returned the goblet to the table. "I'm not sure which one this outfit is from, Thornton. I fear I visited so many I've forgotten who half of them are."

"Surely there weren't that many." Thornton smiled at her before he turned to his father. "When are the officer's lessons?"

"Oh, Thornton, never tell me you're thinking of following in your brother's footsteps." Brisa's jewelled hand pressed against her throat.

Thornton shook his head. "Never. How could I tear myself away from all these beauties for months at a time?" He raised his goblet, tilting it towards Shadow before he drank from it.

"Tonight and then two nights later. Same each week," Nickel said.

"Does Dore still run them?"

Nickel chuckled. "As if he'd let another hold them."

"And he still trains the most promising new recruits?" Thornton asked.

Nickel nodded. "Why all the questions?"

Thornton smiled. "Oh, you know me." He made a vague motion with his fork before he used it on his meal. "This smells great. I'm hungry enough to eat a pig."

"A pity you're stuck with bull instead," Shadow muttered.

Thornton laughed. "My other favourite meal." He lifted a slice of the roast beef to his mouth. He leaned closer to Shadow, lowering his voice. "Although it's best when you're the one doing the serving."

"Where did you wander off to all day, my lord?" Krisa asked Thornton from across the table. "I haven't seen you since Shadow tripped over her own feet coming out of her room."

Shadow ignored the titters she could hear along the table, but the look of laughter in Brisa's eyes as she pressed her napkin to her lips shot anger through her. "We ate at a tavern in the city where Thornton gave me a letter from Carson."

Brisa's eyes became frosty again. "Carson sent you a personal letter?"

Nickel reached out and patted his wife's hand. "I told you we received a dispatch from Carson today. He and his men are well and we're working on the plan he suggested."

Brisa's lips curved into a false smile, her gaze never leaving Shadow's. "Of course he would have to send you a personal letter. He would have clearly known you would never be privy to any of the army dispatches. We don't trust just anyone to read them."

Shadow had no reply she could make. Instead she nodded jerkily.

Thornton rose to his feet, most of his meal eaten. "If you'll excuse me, Mother, Father." He nodded to each one. "I believe I'll step in on the officer's lessons this evening." He turned to Shadow and held out his hand. "Would you care to join me?"

Shadow rose to her feet and Krisa screeched, her hands covering her mouth. "You're wearing a sword? What on earth will Captain Carson think when he returns home?"

Shadow's hand dropped to her pommel and she fought the urge to draw it from the scabbard. "I can't think he'll complain since he was the one who gave me his sword." She felt Thornton tug on her elbow and allowed him to lead her from the room, satisfied by Krisa's gasp and the sudden whispered conversations that ran around the table.

"Don't do that to me again." Thornton pressed a hand to his heart once they were out of the room. "Are you trying to kill me?"

"Do what?"

"I thought you were going to draw your sword and carve that viper into little pieces."

Shadow laughed. "I thought so too for a minute."

"Maybe you better not wear it to dinner in future."

"Avoiding dinner might be the better choice."

Thornton stopped in the middle of a hallway, turning Shadow to face him. "I'll see what I can do."

"Really?" When Thornton nodded she grinned. "That would be a perfect way to show your eternal gratitude."

"Not riches and wealth beyond imagining?"

Shadow shook her head. "No. Never having to attend another one of those dreadful meals would be a lot better."

"I can't promise never, but I think I might be able to get it down to once a week. Will that do?"

"I suppose so." She sighed then looked along the hallway. "Weren't we going to an officer's lesson?"

Thornton grinned and held out his arm. "My lady, allow me to escort you."

Shadow placed her hand on his forearm and fell into step beside him. When they wound their way through hallways, staircases and past numerous rooms she was glad to have him with her. She didn't know how she would ever find her way back here.

Their destination was a large room with an oval table in the centre, young men seated at it all looking towards a sharp nosed man with hazel eyes that looked like they could see through to a person's soul. His head had dark stubble and his face was clean shaven, his left cheek marred by a three inch long scar. He stopped in mid sentence and all heads turned their way.

Thornton smiled, striding into the room without a glance towards those seated. "Dore." A sharp nod. "Carry on. We've come to be enlightened." His smile widened as he seated himself and Shadow at the oval table.

Dore stared at Thornton for several long moments. It wasn't Thornton who ended up shifting uneasily in his seat, but the other young men. Then Dore repeated the sharp nod given to him by Thornton and picked up the thread of his conversation, gesturing towards the map in the centre of the room.

Shadow watched in fascination as Dore described a battlefield scenario then fired rapid questions at each of his students as to how they would react. She itched to give her opinion, leaning forward with each suggestion. Upon hearing the answers, she leaned backwards, wanting to ask them if they had any experience at all.

Dore pointed at Shadow. "Either spit out what you have to say or sit still."

"It's the battle of Wolf Ridge." It had been the tale most spoken in the tavern, always in hushed whispers with glances towards Gil.

Dore's gaze bored into her then he gave a single,

sharp nod. His gaze skated across the rest of his class. "Haven't the lot of you a brain to share between you? What makes you think you can be officers?"

Shadow felt instant pity for them. "I was raised on the tale." When Dore's gaze fell on her, she added a hurried, "Sir."

He gestured towards his students. "This lot were raised on such tales. Why should you have learned it any better than them?"

"I'm Shadow Morgan."

Dore stared at her. "Gil a relation?"

She nodded. "My Pa."

Another lengthy stare then he reached towards the map and rearranged the wooden counters. He fired out the scenario in short, sharp words then returned his gaze to Shadow.

"The battle of Tun Mountain." Maybe serving drunks hadn't been a complete waste of time, although squiggles in the gravy remains on plates didn't do as good a job as an actual map.

Dore grunted at her then rearranged the map, barking the next scenario.

Shadow bit back a grin, enjoying herself. "Murder Lake."

"I knew that one, sir," one of the young men half

raised his hand, his gaze dropping to the table top when Dore's gaze fell on him.

Dore's narrowed gaze returned to Shadow. "What are you doing here if you know all this?" His hand swept above the table.

Shadow was lost for words. Because I want you to train me didn't seem like it'd work. She glanced towards Thornton who sat forward, about to speak.

Dore held up a hand. "Not you, her." He pointed at Shadow.

"Really, Dore, is that any way to speak to your future king?" Thornton leaned back in his chair, a slight smile on his lips.

Dore's gaze remained on Shadow. "Well?"

"Carson's been training me, but he's not here. I was told you were the best trainer in Crell."

"Girls aren't allowed in the army." Dore's hands went behind his back, his stance widened and he stared down at her. "Ever."

Anger spiked and it was all she could do to remain seated. "Then I have no idea where I've been all these weeks. Felt an awful lot like Carson's company to me."

"I don't tolerate back talking." His gaze momentarily dropped on Thornton. "From anyone."

It returned to Shadow. "No girls are allowed in the army."

Her chin rose. "I didn't ask to join the army. I asked to train. Next time I'd like to have some chance of coming out alive by my own effort."

Thornton spoke up. "They're not about to let elf sight sit at home knitting baby bonnets."

Dore eyed her. "Like your father, are you?"

Thornton chuckled and answered before she had a chance. "In more ways than one."

Shadow sent him a daggered look before she turned back to Dore. "If you don't know how to train a girl tell me so I can find someone who can."

Dore remained silent, his hands still behind his back, his shoulders straight, feet apart. "Your challenge doesn't interest me, but I'll give you one week to show me if a girl is trainable. If I give you a ball of wool at the end of the seventh day I better not see you on my training grounds again." He paused. "Or in this room."

Shadow wanted to shout, dance around the room and grin like a maniac. She did none of them. Holding herself still until the urge passed she gave a single nod. "Deal."

He pointed at Shadow. "Daybreak. If you're late,

you get the wool and you're knitting me a baby bonnet."

She gave a single nod again.

Dore looked around the room. "Dismissed."

His students quickly rose to their feet, saluting before they hurried from the room. Shadow remained seated since Thornton did.

Dore's gaze flickered between them, remaining on Thornton after a moment. "Was there something else?" His tone changed to one of mocking subservience. "My lord."

Thornton shook his head, a lazy smile forming. "No, I like to watch all the rabbits scurry. How are they going to gain a backbone if you whip it out of them?"

"I never raise a whip to my soldiers."

Thornton chuckled. "I hear it raised all the time. I'm surprised they ever have any skin left on them once you've given them a tongue lashing."

"And yet you still brought me another student." His gaze fell on Shadow before it returned to Thornton. "What were you expecting?"

Thornton rose to his feet, holding his hand out to Shadow, his smile directed to her. "This one has a backbone of willow. I have no fear for her."

"I believe the term is steel," Dore corrected.

Thornton shook his head. "No. Willow. Steel will eventually break." He flashed a smile at Dore. "I'm curious as to what you'll do with the ball of wool when you can't give it to Shadow."

"I only ever have five in my squad at a time. Someone will be knitting me a baby bonnet next week." With a sharp nod Dore strode from the room.

Shadow dropped back into her seat, her head into her hands. "What have I done?"

"I believe you got yourself the best trainer in the city."

Shadow shook her head, dropping her hands to look up at the prince. "No, I've ruined some young man's life."

Thornton threw back his head and laughed.

Frowning, Shadow rose to her feet and glared at him. "Oh shut up."

His laughter became a smile. "Did you ever think it might be you getting the ball of wool?"

Shadow shook her head, an image of serving drinks in the tavern as an old woman coming to mind. "No. Never."

Thornton dropped an arm around her shoulders. "Come along, my willow. Let me escort you to your room. You have an early day tomorrow."

"Why willow?" She walked along the empty hallway with him.

"Because willow can bend when necessary."

Chapter Thirty-Two

Shadow rolled out of bed, wide awake. Energy coursed through her as she pulled on her trousers and shirt, automatically tipping out her boots after so long on the trail. She buckled on her belt, running her fingers down the pommel of her sword and wishing Carson was here. Her first day training with Dore and she wasn't going to be late.

She hurried through the hallways and stairwells, making her way to the kitchens first for some freshly cooked pastries to take with her. She was one of the first at the castle training grounds, stopping in the area Thornton had told her Dore held his lessons. She slowly ate the still warm pastries as she leaned against a hitching post waiting for Dore to arrive. By the time he did, there were five young men standing around the area with her.

Dore strode towards them, bellowing, "Fall in, lads."

Shadow lined up with the five new recruits. She didn't care what he wanted to call her as long as he trained her. She glanced at those beside her and clasped her hands behind her back, widening her stance like they did.

Dore slowly strode along the line, tossing a ball of grey wool up in the air. Each time he caught it, he'd glance at the person he was next to, then gaze straight ahead, he'd walk on, tossing the ball into the air again. Finally he came to a halt in front of the middle of the line and turned to stare at them. "I only ever have five in my squad at a time. Look around you lads. Who here can count?"

One of them raised his hand and quickly dropped it at Dore's withering stare.

"What a marvel. Only one of you can count. Good job, Vin, amazing trick."

There was snickering in the line. It drew Dore's attention.

"Is there a problem, Jurn? Maybe you need a lesson in counting? Possibly showing me you can count to twenty by the amount of push ups you can do."

"No Sergeant. There's six here. Sir." Jurn's gaze met Dore's.

"Can anyone tell me what this is?" Dore held up the ball of wool. When there was silence, he gestured towards one of them. "Marsh. What am I holding?"

"Wool, sir. A ball of wool." Marsh nearly shouted the words.

"And what is wool used for." Dore pointed the ball at his next victim. "Wirrin?"

"Ladies use it to knit with, sir," Wirrin said.

"Dalan." Dore pointed the ball of wool at the last recruit in the line.

"Yes, sir."

"Would you like to knit me a baby bonnet out of this wool?"

"No, sir."

Shadow struggled to remain quiet. Did he really need to do this? Was he always this way or was it for her benefit? She wanted to call out enough, but she had argued for this chance. Was that what he wanted? For her to ruin her chance in the first hour? Her lips tightened, her hands becoming fists behind her back.

Dore strode along the line one more time before he faced them. "In one week, I'll be kicking one of you six out of my squad. And that person is going to knit me a baby bonnet." He tossed the wool into the air again.

"But sir, that's a girl," Jurn said.

Dore stepped forward to stand toe to toe with Jurn. "If you can't do better than a girl then you don't deserve to be in my squad. Is that understood?" He raised his voice on the question, his gaze travelling the line.

"Yes, sir." Five voices echoed back.

Dore's gaze stayed on Shadow, who hadn't spoken. The moment spun out then he addressed the entire squad. "Swords off. Pair up for hand to hand." When they didn't move instantly, he bellowed, "Hurry up lads. I'm going grey standing here."

Shadow removed her sword and put it with the rest of them. She turned to find Jurn grinning at her, waiting to partner her. She eyed him up and down. He wasn't much taller than her, but his broad chest and muscular arms were going to put her at a disadvantage. When Jurn cracked his knuckles Shadow had to force herself to remain still. What the hell was she doing here? She must have a death wish. Somewhere deep down, she had to have a death wish.

"Any daggers you have are to remain where they are. Body parts only. Fists, feet, heads, elbows, knees. Does everyone understand?"

"Yes, sir." Shadow joined in.

"I want your opponent on the ground. You have

fifteen minutes then swap partners." Dore moved away from the paired recruits.

Shadow nearly groaned. This was going to be the longest fifteen minutes of her life, if she survived. She kept her gaze on Jurn, waiting for him to move.

"Don't stand around gazing into each other's eyes. This isn't a romantic dinner. I want to see someone eating dirt. Now," Dore bellowed.

Jurn's grin widened and he beckoned her forward. "You hungry?"

Shadow raised her fists. "No thanks. I've already broken my fast, how about you?"

His reply was a swing of his fists and Shadow ducked, slipping to the side. Then there was no time to talk. Limbs flew at her. Fists towards her face and stomach, legs tried to sweep her off her feet. She stumbled as she spun away, feeling a glancing blow on her shoulder. That was going to hurt later. She faced Jurn, wishing she could attack rather than duck and weave. How was she going to make anyone eat dirt?

"Change partners."

It took Shadow a couple of seconds to process the command as she tried to avoid Jurn's fist. His angry glare as he stepped away didn't look good. There wasn't going to be the camaraderie she'd found with

Carson's men, Dore's earlier speech had assured that outcome.

Her next partner was Marsh. He was tall and solid, but not as broad as Jurn. His reach was also longer than Jurn's and he managed to get in several hits before she figured out his reach. Once again she was on the defensive, finding it impossible to even consider attacking. This time Dore wandered amongst them calling out corrections. Then finally the words she waited for.

"Change partners."

Shadow faced Wirrin, a short dark haired lad with more strength in his punch then either of the last two. Unless it felt worse because she was tiring.

"Can't any of you follow a simple direction? Dirt. I want to see someone eat dirt. You're not trying. None of you are." Dore's voice brought them all to a halt. "Did I tell you to stop? No. Now fight. I can't even see blood. The lot of you are a pack of girls. It looks like I should have brought six balls of wool."

Shadow winced as Wirrin's fist connected with her jaw. That was going to bruise, in a major way. She ducked his next fist, striking out with her foot. He jumped out of the way and then she was forced to defend again.

"Shadow. Wirrin. Here."

They joined Dore and watched and listened as he explained what they were doing wrong. Then he gestured for them to begin again. After several seconds he turned away, calling another pair to him.

When Dore finally called a halt, Shadow wished she could drop to the ground. She wasn't anywhere near as fit as she'd thought. Unless a week of castle living had made her soft. She had continued her push ups but there'd been nowhere to do chin ups. Maybe she needed to find somewhere.

Now she was no longer focused on trying not to get beaten into the ground, she noticed there were other trainers and their squads using different areas of the training grounds. Maybe she'd have been better off trying to get one of them to train her. Who was she kidding? She wanted the best, even if that meant dragging herself here a couple of hours earlier than all the other squads.

"Grab your swords and follow me." Dore strode away before any of them had a chance to move.

Then there was a scramble to collect swords and race after Dore. He stopped beside an open chest. Inside were crossbows and bolts. Shadow almost shouted in joy. She wasn't brilliant with a crossbow, but it had to be a lot easier than being pounded into the ground, and she'd done a lot of training with one.

"Choose a weapon, lads. I'll be greyer than a misty morning at this rate. Come on. Grab ammunition then line up in front of the targets. I expect every bolt to hit the target. Anyone who gets a bullseye will not be forced to run around the training grounds twenty times when we stop for a meal. Hurry up now."

Shadow loaded her crossbow and sighted in the target. She hit, missing the bullseye. She frowned. It was different to her crossbow, not as accurate. She tried to think about the adjustments she had to make. A few seconds with her eyes closed and she thought she might have worked it out.

"Bullseye," Dalan called out. He wore only a vest, no shirt. His slim frame covered in wiry muscles, his hair a brown stubble.

She pulled the trigger and grinned when the bolt hit. "Bullseye." She reloaded and aimed again. There might be a chance she didn't fail training after all.

"Bullseye," Dalan called again.

Shadow grinned when her bolt landed. "Bullseye."

Chapter Thirty-Three

After their meal break Shadow endured an afternoon of sword drills. Once it was over, she wanted to curl up in a ball and pretend every muscle, bone and inch of her body didn't hurt. Instead she stood at attention with the rest of the squad, waiting for Dore to finish pacing back and forth in front of them, the ball of wool being tossed into the air.

He stopped abruptly turning to face them. "Dismissed." His finger pointed at Shadow. "Except you."

Shadow kept her gaze on Dore, but she still couldn't miss the glances sent her way as the squad deserted her. She continued to stand at attention, her hands behind her back, her gaze straight ahead, and waited. The moment stretched out, her muscles protested and still Dore stared at her. She bit back her demand to know what he wanted. Was this another one of his tests?

"I should probably thank you."

Her startled gaze flew to his. There was no humour in them, just the same hard stare as usual. "Why?"

"I've never seen them work so hard. If nothing else having you threaten their position in the squad has done wonders for their abilities. This is the first time Dalan hit the bullseye nearly every time."

Shadow waited. Dore continued to stare silently at her. Annoyance twisted through her as she noticed he didn't comment on how she'd matched Dalan at his feat. She pushed away the annoyance and tried to picture the willow Thornton believed she was. It didn't help. All this willow wanted to do was dip her head to the ground, curl up in a ball and never move again. Why on earth had she thought she was up to this? So she'd found the prince, big deal. She'd had help nearly every step of the way.

"Dismissed."

It took her a moment to realise she could move. Then another moment before her reluctant body obeyed. She nodded at Dore and then turned away, surprised to see Jurn jogging around the perimeter of the training grounds. She felt Dore step up beside her, his gaze also drawn to the young man.

"That lad won't be getting the wool in seven days. Not with his dedication."

Shadow groaned when Dore moved away. Jogging? How much more torture did she need to put herself through? She closed her eyes momentarily. She'd made this bargain and she wasn't going to fail. Bringing to mind the image of herself old, decrepit and serving in the tavern she forced her body to obey. Jogging to the edge of the training ground she fell in behind Jurn. He soon out paced her, but she kept up her steady movements. She could do this. She'd done similar before.

An image filled her mind of spinning around a clearing, arms outstretched as she celebrated twenty chin ups. Her jaw tightened and she winced at the bruise. She could do this. One foot in front of the other. It didn't have to be fast. Then Jurn was behind her, passing her again.

He was a few steps ahead of her when he sent her a look of contempt. "You're wasting your time. I'll bring you a pattern tomorrow so you'll know how to knit that baby bonnet."

Her eyes narrowed and her chin came up. "I'll keep the pattern safe for you."

Jurn laughed, a humourless, mocking sound. "Keep dreaming little girl." He pulled ahead of her.

Shadow forced herself to keep to her original pace. Racing ahead would only exhaust her and she'd collapse on the ground. She didn't need to give Jurn anything else to mock.

The sun filled the sky with splashes of orange and red, darkness creeping in. And still they jogged. Shadow breathed through her mouth, ignoring each screaming protest of her body. Why was she still here? Why wasn't she begging one of the servants to draw her a hot bath? Jurn jogged past her again, not looking at her. That was why she was still out here in the dark, wondering what the hell she was doing. Tenacity. Or was it stupidity? Probably both. Another figure came up on her right and Shadow glanced over to see Thornton falling into step with her.

"Should I have had your dinner sent here? Or maybe have a tent set up? Any preference to location?"

She could hear Jurn behind her. This time he didn't pass. She felt like telling Jurn to get lost. Instead she answered Thornton. "And why does this concern you? My lord?"

"Ah, like that huh?" Thornton laughed softly. "I'm hungry and you're dining with me." He glanced behind him and waved Jurn forward.

Jurn jogged past, a respectful nod and a quiet, "My lord."

"Do you think we can call it a night? Before I die of starvation?" Thornton continued to keep pace with her.

She bit back her sigh. Maybe it was time to be a willow. Before she did break and couldn't even crawl back to the training grounds tomorrow. "I wouldn't want that after all the effort it took to rescue you."

"I'll meet you in your room in an hour. That should give you enough time to bathe before we dine."

Shadow laughed. "Is that meant to be a polite way of telling me I stink?"

Thornton grinned at her. "How does pig sound, my lady?"

"Bull would probably be more appropriate."

"I'll see you in an hour." He cut across the training grounds towards the castle.

Shadow started to slow as she watched his guards trailing in his wake at a discrete distance. Then Jurn was beside her, his pace matching hers.

"I was wondering how you'd bought your way into the army." Then he sped up, giving her no chance to reply.

Shadow came to a halt, glaring after him. She'd show him there'd been no buying involved. She mightn't have his strength and obviously not his stamina. Yet. But she wasn't completely unskilled. Look how many times she'd hit the target today. She strode across the training grounds to the castle, heading for her room. By her door stood a servant.

He nodded, "Let me know when you're finished, my lady."

Shadow swung her door open and was about to ask, finished what, when she saw the large wooden tub sitting in her room filled with steaming water. Beside it was a bucket of cold water. With the way she felt there'd be no need for the bucket. With a nod of her head, she entered her room, closed the door and quickly discarded her clothes. She winced at the heat of the water, sucking in a deep breath as she lowered herself in further.

How was she going to survive a week? Ducking under the water, she rubbed at her face, biting back the groan as she touched the bruise. Surfacing, she felt a little better. She could survive. The same way she'd survived the army. One day at a time. One second at a time if need be.

Reluctantly climbing from the tub she reached for the soft linen towel and rubbed herself dry, quickly dressing in another one of her unconventional outfits. She reached for her sword, withdrawing it slightly to run her fingers over the engravings, thinking of Carson.

Her fingers tingled and she saw him, head bent as he wrote at the collapsible desk inside the tent. His head lifted like he felt her gaze on him and he glanced around. He looked real enough to touch. Then the flap of his tent was thrown open and Gil entered the tent with a glare. Carson gave a short nod and the scene evaporated.

Shadow sighed. As if she didn't have enough to worry over. She'd seen that expression on Gil's face numerous times and each time had ended in a fight. There was nothing she could do about it except hope he kept his promise to take care of Carson. She rose to her feet and opened the door to find the servant still standing patiently in the hall.

"I'm finished."

With a nod he took away the bucket and soon returned with several other servants who scooped buckets of water from the tub before they removed the half empty container. Thornton entered as they left and Shadow suspected someone had fetched him.

"A gift." He held out a sealed jar to her.

Shadow stared at it while her hands remained at her sides. "What is it?"

"Bruise balm." He reached out for one of her hands and placed the jar in it.

"Isn't this cheating?" She eyed the jar suspiciously.

Thornton laughed. "You tell me tomorrow who's cheating when each one of your fellow students return to class with not a single bruise on them." There was a tap on the door and he turned to open it. With a smile in Shadow's direction, he said, "Dinner is served, my lady."

Shadow watched as servants brought in a small round table, two chairs and numerous dishes of food that made her mouth water.

Chapter Thirty-Four

A knock on her door dragged Shadow from sleep and brought her to her feet. Still in her nightgown, she grabbed her sword that lay on the floor beside her bed and half opened her bedroom door. A servant stood there with a plate of large biscuits filled with oats and nuts, steam rising from them. In her other hand, she held out a letter.

The servant made an awkward curtsey as she tried to hold the plate steady. "My lady, I had orders to bring these to you before you left for training."

Shadow leaned her sword against the wall by the door and took the plate and letter. The servant curtseyed again, more graceful this time, before she turned and fled. Shadow smiled. It seemed to be a common reaction among the servants. She closed her door with a bump of her hip and returned to her bed, sitting the plate beside her so she could open the letter.

'Shadow, One of my favourite memories as a child was sneaking out of the nursery early in the morning while only the servants were awake and going to the kitchen, which was filled with the smells of freshly, baked bread, pastries and biscuits. The cook always made my favourite ones when she knew I was home. Filled with oats, a mixture of nuts and sweetened with honey. It's a different cook now, her daughter, but still the same recipe. I hope you enjoy them as much as I do. And did you like your gift? How many people have you pestered so far to teach you how to use it? I wish I was there to show you. Love Carson.'

She smiled as she took a bite of one of the biscuits. She hadn't pestered that many people. Yet. She glanced towards her window. If she didn't hurry and get ready she'd have to find someone else to pester because Dore would fail her.

When she reached the training grounds it was to find the other five already there. A quick search of the area showed Dore hadn't arrived. She finished off the last of her biscuits and dusted the crumbs on her trousers as she eyed her silent companions. Not a single one of them showed any signs of the bruises they had sported yesterday afternoon and she bet like herself all their aches and pains were gone. She reminded herself to thank Thornton later then joined the line the lads started to form when Dore strode towards them.

Before Dore reached them, Jurn pressed a piece of paper into her hands. She glanced at it to see a knitting pattern. Tucking it into her belt pouch she said softly, "Don't worry, I'll keep it safe for you."

Jurn ignored her, but that could have had something to do with Dore arriving and shouting at them to choose partners. She nearly groaned when Jurn turned to her, a look of retribution in his eyes. Today she was going to eat dirt if he had anything to say about it. Her chin came up with her hands and she waited for him to throw the first punch.

The rest of the day continued like it started. Jurn choosing her as a partner whenever possible. It was close, but she didn't eat dirt. She had more bruises and plenty of aches and couldn't wait to use her bruise balm, and then the moment she'd been waiting for arrived and they were standing to attention in front of Dore, the day nearly over.

He stood in front of them, stance wide, glare firmly in place. "Officer lessons tonight." His gaze dropped on Shadow. "For anyone who thinks they have the balls to reach that level."

Her chin rose. Screw being a willow. "I'll see you there, sir."

Jurn stood beside her. "Yes, sir."

Shadow felt like groaning. Or shoving the knitting pattern down Jurn's throat. And they called her Shadow.

"Dismissed," Dore barked before he strode away.

Shadow watched as the squad moved away, Wirrin, Dalan and Marsh falling into step together, Vin hurrying away on his own and Jurn to jog around the training grounds. Shadow suppressed a groan and joined him, ignoring the protests of her body. She watched as he pulled away from her, his longer legs making it seem effortless. She glared at his back, her boots hitting the ground as the distance between them grew. A sparkle in the air ahead drew her attention.

A man stood, his back to her, watching Jurn run past. He was magic hid, his solid frame clothed in rich dark colours, his brown hair, with several streaks of grey, tied at the base of his neck in a stubby pony tail and a hand on his hip. Shadow met his dark eyes when she jogged past and he took a step back. When she would have had to turn around to watch him, he gave her a nod and strolled away. She stopped and watched him, standing there long enough for Jurn to pass her with a sneer.

Her sympathy evaporated. "Who was watching you?"

Jurn stopped to face her. "What?"

"The magic hid man with the pony tail and dark eyes. Had his hand on his hip as he watched you."

His face tightened and he turned away, starting to jog again.

"I guess I could ask around." She began to follow him.

Jurn slowed until she was beside him. "My father, Hurrin."

"Your father's a wizard?"

"Yes." There was a wealth of bitterness in his tone. "One of the most powerful wizards in the country. And I haven't an ounce of magic."

Magical talent, like elf sight was hereditary. But unlike elf sight, each descendent usually had at least a little skill. Shadow momentarily closed her eyes. She didn't want to feel sympathy for Jurn, but what must his life have been like to be born to a famous wizard when you had no magical talent? If the disappointed expression on his father's face was anything to go by, it hadn't been pleasant.

She watched as Jurn pulled away from her again,

promising herself once more around the grounds before she left to get ready for the officer lessons. Jurn finished before her. She watched him leave, trying to ignore the sympathetic feelings that flooded her. He wasn't interested in friendship and he was determined she'd fail. She had to continue to treat him the same. He wouldn't welcome her sympathy.

When she reached her room, the same servant stood at the door. She nodded in greeting before she stepped inside to use the bath waiting for her and eat the tray of food on a small table set against the wall. She pitied the servants forced to lug the furniture around for her convenience. As she was about to leave her room, she recalled the pattern in her belt pouch and dropped it inside the chest at the foot of her bed. She stared at the chest a moment before her lips curved into a smile.

Pulling the door open, she asked, "Can you get me knitting needles?"

"Yes, my lady." The servant nodded.

"Now?"

Another nod.

"And I need someone to show me where the officer's lessons are held."

"If you meet me in the main hall I can fetch the needles and lead you from there," the servant offered.

"Thanks." She started to turn away then stopped. "What's your name?"

"Radler, my lady."

"You've been here twice. Were you assigned to serve me?"

"No, my lady."

"Then why are you here?"

"I serve the Captain when he's home, my lady."

"That doesn't mean you have to automatically serve me. And quit calling me my lady. It's very annoying. Shadow. It's simple enough to say."

"Yes, my… yes Shadow."

"What's going on here? Evasive answers and eyes that look everywhere but at me. I'm not an idiot." Her hands went to her hips and she stared at the man until his green eyes met hers. He couldn't be much older than her, maybe Carson's age. His narrow freckled face was topped by a mess of sandy blond hair. "I'm waiting. You're going to make me late."

Radler sighed. "I should have known a lady of the Captain's was sure to be difficult. Prince Thornton came to the kitchens and said there was to be a bath in your room for you when you finish training. And the nights he isn't to dine with you, a meal."

"So you took it upon yourself to follow his orders?" Radler shook his head.

Shadow grinned. "Let me guess. No one else was willing."

"There was a suggestion from someone else you might prefer to seek your own bath and meal since you're so independent."

"Someone else?"

"Yes, my lady."

"Shadow," she said automatically as she continued to stare at Radler. He only nodded, volunteering no more information. Right now she could have done with being able to read minds. Elf sight and the odd vision weren't that helpful sometimes. She nodded slowly. "I'll meet you in the main hall, Radler."

"Yes, my lady."

"Shadow." She said it sharper this time.

Radler's grin was fleeting. "Yes, Shadow." He hurried away and Shadow stared after him. With a shake of her head she strode towards the main hall.

She wasn't there long before Radler joined her, handing over the two polished wooden knitting needles. After staring at them for a moment she tucked them down the side of her boot that didn't contain a sheathed knife and gestured for Radler to lead the way. He led her quickly through the warren of the castle, pausing several steps away from the room she'd visited two nights ago.

"Thank you, Radler."

"I'll return for you, my lady." He glanced towards the person walking along the hallway before he nodded deferentially and left.

Shadow turned to see who was there and her lips curved into a smile when she saw Jurn. His steps slowed at her expression. "I brought a present for you. After all the effort you went to in choosing one for me I wouldn't have considered forgetting to get you something."

He halted in front of her. "You wasted your time. I want nothing from you."

"You'll want this." She reached for her boot and saw Jurn tense, his hand going to the pommel of the sword hanging from his belt. She withdrew the knitting needles and held them out to him, her smile firmly in place.

Footsteps sounded in the hallway behind her and Jurn's gaze flickered over her shoulder before he reached out and took the knitting needles, sliding them down the side of his boot. "I'll keep them safe for you." He spun and entered the room.

Chapter Thirty-Five

Shadow turned to see Dore. With a nod in his direction she entered the room and found herself a seat. As well as all who had been there last time there were three new people. Only two of them she knew. Jurn and Vin. Neither of them met her gaze when it fell on them and she turned towards the front of the room when Dore strode to his usual place.

His hands went behind his back and his stance widened. "Each of you take paper, quill and ink from those in the centre of the table. There won't be enough. I expect you to pair up. If you can't sort it out amongst yourselves I'll do it for you. Tonight you'll be feeding troops on campaigns. Ask plenty of questions because at the end each team will be given a scenario. You fail that, I don't want to see you back."

Shadow looked to the young man on her right. He spoke to the one on his other side. She turned to her left and had the same problem. A quick look around the table showed only one without a partner. A young man who swallowed visibly when he came to the same conclusion. His gaze darted to the door. Shadow's lips thinned as she glared at the young man. Anyone would think she was contagious. She rose from her seat and started around the table, taking her chair with her. The young man also rose, his gaze darting between her and the door.

"Sit down, Dan. Only one of you needs to relocate." Dore glared at him.

"Oh… ah… I was…" Dan gestured towards the exit.

"Sit."

Dan dropped into his seat at Dore's command.

Shadow looked to each side of Dan. On one side was a stranger, the other was Jurn, a mocking smile on his lips. Eyes still narrowed, she stepped closer to Jurn, pushing her chair towards the table. He met her gaze, making her stand there long moments before he shifted along to give her the barest amount of space.

Shadow leaned towards him as she sat, her voice soft enough for only Jurn to hear. "I didn't realise how keen you were to be close to me. No wonder you single me out as a partner every morning." She smiled up at him and managed to prevent her smile from widening when he scraped his chair across the timber floor giving her more space.

"You will need to take into account the terrain, what is expected of your troops and the weather. These will all have an effect on how much your troops eat."

Shadow's smile faded as she concentrated on Dore's words. When he started giving amounts and her partner was the only one not writing she tried to take the quill he tightly gripped. Dore sent a glare in her direction and she let the quill go. A snicker on her other side made her want to draw her knife and stab Jurn. Or better yet have kept the knitting needles and jabbed him with them. Still trying to listen and retain the information Dore was sprinkling through his explanations, Shadow slid the knife from her boot and pressed the sharp blade into the back of Dan's knee, leaning close to him.

"Drop the quill or I'll make you lame."

He made a sound halfway between a squeak and a gasp, but he dropped the quill and Shadow sheathed her knife and hurriedly started to write the information she needed to pass tonight's test. When the question and answer portion of the evening was over Dore handed out scenarios for them to read.

Shadow read the paper she held, Dan sending her

frequent nervous glances. He wasn't going to last long. It was a wonder Dore hadn't kicked him out long ago. She placed the paper in front of Dan so he could read it and began to scribble notes on a clean page.

Dan's finger pointed to her second line of writing. "That's wrong."

"No it's not."

A whispered and heated argument followed until they figured both had been wrong. When they finally finished and handed their answers to Dore, Dan muttered to Shadow, "You cut my trousers."

"Oh shut up."

"How am I meant to explain that?"

"You caught them on something?"

"And the blood? You cut me."

Shadow smiled at his petulant expression. "Must have been a nail sticking out of something."

"And what about you? How do I explain this? My father'll kill me when he finds out I talked to you."

"Don't be such a baby," she hissed, her glare destroying her smile.

"You don't know what it's like. So he mightn't kill me, but I'll wish he had by the end of it."

Shadow sighed. She did know. "Sorry. Tell him

Dore made you partner me. That you hated every minute of it."

"That won't work."

"Why not."

Dan stared at her a moment, swallowing visibly. "He can tell when I'm lying."

Shadow met his stare, wishing she hadn't pushed him into being her partner. "Tell him you were terrified Dore would throw you from the room if you disobeyed. Think you can tell that convincingly?"

Dan nodded. Then turned to face Dore when he slammed his hand on the table.

Dore raised his other hand to point his finger at two young men across the table who visibly paled. "You. You. Out. Your troops are dead. Don't come back." He straightened, his hands going behind his back. "The rest of you go home. I'll see you next week."

"Yes, sir." The words rang out around the room as Dore strode from it.

Shadow started to rise, but Dan placed a hand on her arm. She turned to him with a questioning look, but he was watching the doorway with everyone else. Then as if a signal unheard by her was given, there was a scramble for the reports in the middle of the table. She watched silently as the report from the two who had failed was dissected. It was only once this was done students drifted from the room.

"Thanks." Shadow said softly to Dan.

"Don't mention it. And I mean that seriously. Never, ever mention it." He kept his voice equally soft. "And please don't talk to me." He sent a nervous glance around the room before he hurried away.

Shadow saw Vin and Jurn huddled by the door, arguing in hushed tones, Vin shaking his head. When he saw Shadow watching them, he spoke to Jurn who turned to meet her gaze. His eyes narrowed and he pushed Vin out the door, dragging him along the hallway with him. She strode to the doorway and watched them leave, wondering what they were planning. Hoping it had nothing to do with her, she turned towards Radler. Maybe she was getting too suspicious.

"My lady? Is everything fine?"

"My lady?"

Radler smiled fleetingly. "This way. Lady Shadow."

She followed him, unable to resist smiling. Her smile faded when she reached her room and closed the door as Radler left. She took a deeper breath, closing her eyes. The scent was faint, but familiar. Frowning, Shadow stepped further into her room and looked around. Nothing seemed out of place. Reaching out, she placed a hand on the chest and felt a tingle in her fingers as she tried to see what had happened while she was gone.

Krisa slipped into her room, Lani, one of her friends, staying as lookout at the door. Krisa glanced around the room, distaste on her face. "How can she live like this? It's so basic." She opened the chest and stared at the contents.

"Hurry up, Krisa. We don't want to get caught." Lani glanced into the room before she returned to peering up and down the hallway.

"It doesn't matter. I have that sorted. If we're caught I'll say I'm leaving her one of my lace hankies. Poor girl has none of her own. Why, she doesn't even have a decent dress to wear if her current attire is any indication." She laughed at her false tone of sincerity as she touched the material of the folded clothes in the chest. "This isn't even silk. She's clueless." Next she picked up the knitting pattern and looked at it. "Lani, come here."

"What if someone comes?"

"Lani." There was a threat in her tone that brought Lani immediately to Krisa's side. She held out the pattern. "Who wrote this?"

Lani read it over. "It looks like Jurn's writing."

Krisa smiled. "I thought so."

"What are you going to do?"

Krisa dropped the lid of the chest and tucked the pattern into her reticule. "My mother did not go to the effort of making my name similar to the queen's and pandering to her all these years to let some upstart come in and steal my place. Even if everyone else doesn't realise it, I know the queen will eventually accept her when the captain returns."

"How are you going to stop her?"

Krisa linked her arm through Lani's. "Is that palace guard still madly in love with you?"

Lani nodded as they walked towards the door.

"And he'll do whatever you want?" Krisa paused in the doorway.

"Of course."

"I have the most delicious plan. You're going to love it." Krisa closed the door, a sly smile curving her lips.

Shadow sat on the top of her chest as the vision faded. Didn't Krisa realise she wasn't interested in taking her place? And the queen probably hated her more than Krisa did and would never accept her. She felt alone. Completely alone. She hadn't even seen her brother in days. Sliding her sword out of the scabbard she sat it across her lap, feeling the engraving. When her fingers tingled again, she closed her eyes and sank gratefully into another vision.

Carson peered into a fire, his hands wrapped around a mug he sipped from. The sounds of murmured conversations drifted to him, but he sat alone. Across the fire was Gil, head tilted back as he stared into the starlit sky. Carson looked around and Shadow wished there was a way to tell him she could see him. Hear him.

Carson rose to his feet and strode over to Gil who took his time watching the sky before he finally gave his attention to Carson. "Are you sure there's no one magic hid around here?"

Shadow watched as her Pa rose and slowly turned, checking his surroundings. He frowned and rubbed the back of his neck. "If the old girl weren't dead I'd think it was Gennie's Ma checking up on me. She had a lock of Gennie's hair she'd use to check what we were up to. It didn't always work but she could call up visions of the near future, the present and the not too distant past. Gave me the creeps."

"Your wife or children don't have it, do they?"

Gil shook his head. "Gennie said she wished she did when I was lost. She tried every day but not a single spark."

"Your children?"

Gil started to shake his head then swore. "Anything's possible with that bloody Shadow."

Carson grinned. "That's certainly the truth." He paused a moment. "These visions. What are they like?"

Gil shrugged. "The old girl reckoned she could see and hear as clear as if she stood there when she was having a good one. Sometimes they were hazy and muffled. Or didn't come at all. Why?"

"Just wondering." He paused. "Thanks." A nod and he strode away from the campfire to stand alone among the trees. Silence filled the night and Shadow was about to let go of the vision as it was becoming harder to hold.

"Shadow." The word was spoken so softly she almost didn't hear it.

She fought to hold onto the vision.

"I miss you, Shadow. Check on me any time you want."

The vision evaporated and Shadow wanted to scream in frustration. She ran her fingers back and forth along the engraving. Nothing happened. She ran the back of her hand across her eyes when they blurred and was surprised by the dampness. Rising to her feet she sheathed her sword. There was no way she'd be able to sleep. Her hand rested on her pommel and she quickly came to a decision.

When she reached the training grounds she was surprised to find Jurn there, his sword slashing imaginary foes. If his movements were anything to go by, he was helplessly outnumbered. She drew her sword and he turned at the sound. He watched silently as she stepped forward.

At his sharp nod she attacked. He met her blows, the sound of metal singing in the night air. Time became meaningless, measured only by the collision of metal and the sharp breaths of exertion. When Shadow's sword eventually landed on the ground, Jurn stepped back and gestured towards it.

She watched him a moment before she cautiously bent to retrieve it. He beckoned her to come at him again. Another watchful moment before Shadow complied. She was beginning to tire, her arms a burning ache, but still she continued. Her movements slowed and she concentrated on defending, attacking beyond her. And still Jurn came at her, his movements full of fury. When Shadow's sword landed on the ground again, Jurn held his sword at her throat.

Her gaze met his, refusing to flinch away from the anger in them. There was little true darkness in the castle and its grounds. Lanterns dispelled any chance it had to take hold so there was no mistaking the equal parts of anger and venom. She held herself still, ready to move if he continued to attack. Not to run, she knew she couldn't outrun him, but maybe grab the knife from her boot. Then he lowered the sword and spun away, sheathing it as he left.

Shadow watched him walk towards the castle before she collected her own sword and sheathed it. Her steps were slower as she headed to the castle, wondering if Jurn was one of the many people who lived there.

Chapter Thirty-Six

Shadow was doing push ups on her bedroom floor when there was a knock at her door. She jumped to her feet, grinning that she felt no aches after last night's practice session. Or had it been a fight she'd twice lost? Either way, she never wanted to run out of bruise balm. She swung the door open and took the well folded paper Radler handed her, her name scrawled across the front. In his other hand was a basket covered in a cloth.

"Enjoy your breakfast, Lady Shadow." He held out the basket.

"Thank you." Once she took it from him, he turned and headed down the hallway. Shadow was surprised to see her brother coming towards her, yawning. "What are you doing up so early?"

He grinned. "I'm not up. Or should I say I haven't

gone to bed yet." He yawned again. "Not everyone wants a daily dose of the torture they call army."

"Who told you?"

He shrugged. "There's rumours everywhere. Most of them are about you failing. You better not." He pointed at her in warning. "I've got a lot of money riding on you."

"You're betting on me to win?"

"I'm not stupid enough to think you're going to lose."

"No, I mean-" she broke off, waving the rest of her words away with her hand. "Oh forget it. I should be used to you gambling on everything possible."

"Only on a winner." He grinned and reached out to check under the cloth draped over the basket.

Shadow dragged it away from him. "Mine."

"Heartless wench. I'm off to bed." Irlan started to move towards his room.

"Irlan." She waited until he turned towards her. "You're fine? Everything's well?"

Irlan grinned. "Couldn't be better. Who'd have imagined we'd end up at the castle? Not bad little sister. I'm looking forward to your next miracle."

"There aren't going to be anymore miracles." She emphasised the last word.

"Of course there will. In four days." He grinned.

"Night." His grin remained in place as he turned and strolled towards his room.

Shadow shook her head as she stared after her brother. Miracle. Not likely. It was going to take a lot of hard work. She closed her door and sat on her bed, pulling back the cloth from the basket to find a mix of pastries and Carson's favourite biscuits. She took a bite of a biscuit and dropped it in the basket so she could undo the string holding the letter closed. It was folded up several times and she quickly found the reason. A lock of Carson's hair.

'Shadow, I hope this will make it easier for you. I wish I could do the same. I guess I will have to wait to find out what chaos you're creating. Love Carson.'

With a smile, Shadow tucked the letter into her belt pouch along with the other two. With Krisa thinking she could wander into her room there was no way she'd even think about leaving them behind. She touched the lock of black hair and focused on Carson. She felt a tingle and closed her eyes as the vision sharpened. He walked along, leading his horse, two of his men in front of him.

Carson looked up from the ground he studied. After a glance around, he smiled, pressing the fingers of his right hand momentarily against his heart. His glance had shown Shadow the rest of the soldiers and her Pa following him.

One of the men looked back and stared at Carson for a moment. "What are you grinning about, Captain? We've been dancing through these hills too long to find anything worth celebrating. How long's it gonna take to get that army together?"

"A couple more weeks. Maybe a little longer and then we can head home," Carson said.

"Grinning?" Gil came alongside him. He rubbed the back of his neck once he came into Shadow's viewing area. "I thought so. You better watch out for that brother of yours, Shadow. You owe me for this, girl."

"For what?" Carson asked.

Gil shook his head. "That's between me and my girl."

"The pair of you have cracked," the soldier said, hurrying ahead. "That'll teach you for playing cat and mouse with an army too big to take on."

Carson chuckled. "I wasn't the one talking to people who aren't actually here."

"She might as well be," Gil grumbled. "Take up embroidery or something. Try and stay out of trouble for once."

Farnell joined them. "How can you be certain it's

Shadow? It could be anyone spying on what we're up to."

"You need something personal to view over long distances, or be very attached to the one you're viewing. How many people are running around with locks of his hair?" Gil nodded towards Carson.

"One," Carson answered.

Shadow almost groaned when the vision slipped from her grasp, but a smile still formed when she thought of his answer. One. That had to be her. She slid her hand into her belt pouch and reluctantly let go of the lock of hair. And no one else was going to get hold of it. No wonder people threw their hair into a fire when they had it cut. She thought of the hair she'd left behind for her Ma to find. Usually.

Shadow did groan when she realised how much time had passed. She'd have to rush to get to the training grounds before Dore. Grabbing a handful of the food from the basket she slid her boots on and raced through hallways, ignoring muttered curses from the few people she passed. Once she stepped outside she slowed her pace, arriving at the training grounds minutes before Dore.

They fell into place before him and he glared at them, holding up a page. Shadow stared at the pattern, keeping her gaze on it when she would have preferred checking Jurn's reaction.

"Well? Anyone going to tell me what this is?"

"It's mine," Shadow said at the same time as Jurn said, "It belongs to me."

She had no idea what Krisa had instigated, but it wasn't fair to let Jurn take the blame when it was her Krisa was trying to harm. "You can't take it back, Jurn. It's mine."

"He gave this to you." Dore faced Shadow.

Shadow nodded.

"Why?"

"How did you get it?" Shadow stalled for time.

"I ask the questions. You answer." Dore's gaze bore into her.

Shadow was tempted to tell him her Pa could teach him a few lessons on how to have a person quiver in their boots with just a look. "It was a joke. I gave him knitting needles."

Dore stared at her a moment longer. "You." He pointed at Shadow. "And you." His finger aimed at Jurn. "Follow. The rest of you." His gaze fell on the rest of the squad. "Push ups."

No one dared to groan as Dore strode away. Shadow and Jurn followed him.

"What do you think you're doing?" Jurn hissed.

"Don't blame this on me. It's all Krisa's effort."

"What did you do to her?"

Shadow couldn't resist grinning. "She's threatened by my stunning beauty and worried I'll steal all her love struck followers."

Any words Jurn might have spoken were prevented by Dore. "Wipe that grin off your face. There's nothing amusing here. Or is that the plan? Get rid of the toughest competition."

"Maybe you should be telling us what's happening. We're the ones confused," Shadow said.

Dore's eyes narrowed further until he looked like he might draw his sword. "A palace guard brought this to me this morning." He shook the paper. "The queen is not impressed her protégée is the brunt of these unamusing jokes and would like the soldier at blame to be punished for his poor attempt at humour." His gaze turned to Jurn. "Can you imagine how severe that punishment would need to be, soldier?"

"Yes, sir." Jurn held his gaze unflinching.

"I started this," Shadow said.

"This is your writing?" Dore waved the paper at her face.

"No, sir. Ask him where the knitting needles are I gave him."

Dore turned to Jurn. "Well?"

Jurn pulled the needles from his boot and held them out. Each wooden needle had been sharpened to a point, looking more like weapons.

"When did you get these?" Dore pointed towards the needles.

Shadow answered before Jurn could. "We swapped gifts yesterday. Sir."

"Did I ask you?"

"No, sir." Shadow shook her head.

Dore turned back to Jurn. "Well?"

"We swapped gifts yesterday, sir." Jurn repeated Shadow's words.

"Then what's going on?" Dore roared.

"I guess the queen was misinformed about the joke, sir." Shadow shrugged. "It happens. You know how many mouths every comment goes through. I'm surprised it wasn't even more garbled by the time it reached the queen's ears."

Dore stared at her a moment longer. "And what do you suggest I do with this?" He waved the pattern at her again.

Shadow remembered Iain's words about how she should act around Dore. She took a steady breath and tried to remain relaxed. "Maybe you should keep it for the one who wins your ball of wool. Sir."

Dore pulled the ball of wool from his belt pouch and held it out to her. "Maybe I should give both of them to you right now. And those knitting needles."

Jurn held the needles out to Dore again.

Shadow was tempted to thank him for his help. Right before she stabbed him with one of the needles he'd sharpened. "That was a quick seven days, sir."

Dore glared at her a moment longer before he turned to Jurn, shoving the pattern at him. "Fifty push ups. The two of you." He strode back to the rest of the squad.

"That's mine." Shadow snatched the pattern from him and folded it to fit in her belt pouch.

"How did Krisa get it?"

"She obviously believes people welcome her going through their things and helping herself to whatever she wants."

Jurn slid the needles into his boot before he dropped to the ground and started doing push ups. "This changes nothing."

Shadow joined him. "What do you mean?"

"This is your fault. I owe you nothing."

She was about to make a reply she was sure she'd regret later when a glitter caught her attention. Jurn's father was at the edge of the training grounds, watching. "Why does your father trail after you?"

"Where?"

Shadow described the location and was surprised when Jurn didn't even look in the direction. "Does he do this often?" When he didn't answer, she said. "I saved your butt. How about we call the answer a fair exchange." Silence stretched out and she began to think he wasn't going to answer.

"Must do. Or at least someone regularly follows since he knows everything I do."

They fell silent, both doing their push ups. Jurn finished first. She watched him walk away then glanced to where his father still watched. She was beginning to think Gil was the better father and that was a scary thought.

When Shadow rejoined the squad, Dore called them to attention, ending the hand to hand training early. He clasped his hands behind his back and waited until they were neatly lined up. "Dagger throwing. You better all be carrying one. No soldier wanders around with a single weapon." He was silent a moment. "Well? Where are they?"

They all reached into their boots and pulled out daggers, looking towards the targets they usually used for crossbow training when Dore pointed in that direction.

"Well? What are you waiting for? My funeral?"

When they started to move away, Dore pointed first to Jurn, then Shadow. "Not you two." He paused while they came to a halt in front of him. "I believe you both have another weapon you prefer." His gaze fell onto Jurn's boot he'd tucked the knitting needles into. "Well?"

"Yes, sir." Jurn tucked his dagger into his boot and pulled out the needles, handing one to Shadow.

"Sir."

"What?" Dore snapped at Shadow.

"Why does Jurn's father watch us while he's magic hid?"

"Where is he?" Dore growled. "Exact location without staring at him."

Shadow nodded and with a glance from the corner of her eye did as she was ordered.

"Tell me if Hurrin moves." Dore readied his crossbow that had been slung on his back. "Well?"

Another quick glance. "Still in the same location, sir."

Dore fired his crossbow and a bolt embedded itself in the ground at the wizard's feet. He turned to Shadow. "Well?"

"He's leaving sir."

"Good. Now start practicing." His gaze fell on Jurn. "Both of you."

Chapter Thirty-Seven

Jurn walked beside her. "Did I ask for that?"

"It wasn't for you."

"Who was it for?"

"Me. It was distracting all that glitter in the air." She threw the needle at the target and glared as it fell far short. She almost cheered when Dore finally told them to use crossbows. But that was the last time she felt like cheering. After their meal break Dore paired her with Jurn for sword practice and he wasn't giving any quarter. Four times her sword landed in the dirt. The fourth time she did too. When she rose from the dust it was to see the entire squad watching her.

Her gaze narrowed and she picked up her sword and held it ready. This time she concentrated on defence. There was no way she could attack with the mood Jurn was in. He seemed out for blood and hers looked to be on the top of his list. There was no way she could draw blood with her sword, but there were other ways to wound.

"When did you first pick up a sword?"

"You don't seriously wish to talk right now." Jurn looked at her in disbelief, his sword barely slowing.

"Oh, I see, it's a secret."

"How would I know? I was little. Maybe five. Six. Something like that."

"That long ago? Huh, I'd have thought you'd be better than that then."

It was Jurn's turn to narrow his eyes. "You're the one who lost four times today."

She blocked. Barely. "What do you expect? I only picked up a sword two months ago and most of my training's been with a dagger." She almost laughed at the renewed speed of his attack. At least she would have if she'd had the energy. Her sword landed in the dirt again, Jurn's at her throat. She met his gaze. "Only five times."

There was an unreadable flicker in Jurn's eyes and he turned away. "Can't I be paired with someone more my level. Sir?"

Dore stood watching with the rest of the squad. "Fall in." He waited until they were lined up, Shadow collecting her sword before she joined them. "Just because tomorrow's a rest day doesn't mean I'm not still counting it towards the seven days. I'll see you all the day after. Dismissed." His finger pointed at Shadow. "Not you."

She nearly groaned. Now what. She managed to hold back that comment. "Yes, sir."

Dore waited until the squad had moved away. "When was the first time you used a weapon?"

"Two months ago, sir."

"And you think you can outdo one of these lads."

"Who are the three best at the crossbow amongst us?"

"That isn't the only ability I'm judging. You lost your sword five times."

Shadow could have happily remained silent, but that had never helped her. Only kept her serving at the bar. "Against Jurn. Who'd you say is the best at sword fighting in the squad?"

"Don't back talk," Dore growled.

"I expect a fair chance. Against each of them. On the seventh day we should be tested against each other. With the amount of bets I hear are riding on the outcome you wouldn't want someone to claim the outcome unfair."

"I don't need you telling me how to do things, girl."

Shadow nearly smiled. He sounded like her Pa with

the way he said girl. Annoyance, exasperation and probably a desire to clip her across the ear. She wondered if he'd roar too when she ducked out of the way.

"Dismissed."

Shadow nodded and turned away before she ended up in more trouble. She should skip jogging today for the same reason. She spotted Vin and Jurn arguing. Heading towards the castle, she wandered closer to them so she could hear.

"I can't," Vin said.

"You want to fail?"

"You know I-"

"Forget it. You can fail for all I care." Jurn turned away from Vin.

"Jurn-" Vin broke off at the gesture from Jurn.

Jurn sent a glare towards Shadow before he looked around. Vin looked between them, Shadow having stopped to watch, before he ducked his head and hurried away.

As soon as no one else was close enough to hear, Shadow said, "He's not here. Or anyone else magic hid."

"I wasn't looking for him."

Shadow shrugged. She was tempted to call him a liar, but she was surprised by the relief in his eyes. She watched him a moment longer before she continued towards the castle, wondering what was going on. She was nearly at the castle entrance when she saw the crowd. Krisa was amongst it, fawning over Brisa. There was no way she wanted to get caught up in that drama. She headed towards the gardens, stopping to sit on the edge of a fountain. Her fingers tingled against the stone and she let the vision come.

It was night, a lantern casting dim light over the fountain, creating shadows out of the two figures that stood there. Both were hooded. "It's too soon." The voice was a harsh whisper. "Tell our mutual friend it'll take time to plan again."

"He's running out of patience. With both princes. You've been no help in finding out what the army's doing and you know what he's like when he runs out of patience." The second hooded figure's voice had a slight accent. Shadow couldn't place it.

"Don't threaten me. I'm stronger than the two of you. You can barely hide yourself let alone do anything more powerful. I'll let you know when it's time to set a new plan in motion. But it'll be soon. Before they have time to fully recover from the last attack."

"You know where to find me." The man started to move away.

"Yes. You better remember that." There was no mistaking the threat.

Voices dragged Shadow back from the vision and she cursed, words she'd learned from the soldiers. She headed further into the gardens, not wanting to encounter anyone. She needed to see Thornton. That vision was too insistent for it to be old, a night or two at the most.

Taking a circuitous route, she made her way inside the castle and after asking several servants, finally found Thornton. He lounged with two other men, sipping from goblets and talking.

"My lord, could I have a moment of your time?" Shadow's eyes begged Thornton to agree.

"Surely you could have washed the dirt of the training grounds from you before bursting in here," one of the other men said. "Soldiers have no sense of propriety."

Thornton rose to his feet. "As many moments as you'd like, my lady." He smiled when she glared at the way he addressed her.

Shadow nodded and spun on her heel, heading for the door. She heard Thornton tell his companions he'd be back later and then he was beside her.

"What's wrong?"

She waited until they were clear of anyone who might hear. "Where did they kidnap you from?"

Thornton came to a stop, pulling Shadow back to him. "What's this about?"

She shook her head. "Where?"

He stared at her a moment. "My suite."

"Can you show me?"

Thornton grinned. "You love making the rumours fly, don't you?"

"You dine in my room regularly, what's the difference?"

"Never mind." He shook his head. "When?"

"Whenever you're ready."

Thornton nodded. "How about now?" He leered at her. "I can't wait to drag you back to my room."

She laughed. "Bull."

Thornton escorted her to his suite, his guards remaining outside. They walked through a sitting area and into a bedroom, a large bed dominating the room. She crossed the room, resting her hand against the smooth covers of the bed. When her fingers started to tingle she closed her eyes. An image of Thornton, limbs tangled with those of a smiling blonde filled her mind. Her eyes flew open as she quickly pulled her hand back, heat filling her cheeks. Her gaze met Thornton's.

He took a step back, a hand held up. "Look Shadow, I don't think this is a good idea. Why don't we–"

Shadow shook her head, firmly putting the image from her mind as she interrupted Thornton. "Where'd they come in?"

He gestured to floor length curtains. "The balcony." When Shadow strode towards them, he continued. "There's always two guards out there now."

She nodded, pressing her hand against the door before opening it. Night had fallen while she'd been looking for Thornton.

Chapter Thirty-Eight

Ignoring the guards, and Thornton who trailed behind her, she wrapped both hands around the balcony rail. The smooth stone was cold to her hands and she slid them along until she felt a tingle. Closing her eyes, she was drawn into a hazy image of four magic hid, black clad men sliding down ropes from above. Within seconds they were going through the balcony doors then returning with Thornton, his body wrapped and struggling. Two of the ropes were tied around him and he was drawn upwards, magic hid figures climbing up the other two ropes, which were hanging down.

Shadow opened her eyes and turned to face Thornton who had followed her. She pointed to the castle walls rising above them. "What's up there?"

"More rooms." He shrugged. "Are you finished here?" He returned inside.

Shadow followed, frustrated by his answer. She glanced towards the bed before she stepped closer to Thornton and lowered her voice, conscious of the guards on the balcony. "You can do better than the blonde."

It was Thornton's turn to have a flush spread across his cheeks. "You saw?"

"Now tell me, what's on the floors above you."

"How did you see? And what's all this about?"

Shadow shrugged. "I'm not completely sure, but I see things."

"I know. Magic hid things."

"No. Things. Visions." She glanced behind her to the balcony doors, wondering how safe it was to speak here.

Thornton nodded and led her to another door that led off his room. He closed it behind them. "What did you see?"

Shadow glanced around the room, noting the many garments hanging along one wall and the large tub waiting for Thornton. She took a deep breath and told him about the episode at the fountain and the one on his balcony. "So they're still here, whoever kidnapped you. And they're wizards."

"Are you sure you didn't see a face? Or hear a name?" When Shadow shook her head Thornton sighed. "I can't lock up every wizard in the castle. There must be several dozen of them."

"Who are the most powerful?"

"That doesn't help. He only has to be more powerful than the other two. Which wouldn't take much for the one who can barely hide himself." He swore. "I'll have to tell my father."

"Does he have to know about my visions?"

Thornton grinned. "He won't believe I'm the one having them. Why didn't you tell us earlier you could do this?"

"I only did it for the first time when I was trying to find Irlan. That's how my Gran started, one of her siblings wandered off. Something has to trigger it. And I've been using it a lot lately so I guess they're coming through easier."

"Why've you been practicing?"

"I haven't exactly." She glanced away.

Thornton laughed. "You've been spying on my brother. I hope he's been behaving himself."

"He knows."

"How?"

Shadow shrugged. "What are we going to do about your kidnapper? I can't exactly go around touching every inch of the castle hoping to figure it all out. Things that are handled by too many people don't work. And the longer ago something happened the less clear it is."

"I'll have a talk to my father and see what we can figure out."

Shadow nodded. She looked towards the door. "Do you think you can have someone show me to my room? I don't know how to get there from here."

Thornton nodded and had one of the servants hovering in the hallway outside his suite show her the way through a maze of hallways and staircases.

With a nod to Radler, Shadow stepped into her room. She smiled when she saw the bath and food. She started to put the pattern in her chest, then hesitated. She thought of the expression on Jurn's face and was about to return it to her belt pouch when her fingers tingled. She sunk into the vision, gasping when she saw Jurn's father hit him.

They were in the training grounds and Hurrin was magic hid. Jurn closed his eyes, trying to hear the blow before it hit him. He had no luck. He landed on the ground, picking himself up and slowly turning as he tried to anticipate the next attack.

"You're a disgrace to the family. Stay away from the girl. Do you hear me? She'll drag you down with her."

Jurn faced his father's voice. "I know why you

don't like her. Elf sight." He doubled at the blow to his stomach. Straightening, he grinned. "You can't hide from elf sight. Ever. You're powerless around her."

Hurrin rained several blows on Jurn. "I am never powerless. Remember that. You fail and I'll cast you from the family. Failure will not be tolerated. If you're the one thrown from the squad don't bother coming home." Hurrin turned and walked away.

Jurn continued to stand there, looking around like he expected another attack.

Shadow dragged herself from the vision, pushing the pattern into her pouch. She flung the door open. "Radler, can you get me a small jar of bruise balm? One small enough to carry in my belt pouch. I need to go out."

"You're going now? Without your dinner? Or bath?"

Shadow nodded.

"I'll meet you in the main hall with a small jar of bruise balm, Lady Shadow."

"Thank you." She hurried away, to pace in the main hall as she waited for Radler. People gave her a wide berth and she was relieved. She wasn't in the mood for conversation. There were too many unanswered questions. When Radler arrived he handed her a small jar and with a nod left as silently as he'd arrived. Shadow tucked the jar into her belt pouch and strode towards the training grounds. Once again Jurn was furiously training.

He spun to face her. "What are you doing here?" He glanced around before his gaze returned to Shadow.

She tossed him the jar of bruise balm. "Use it. I wouldn't want you to say I took unfair advantage of whatever fight you got that bruise in." She pointed towards his jaw that was colouring quickly.

"Who says I want to train with you." Again he looked around.

Shadow slowly checked the area. "It's only us. Magic hid stand out brighter than someone normally hidden to me."

Jurn stared at her a moment before he sheathed his sword and applied the bruise balm to numerous places including his stomach and jaw. He tossed the jar back to her once he was finished. "What are you doing here?"

"Training. I thought that was obvious."

"And the bruise balm?"

"What about it?"

"Convenient."

Shadow grinned. "You'd be surprised what I have

in my belt pouch. Are we going to stand around all night or train?"

Jurn pulled out his dagger. "Didn't you say this is what you've trained in the most?" When Shadow nodded Jurn spoke again. "Come on. I wouldn't want you to say I'd taken unfair advantage of you."

She laughed at hearing her words thrown back at her. "Fine." She pulled out her dagger and prepared to eat dirt.

Surprisingly she didn't eat dirt as much as she'd expected and even managed to land Jurn in the dirt once. Eventually they both stood there, exhausted. Jurn's stomach growled in the quiet night.

Shadow returned her knife to her boot. "Dinner?"

"What?"

She glanced upwards. "Maybe it's supper by now. I wouldn't have a clue what time it is."

"You're inviting me to eat with you."

"You do eat, don't you? Normal food, not poached babies or something equally strange. My Pa always said wizards were demons masquerading as humans and probably ate poached babies. So, do they?"

"I'm the wrong person to ask. I have no magic. At all."

"You live with a wizard, don't you?"

"No babies were served that I know about, but

the demon part's probably right." He stared at her a moment. "Why are you here?"

"Training."

Jurn shook his head. "No. Trying to get into the army."

"It's where I belong."

Jurn stared at her again before he nodded. "Me too." He was silent a moment. "I can't be seen anywhere with you. I still live under my father's roof."

Shadow nodded. "Keep me in sight then." She headed for the castle and her room. Once she arrived she sent Radler to bring her a new meal, this time for two.

Jurn arrived at her door once Radler had left. "They really don't like you, do they?" He stepped into her room.

"Why do you say that?"

"This room." He waved a hand. "These rooms are farthest from everything and the smallest ones available. Most people are given suites. And they're not even close to running out of suites."

Shadow shrugged. "This is better. I don't want a room near everything. I'd be tripping over people all the time." She went to answer the knock on her door and took the plates from Radler, not letting him enter.

"Is there anything else you'll need tonight, Lady Shadow. Maybe the room across from yours prepared?"

Shadow turned to Jurn with a question on her face. He shrugged and she turned back to Radler with a nod. "I don't want a big fuss made about it, Radler."

"Of course not, Lady Shadow." With a shallow bow he took his leave.

Shadow closed the door with her hip and handed one of the plates to Jurn who crossed the room to her.

"Why are you doing this?"

"Feeding you isn't much of an effort."

"Don't play dumb. How long were you at the training grounds tonight?"

Shadow sighed and sat on the floor, the table and chairs no longer in her room. "I'm not doing this out of sympathy."

"How long?"

She met his gaze. "How can I feel sympathy for someone who refuses to give in? I wanted to cheer each time you faced him, even though you couldn't see him. I've been told I have an excess of tenacity too. But I don't see how that can be a bad thing."

"You can't fight what you can't see."

"You can. You did."

Jurn held her gaze a moment before he nodded and turned his attention to the food. Shadow waited a moment to see if he'd speak again. When he didn't she quickly ate her meal, long past hungry.

Chapter Thirty-Nine

Shadow staggered out of bed to answer the knocking on her door. "What?" She glared at Jurn.

"You wear a night gown to bed?"

She started to close the door again.

"Wait." He pressed a hand against the door. "Sorry. I thought you wanted to be a boy or something."

"No. Was there a point to knocking on my door or did you just want to interrupt my sleep?"

"Train? I know it's a day of rest, but I always train. Usually Vin joins me but his family had other plans for today."

"That's what you were arguing about?"

"Yes." Jurn looked along the hallway and cursed, stepping away from her door. He bowed. "Good morning, Prince Thornton." He turned to Shadow. "I'll see you later."

"Wait. Yes." At his look of confusion, Shadow said, "Training, the answer is yes."

"I won't be long. Just playing delivery boy." Thornton held out a letter. "And reminding you everyone of importance is expected to attend dinner on rest day. No excuses. Well, other than being on your death bed or too far from the city." He paused. "Come to think of it, I'm not even sure being on your death bed would be an acceptable excuse. It'd have to be the grave."

"Thank you." Shadow glanced at the letter.

"I've got a lot of people I want you to meet tonight," Thornton warned.

"People?"

Thornton nodded. "Maybe you'll recognise a voice or two."

Shadow smiled when she realised what he meant. "Maybe."

"I'll see you this evening. Don't be late." Thornton sent a glance to Jurn before he strode away from Shadow.

"Does the prince often visit you without warning?"

"Warning?"

Jurn nodded. "He usually sends a servant to warn people he intends to visit."

"Oh. I didn't know."

"You're friends with the prince." Jurn stared at her. "Real friends."

"Yes." She held up a hand to stop more questions. "Give me a minute to dress and read my letter."

"Why would the prince deliver your letter?"

Shadow grinned. "Because it's from his brother." She laughed when Jurn's mouth dropped open and he stared at her. She stepped into her room, closing the door. She hurriedly dressed and sat on her bed to read her letter.

'Shadow, Only follow the map if it's well before sunrise. I want to share one of my favourite places with you. A place I go to escape all the chaos. But it's best seen at sunrise for the first time. Love Carson.'

She looked at the next page, frowning as she tried to figure it out. Still clueless she opened her door and handed the map Carson had drawn her, to Jurn. "Can you find this?" At his nod, she asked, "Before sunrise?"

"If we hurry."

"Come on then. Run if you have to. Just don't leave me behind."

Jurn grinned. "You run, I'll walk." He hurried along the hallway.

Shadow kept pace with him, her legs barely keeping up with his long legged stride. He led her along hallways and up staircases. They burst out onto the battlements as the sun was rising, colour splashing across the land. She circled the tower that shot into the sky in the middle of the battlements. On one side the world was in darkness, on the other light painted every object it fell on.

Past the city Shadow could see the harbour, ships tied up at wharfs that stretched into the sea. The city was already stirring, people and animals moving about. She clutched the map to her chest and thought of Carson. Her fingers tingled and she saw him standing watching the sunrise. He grinned and pressed his right hand to his heart.

"Are you there? In my favourite place? What do you think, Shadow?"

She wished she could tell him she loved his favourite place. Frustration arrowed through her at everything she wanted to say but couldn't.

"We'll go there together when I return home and watch the sun rise."

Yes, she wanted to tell him. Absolutely.

"Shadow. Shadow."

The insistent voice dragged her away from her vision and she was tempted to hit Jurn. "What?" she snapped.

"Are you fine?"

"Of course."

"Are you sure? I called your name a dozen times before you answered. What happened?"

"Nothing."

Jurn's eyes narrowed. "I'm going to the training grounds."

She could almost see him retreat behind his shell of anger. "A vision."

He stopped, his back to her.

"I wasn't at the training grounds last night. I was in my room. I saw a vision of what was happening. It's always in the present or the past. I can't see the future. At least I haven't yet."

"What did you see this time?"

"Carson."

"You can see what people are doing even when you're not with them?" Jurn turned to face her.

She shook her head. "Not everyone. It's easiest with a lock of hair. I was holding the pattern last night when I had a vision of you. Something personal helps it work."

Jurn stared at her then nodded. "Do you want to stay up here longer, or train?"

"A few more minutes." When Jurn nodded she moved to lean on the rail that ran along both sides of the battlements. Below the castle and city spread out before her. She tried to see Carson again, even touching his lock of hair. Nothing helped. Giving up, she turned to Jurn. "Can we stop at the kitchens on the way to the training grounds?"

He nodded and led the way.

The two of them spent most of the day at the training grounds. Only once did Shadow see someone magic hid coming towards them so she used Dore's method of getting rid of them. Her bolt didn't hit the ground as close since she wanted to scare the man off, not accidentally kill him.

They didn't stop training until it was nearly time to ready themselves for dinner. Shadow was horrified to learn that rest day's dinner took place in the banquet hall since the dining room wasn't large enough to accommodate everyone.

"And this is every rest day?" she asked Jurn.

He nodded. "Don't seek me out down there."

Shadow couldn't resist smiling. "Unless it's a dark corner and no one can see?"

"Everyone always sees. Especially in the dark corners." Bitterness filled his tone.

Shadow kept her expression neutral. "I'll see you tomorrow. You better get back to your father's suite to dress." She eyed him up and down. "I don't think the queen would appreciate you turning up in the dust of the training grounds." They stood at her door, Radler pretending to be invisible.

Jurn nodded. He started to turn away, then stopped. His gaze still in the direction he had to go. "Thanks for the bruise balm."

"Any time." She watched him walk away before she slipped into her room to the waiting bath.

Once she was clean she reached for a dress. Her hand hovered over the material before she closed it. No. That wasn't her. No matter what the function, she was wearing trousers. If they didn't like it, she didn't have to go to their stupid dinners. She grinned. That'd suit her just fine.

When she was dressed, Radler led her to the banquet hall. She paused in the doorway, trying to keep her expression neutral. There were more people crammed in this one room then she'd probably seen in her entire life. Well, maybe not quite, but she'd never before seen such a large gathering. Already rethinking her choice of clothes, she fought the urge to run. Her gaze landed on Krisa and that urge changed to a rush of anger. If Krisa's glare was anything to go by, she knew her plan had failed. Looks like the army wasn't the only place battles were fought.

She nearly grinned when Iain's words came to her.

Them or us. Tilting her head up, she strode into the room, ignoring the abruptly ended conversations that restarted behind her in whispered tones. Maybe she was paranoid, but she didn't think so. She'd wager those conversations were about her.

A servant stepped up to her. "My lady, Prince Thornton requests your presence."

Shadow nodded and followed through the press of bodies to where Thornton was standing with a group of men. Amongst them was the glitter of magic even though none were hidden. There were other uses for magic.

"Shadow. I had hoped you'd arrive before we all sat down for the meal." Thornton reached out for her hand and tugged her to his side. "I'd like to introduce you to some of the castle's residents."

She was tempted to ask, do you have to, but managed to nod instead. The next half hour was filled with a blur of names, many of them wizards. It didn't help, not a single voice sounded familiar. Many were the right height, but that wasn't enough evidence to accuse a man.

When it was time to be seated for dinner, the crowd moved to the various tables set up throughout the banquet hall. Thornton led Shadow to the royal table where his parents and several lords and ladies were seated. Irlan wasn't at the table and she searched the room until she spotted him in animated conversation several tables away. Her gaze moved on and she spotted some of Dore's squad at different tables, including Jurn beside his father. Her jaw tightened when she saw the black eye Jurn sported.

"Is everything well?" Thornton leaned close to her.

Shadow nodded. "It will be." She glanced towards Hurrin. "How are rooms assigned in the castle?"

"Do you want a different one?"

"No. I just wondered."

"Are you sure?"

Shadow nodded. "Don't even think about putting me in a different room." She met his gaze. "I'm not moving."

Thornton grinned. "I didn't realise you hated it that much." He became serious. "What are you planning?"

"I don't know." Her words were soft and she glanced towards Jurn before she turned back to Thornton. "The rooms around Irlan and me are empty, aren't they?"

Thornton nodded slowly. "Are you sure you aren't planning anything?"

Shadow smiled at him. "Me?"

Thornton laughed. "A little warning before all hell breaks loose would be good."

"I'll see what I can do."

"What did you think of all the people I introduced you to?" His voice was still low.

"I wish I could give you an answer."

Thornton sighed. "There are more. Maybe you haven't met the right people."

"More?" Shadow momentarily closed her eyes. "Please tell me you're joking."

"I wish." Thornton was distracted by the man seated on his other side.

Shadow silently ate the meal in front of her, letting the many conversations wash over her. She was ignored by the rest of the people at the royal table and was more than happy about it. She was even happier when the king and queen finally retired and everyone else was able to leave. Instead, many of them clustered in groups talking and drinking. Shadow wasn't interested in staying and bid Thornton goodnight.

As she left the banquet hall she looked around for Irlan and Jurn. She saw neither of them. She did see Dan, but when he spotted her, he veered off in a different direction. Her right hand curled into a fist and she forced it to relax. She didn't need any of them. Keeping her gaze straight ahead, she left the banquet hall and headed for her room. Her steps slowed when she saw Jurn leaning against the wall opposite her room. She came to a stop in front of him and pulled the bruise balm from her belt pouch, throwing it to him.

He caught it. "Thanks."

"I'd say any time again, but you might think I was encouraging you."

Jurn grinned as he rubbed the ointment over his black eye. "I think you're talking to the wrong person." He tossed the jar back to her, the bruise fading away. "Do you think anyone'll mind if I crash here again?" He nodded towards the room he'd stayed in the night before.

Shadow shrugged. "No one'd probably know anyway." She hesitated. "Why not grab your gear from your father's suite and move in until someone complains?" When Jurn looked away, she added. "I can help you tomorrow. During our meal break or after training."

Jurn's head whipped back to face her. His eyes narrowed. "I'm not afraid of him."

"Good for you. He scares the hell out of me."

Jurn's lips twisted into a wry smile and he gave a single nod. "During our meal break." He paused. "Night."

"Night." She turned and entered her room, closing her eyes as she breathed deep. There was no unwanted lingering perfume. She pressed her hand against the door, trying to dredge up a vision. Nothing. The same happened when she pressed her hand against the chest and her bed. She hoped it meant no one had been messing with her gear and not that her visions were failing.

With a last searching look around the room she readied herself for bed, taking her belt pouch to slide it under her pillow and her sword on the floor beside the bed. She slid her fingers into the belt pouch and felt around until she found the lock of hair. A smile formed when she felt the tingle in her fingers. She let the vision unfold, closing her eyes.

Carson, Farnell and Gil poured over a map, arguing. Carson and Gil stopped mid argument and Farnell looked around the tent.

"What's wrong?" Farnell demanded.

Carson smiled. "Nothing." He touched his fingers to his heart.

"She's watching us?" Farnell looked around the tent again.

"Bloody rude if you ask me," Gil muttered.

"Then why are we bothering sending messages the

hard way? Get Shadow to pass the message along to Thornton," Farnell said.

"It mightn't come through clear," Gil said.

"Shadow." Carson paused. "Tell Thornton to send the troops to Storne. Tell him tonight. Our message won't reach him until daybreak. Those extra hours will make a difference."

She wanted to be able to tell him she heard. The only thing she could do was end the vision and hope he understood. Quickly rising and dressing, buckling on her sword before she left the room, Shadow hunted for Thornton. When she found him alone in the gardens she looked around for his guards.

"Are you crazy? Where are they?"

"I gave them the slip. Don't start, Shadow. It's been a long day."

Shadow withdrew her knife from her boot and held it out hilt first. "I want a lock of your hair."

"Why?"

"Because I spent ages searching for you with a message from Carson."

Thornton took the knife. "What did he say?"

Shadow repeated the message then took the knife and lock of hair he handed her. "I don't suppose you've got something I can wrap your hair in."

Thornton handed her a plain linen handkerchief. "I'll send them now." He started to walk away.

"Thornton." She waited until he turned back to her. "It's not safe to be alone. They haven't given up."

"I know. But it's not safe for those around me if I don't get some time alone. Completely alone, not just the illusion." He turned away and headed to the castle.

Shadow watched him leave, sitting on the wooden bench in a dark arbour. Her fingers tingled and she let the vision come, releasing it instantly when she saw two lovers entwined on the bench she now sat on. She considered running after Thornton and asking him to send a letter for her, but what could she tell Carson other than she missed him? And if he didn't know that with how often she spied on him then he wasn't smart enough to be a captain. Rubbing at her eyes she yawned. Sleep. That's what she needed. Desperately. She didn't want to give Jurn any further advantages during training.

Chapter Forty

Shadow walked beside Jurn who seemed closed off again. Silent, unapproachable and radiating anger. She remained silent, hoping Hurrin wasn't home. Jurn had said their meal break was the best time since his father was rarely home during the day, but she guessed he worried too. When they reached the suite Jurn stood there staring at the door. Shadow was tempted to ask if he was waiting for his father to return. Not to mention that they couldn't be late back to training or Hurrin would be their least worry. Dore would be out for their blood.

Jurn turned to her. "You wait in the entrance room. I won't be long. I don't have much I want to take."

Shadow nodded and followed him inside. She looked around while Jurn hurried through one of several doors that led off the entrance room. Her attention was drawn by the glow of magic from under a door. She crossed the room and peeked inside. The desk glowed with magic hid objects. Curiosity dragged her across the room and she pressed a hand against her mouth but couldn't stifle the gasp that escaped. She reached to pick up one of the letters scattered across the desk.

"What's wrong? What do you see?"

Shadow turned to find Jurn in the doorway, a bag slung over his shoulder. "More than you. A lot more than you." Pain twisted in her at what she needed to tell him.

The front door burst open before she could speak and Hurrin entered. Jurn spun to face his father and his bag dropped to his feet. Hurrin swore and strode across the room to grab his son by the front of his shirt. "I told you to stay away from her. You idiot." He pushed his son from him and turned to Shadow, a ball of flame appearing in his hand.

"No." Jurn shoved at his father, throwing him off balance so the fireball hit the floor.

Shadow grabbed a handful more of the letters and ran across the room as she bundled them up. "Jurn. Run."

They didn't even make it to the front door that slammed shut, a glimmer of magic visible to Shadow.

She turned to face Hurrin who was now magic hid, his gaze on his son as another fireball started to form in his hands. The letters held in one hand, she reached for her knife.

"He's warded against metal." Jurn's gaze flickered around the room.

"You'll pay for your disloyalty." The ball of fire was fully formed in Hurrin's hand.

"I have already. For years."

Shadow threw herself at Jurn as the fireball flew through the air. They landed together in a tangle of limbs. She quickly scrambled away, still holding the letters and knife. She slid the roll of letters through her belt at the small of her back, watching as another fireball started to form. "Another fireball's coming."

"Where is he?" Jurn was on his feet. He pulled out the knitting needles, holding one out to Shadow. When she took it, he took her knife.

Shadow described the location, then yelled, "Fireball." They both dived out of the way.

Jurn pressed Shadow's knife against his inner arm. "Catch." He tossed the knife to her. "I hope that's personal enough. Use the needle on the door. Run." He threw himself at his father, the needle held out like a dagger.

Shadow flung herself at the door, running the

wooden knitting needle across the magic, pulling the door open as it evaporated. Behind her she heard Hurrin roar and the sound of flesh hitting flesh. A cry of pain from Jurn followed her into the hallway as she raced away, the knife and needle both clutched tightly. She slid the needle into her boot, reaching for the lock of Thornton's hair in her belt pouch. With a glance behind her, she let the tingle in her fingers take her into a vision. The moment she saw where he was she let it go, racing through hallways.

She burst into the room where he sat playing cards at a table with three men, his guards rushing towards her. "Thornton." She pulled the knife back when a guard would have grabbed it. "Call them off."

Thornton rose to his feet, waving the guards away, striding towards her. "What's wrong?"

Shadow pulled out the magic hid letters. "Who can make things visible again? Where can we talk? Alone."

Thornton turned to the three men. "Leave. Now."

They didn't even protest, scooping up their gold as they rose to their feet and hurried from the room.

Thornton waited until they'd left. "What's wrong?"

Shadow moved to the table, words pouring out of her as she laid the letters down. She rubbed the back of her hand across her face, surprised to find tears. "We have to save him, Thornton."

Thornton pointed to the table. "Read them to me."

"We don't have time."

"The important bits. The sections that made you realise Hurrin was behind my kidnapping."

Shadow shuffled the letters, the knife still clutched tightly in one hand. She read through the relevant sections then turned to Thornton. "Hurrin, his brother Alton who's chasing Carson and his brother-in-law Demas all have to be stopped. But Jurn's not part of it. Hurrin attacked him. It was because none of their children have magic. They wanted to make sure their family remains powerful. Vin isn't part of this either." She had found out that Vin was Demas' son and Jurn's cousin. "We have to help Jurn."

Thornton turned to one of his guards. "Fetch my father, Dore and the advisers. Urgently."

Shadow paced while everyone was collected. She glared at them when they finally arrived and spent too long arguing. She pressed her fingers to the blood drying on the knife and sunk into the vision when her fingers tingled. She gritted her teeth when she saw Jurn was unconscious and thrown over a horse like a sack, blood dripping into the puddles of water they walked through in a narrow tunnel.

She turned to Thornton. "Where do I find a tunnel tall enough for a man to walk through leading a horse beside him, puddles of water, and barred gates at regular spaces?"

"There's tunnels under the city, but all the entrances and exits should be guarded," Thornton said.

"How do I get in them?"

"You can't go alone. We're sorting this out." Thornton stepped towards her. "Be patient a little longer, Shadow."

She shook her head. "He's dying. Losing blood constantly. He saved my life so I could tell you. Are you going to let him die too?" She met his gaze, not feeling even a little guilty when she saw him flinch.

"You'll get him killed if you rush in unprepared," Dore warned.

"You won't see them without me. Guards will be useless and he's protected against metal. There's only three of them. Hurrin, Jurn and a woman." She described the woman.

"Lida, Hurrin's wife. She has magic skill too," Dore said.

"How do I get into the tunnels?" Shadow demanded.

Dore stared at her a moment longer. "The moment

he sees you, he'll know we're there. You'll get Jurn killed."

She shook her head. "No. You have to remain hidden. I'll find a way to show you where he is. He won't expect you. I'll tell him no one believed me because his letters are still magic hid and no one could see them."

"Which tunnel are they in?" an adviser asked.

"How would I know?" Shadow asked.

"Each gate is different. At the top. You need to tell me what's at the top of a gate," Thornton said.

Shadow nodded and touched the blade of her knife. It took a moment for the vision to start and several minutes before Hurrin led his horse through a gate. She let go of the vision. "A metal leaf with a curved rod of metal under it."

"I know where that comes out," Thornton said. "A clearing in a thickly wooded area. But the sun will be in our eyes. He'll have the advantage."

"No he won't." Shadow stared at the knife and a smile slowly formed. "The shadows will be long. If I come at him from the right angle and threaten him with my knife I can mark the ground where his feet are."

Dore clapped her on the shoulder. "You mark him, I'll kill him."

"It'll have to be with wood. He's warded against metal," Shadow reminded him.

"Never thought I'd see the day when I wanted a knitting needle."

Shadow grinned at Dore and withdrew the sharpened one from her boot. "I only have the one, but I guess you're not planning on making a baby bonnet."

Dore chuckled before he beckoned a guard forward. He gave him orders to have Hurrin's brother-in-law found and imprisoned and horses readied. Within minutes they were racing towards the location. Shadow, Thornton, Dore and a handful of soldiers. Shadow wished Iain was with them. She didn't know the soldiers she waited with, didn't know if they were trustworthy.

When the sound of the grate opening reached her, Shadow rushed into the clearing, the knife at her side. "Let him go." None of her fear touched her words.

Hurrin stopped in mid stride, dropping the reins of the horse to bring his hands up. "Tell them to come out or I'll kill him." He nodded towards his son as a fireball formed in his hand.

"They didn't believe me, but I don't need them." She raised the dagger, letting the tip of its shadow touch Hurrin's feet. "I'm going to kill you all on my own."

Hurrin laughed, the sound cut off by the knitting needle piercing his stomach. He swore and pulled it out, throwing it on the ground, but it was enough to break the spell. Dore and the soldiers poured out of the trees and quickly disarmed Hurrin and tied him up.

Shadow ignored everything to check on Jurn, tugging him from the horse and struggling to lower him to the ground. It wasn't as gentle as she'd hoped, but it jolted him awake and he groaned, blinking up at her. "You're alive."

Jurn groaned again. "I won't be if you keep throwing me around."

Shadow couldn't resist smiling at him, her finger tentatively checking the cut on his forehead.

Jurn hissed and pulled back from her. "Watch it."

"Shadow." Dore stopped beside her. "We need you to find Lida."

"But Jurn-"

"Now." Dore turned to a soldier. "Watch the lad. Protect him."

Shadow started to rise, but Jurn grabbed her hand and tugged her to him. "She causes pain. That's her speciality. Don't get close. She isn't protected from metal."

"Thanks." Shadow rose to her feet and hurried after Dore. It wasn't hard for Shadow to find Lida in the darkness of the tunnel. The glow of her magic was a beacon. "Lida." The woman turned at the sound of her name.

"I didn't know." Lida spread her hands in front of her, slowly walking towards Shadow. "I wasn't part of this."

There was no sun to help her show Dore where Lida was. "Don't come any closer."

"Show yourself," Dore ordered. He handed the crossbow to Shadow. "Or I give the order to shoot you in the leg. She's hit nearly every bullseye, but there's been a few that have landed astray. So I can't guarantee you'll survive the order."

Lida took another step forward. "I had to go with him. He stole our son. What else could I do?" Her hands spread further apart and tilted slightly forward.

Shadow wasn't taking any chances. "One more step and I don't wait for the order to shoot."

"One more step and you can shoot," Dore said.

Lida smiled, leaping at them, forcing her hands forward as if she threw something. Shadow fired at the movement, the bolt embedding itself in Lida's hip a second before the pain hit Shadow and Dore.

Dore roared for soldiers, Shadow gasped as she struggled to hold onto the crossbow. The pound of feet behind her made her press herself against the cold damp wall of the tunnel so she could keep an eye on Lida and see who ran towards her. Two soldiers raced past to grab Lida who lay screaming in the puddles, blood darkening the already dark liquid. The lanterns the soldiers carried sent crazy splashes of light in all directions.

Shadow held the crossbow out to Dore as the pain started to subside and when he took it she forced her feet to carry her outside.

"You're fine?" Thornton reached out to her.

She pushed him away, shaking her head, then nodding. Her gaze sought out Jurn. She stumbled to his side and dropped down next to him. "She's still alive."

"They were both in on it. I heard them in the tunnels. That's why he pushed me so hard. They needed a soldier loyal to them for everything to work. Why would they think I'd be loyal to them?"

"Because they don't understand that fear doesn't inspire loyalty." She held out her knife.

Jurn shook his head. "I didn't know if it'd work."

He ran a hand over his short brown hair. "Unless I shaved it there was no way I could give you some hair. Not that I had time for shaving."

"You can't get more personal than blood." Jurn looked behind Shadow and she turned to see Lida escorted from the tunnel. "I'm sorry." She turned back to him.

"You didn't make them do it."

Before Shadow could answer, Dore joined them. "Yours, I believe." He held the knitting needle out to Shadow. When she took it, he moved away.

Shadow looked at the dark stain on the timber. "I'm not sure you'll want this one back."

Jurn reached out and took hold of the needle. He tugged on it when she continued to hold it. "I want this one." He continued to meet her gaze and she finally let go.

Thornton joined them, facing Shadow. "What happened to a little warning before all hell broke loose."

"I'll see if I can arrange that next time."

"I hope next time doesn't come too soon." Thornton turned to Jurn. "Let's get you to a healer. Looks like you might end up with a scar on your forehead." He grinned. "I hear the ladies like a few scars. Ask Dore."

"Don't even think about it," Dore ordered as he reached Thornton's side. He turned his gaze from Jurn to Thornton. "And you need to get back to the city so we can all leave."

Shadow looked at the knife she still held before she turned to Thornton. "I don't suppose you have another handkerchief."

He handed it to her. "Maybe I should start carrying several at a time."

Shadow grinned as she wiped the blood onto the handkerchief, rising to her feet. She couldn't help thinking about the one Krisa had been going to leave her as an excuse. Maybe she should ask her for it. "Hopefully I won't need any more." She tucked the handkerchief into her belt pouch and her knife into her boot before she held out a hand to Jurn.

He stared at her hand a moment before he took it and let her pull him to his feet. "You saved my life. How am I meant to repay that?"

Thornton held his hand out to Jurn who hesitantly took it. Thornton shook his hand. "Welcome to the club."

Chapter Forty-One

Shadow knocked on the door to Jurn's room across from hers. There was no answer. Maybe he was already at the training grounds, but why hadn't he called for her first, like the past days. Was it because it was their last day? She wasn't going to hold it against him that he was better with a sword than she was.

Reaching into her belt pouch she pulled out the bloodstained handkerchief and tried to see where Jurn was. The vision took a moment to form. He was on the battlements, staring at a knife in his hand. His head came up and he looked around. Shadow quickly let the vision fade and ran through hallways trying to find her way to the battlements. She had to ask for directions twice.

She burst out the door, onto the battlements, coming to a halt beside Jurn. "What are you doing?"

"Waiting for the sunrise."

Her eyes narrowed. "You're not planning to kill yourself are you? Don't listen to any of those idiots. Marsh is the biggest idiot of all. People will soon realise you're not a traitor."

"I can't stay here. At the castle. No one's going to forget while I'm here."

"Tell me you're not going to kill yourself," she demanded.

Jurn finally met her gaze. "Why?"

"I didn't go to the effort of saving you so you could kill yourself."

"And that's it?"

She shook her head slowly. "I have no idea what you're asking. I hope you're not expecting me to pledge my love to you because that's Carson's. We're friends. At least I hope so. Although with the way you tried to kill me at training yesterday I'm not completely sure."

Jurn grinned. "Friends. That'll do." He tucked the knife away. "How do you do it?"

"What?"

"The rumours. The conversations that stop when you enter a room. People thinking you're scum."

"Hold your head up." She grinned. "And find someone who'll let you burn up some of your anger in sword and knife fights."

Jurn chuckled. "What are you doing after training today?"

"Not knitting a baby bonnet."

Jurn looked skyward. "Then we'd better move before we're late."

Shadow nodded and strode alongside him as they headed to the training grounds. They arrived with plenty of time and Shadow put a hand on Jurn's arm when he would have answered Marsh's comment with a punch. She looked pointedly at where Dore was walking towards them and Jurn relaxed slightly.

"Attention." Dore tossed the ball of wool into the air as he watched them line up. "I'll be judging you today. Each and every one of you will compete against the other. Hand to hand, daggers, sword fighting and crossbow shooting. We start with the crossbow."

Shadow did well with the crossbow, as she expected. Hand to hand was worse than she thought it'd be, but she did well with dagger fighting. Sword fighting didn't look like it was her skill either, but at least she didn't lose straight away. Then the only one she had left to fight was Jurn and she felt like saying forget it. They all knew what the outcome would be. But she couldn't bring herself to give in.

And then she was forced to wonder if Jurn was

the one giving in. Her eyes narrowed and she moved back, lowering her sword.

"What are you doing?" Dore demanded.

She ignored Dore, stepping forward to Jurn, her sword still lowered. "Don't do this. You're not even trying," she hissed at him.

He kept his voice low. "I owe you this."

She shook her head. "You owe me better than this. I don't want it because you're not trying. I need to earn it. I don't want anyone to say I bought my place."

"Sorry-"

"Forget it. You aren't the only one who's said that. Now fight me. Like you want to win."

"If you two don't start fighting I'm going to fail you both," Dore bellowed.

Shadow grinned. "If you don't fight me like you mean it, I'm throwing my sword down."

Jurn nodded and stepped back, raising his sword. Shadow, still grinning, did the same. Then the real fight began and Shadow could barely keep up. She was forced to defend, attack only directed at her. By the time she was disarmed, they were both breathing heavily, but Shadow was still on her feet.

Jurn stepped forward and held out his hand. He

smiled at her when she shook it. "Give it a couple of years and you might have a chance to beat me."

"Give it a couple of years-" she stopped and shook her head. "Nah, not even then you'd be able to beat me with a crossbow." She grinned as she turned away and picked up her sword.

"Fall in." Dore stood, stance wide, hands clasped behind his back. When they were in line, he brought the ball of wool forward and pointed it at Marsh. "You're out."

"What!" Marsh stared at Dore. "But I beat her at sword fighting and hand to hand. You can't kick me out of the squad."

"She beat you at dagger fighting and crossbow. But that doesn't make you even. There are more important traits for someone in my squad."

"What traits?"

"Being a team. You turned on one of your own." His gaze fell on Jurn. "And for something that was no fault of his. Would you have fought your own father in the service of the king?"

Marsh couldn't meet Dore's gaze.

"That's what I thought. There are other squads you can join. But you're not welcome in mine." He held out the wool again. "And I do expect a baby bonnet within the week. No other trainer will take you on until you've completed that task."

Marsh snatched the wool. "You tried to break up the team by bringing her in." He jabbed a finger in Shadow's direction.

"There's nothing wrong with some competitiveness. That wasn't what you were doing. If you can't tell the difference you shouldn't be here."

Marsh opened his mouth then snapped it shut and started to stride away.

"Marsh." Shadow pulled the pattern from her belt pouch.

"What," he snarled as he spun towards her.

"You'll have to find your own needles, but here's the pattern." She smiled at him as she held out the pattern.

With a growl, Marsh turned away, ignoring the pattern as he left the training grounds.

Shadow shrugged, her gaze meeting Jurn's as she returned the pattern to her belt pouch. "I guess he must have his own."

Jurn grinned. "But I bet he doesn't have needles as good as mine."

"Attention." Dore waited until they were all lined up. "The day's not ended yet. Horse riding. Stablehands are bringing five horses in a minute. You need to practice guiding them with your legs. You can't always use your reins in battle."

Chapter Forty-Two

It was nearly two weeks since Marsh had been thrown from the squad. Vin and Jurn were the only ones who accepted her. The others were polite, but distant. Similar to the young men at the officer lessons. Polite, but distant, except Dan, who'd decided that if he couldn't stand up to his own father then he wasn't going to make much of an officer.

People were fairly divided when it came to accepting her. Brisa treated her to the same frosty manner, but Nickel was friendly. Most of the court weren't sure who to mimic so many avoided the issue and her altogether. Which suited Shadow fine.

It was late afternoon and as usual Shadow was in the training yards. She was having trouble concentrating since that morning Carson had told her they were getting closer to Crell and she couldn't wait to see him. It felt like it had been forever.

Dore waved towards the stablehands who held five horses. They stepped forward, dropped the reins on the ground and hurriedly moved out of the way. "All right, lads. The enemy is bearing down on you. Mount up! I expect each of you to hit a target five times or I'll want to know the reason why," Dore bellowed. He still treated Shadow like she was one of the lads.

Shadow ran with her squad for the horses, her sword in a scabbard on her belt. She grabbed her readied crossbow, leapt on her horse, turned it and raced for the targets set up at the end of the yards. Reins in one hand, she aimed at the target rapidly coming closer to her. She fired, not bothering to see if she hit, wheeling around to come back at the target. On the way back she was relieved to see she'd hit the first time. Not in the middle, but a hit all the same. She quickly wrapped the reins around the saddle horn, loaded the crossbow, grabbed the reins, fired again and turned the horse. Five hits and she urged her horse back to where Dore stood. Dalan was already there and the others soon joined them.

"Leave your horses with the stablehands. Let's see what you've done," Dore said.

They dismounted as one and followed behind Dore without protest.

"Looks like we might get you to follow orders yet," a familiar voice said from behind Shadow.

She turned and ran towards him, grinning as she called out, "Carson!"

"Get back here, soldier," Dore bellowed.

Not paying attention, Shadow threw her arms around Carson and kissed him when his lips met hers. She pressed her body against his, her arms tightening. "When did you get back?"

"Minutes ago," Carson said.

"Now soldier! Or you can forget about returning," Dore bellowed.

Shadow grinned up at Carson. "I won't be long. We're nearly finished for the day. Although he's probably going to keep me afterwards for a lecture." With one last kiss, she raced towards Dore who stood beside the targets. "Sorry, sir." She didn't look sorry though, she was grinning.

"Wipe that look off your face and pay attention, soldier," Dore ordered.

Shadow tried not to grin. Instead, she dropped her head and hoped her grin wasn't as noticeable. She ignored Jurn's snicker and didn't look at him because she knew it'd only make her grin harder. She listened with half her mind as Dore told them where they'd gone wrong. Wirrin had to repeat the exercise until he got his bolts in the target every time. He walked reluctantly back to his horse that was being walked by a stablehand.

"The rest of you are dismissed until tomorrow. Except you." Dore pointed at Shadow. "Over there. Wirrin needs to use this area." Dore walked back to where he'd watched them ride and Shadow followed.

She hung her head appropriately and listened to Dore's lecture on suitable behaviour and not being distracted during battle and keeping your mind on the job so you didn't get your fellow soldiers killed.

"Understand?" Dore demanded.

"Yes, sir," Shadow said automatically.

"You know, I was reluctant to have you here, but you've surprised me. Don't let me down." Dore gave her a hard look.

"No, sir." A rush of pleasure filled her. Dore rarely gave praise.

"Dismissed, soldier."

Shadow saluted before she turned away. She glanced around and spotted Carson who still stood at the edge of the training grounds. Jurn was jogging around the perimeter, grinning at her when he caught her eye. She smiled back at him before she hurried over to Carson, the smile still on her face.

"So, why here? I expected to find you in the castle

relaxing and enjoying yourself, hassling the odd soldier or two for some lessons. Weren't you looking for a quiet life?" Carson draped an arm around her shoulders.

"I couldn't stand being stuck inside all day after living on horseback so long and I sort of missed the army." Shadow walked beside Carson, sliding her arm around his waist. "Not to mention the fawning."

"Fawning?"

"Yes, everyone treats your parents like… well… like…" Shadow was lost for words.

Carson grinned. "Royalty?"

Shadow frowned at him. "Well, it was annoying. They were so fake it was sickening. And all the backstabbing. Everyone's trying to make everyone else look bad."

Carson nodded. "It wears on you sometimes. Why do you think Thornton and I argue over who's to become king?"

"I don't blame you. Now, what happened," Shadow demanded as they walked towards the castle, arms around each other.

"We managed to play cat and mouse with the army for a while. Your father's good at that. Best damn tracker I ever met, not to mention good at hiding tracks. We finally managed to lure them to where we had our larger army meet us. Thanks for getting them to Storne earlier. They didn't stand a chance once Gil took out their wizard. Great shot with a crossbow," Carson explained as they entered the throne room.

"You'd better remember that and unhand my daughter," Gil growled from just inside the door.

Shadow ran forward to hug her Pa. She might deplore his views on child raising but he was still her Pa and she loved him. Although sometimes she feared that love bordered on hate. "You're back."

Gil sent a glare towards General Farnell who was speaking with the king and queen. "They weren't leaving me behind this time."

"The General's offered Gil a permanent position with the army," Carson said.

"And I wasn't fool enough to accept it," Gil growled.

"My father's beckoning. We'd better see what he wants before he sends someone over to drag me before him," Carson said.

"Oh Carson," Brisa wailed. "We were so worried for you." She rose gracefully and went to her son. Carson stepped forward for her hug and kiss, and then moved back to Shadow's side. Brisa frowned slightly. "You could have come and seen us when you returned. We'd have liked to have seen for ourselves you were well."

"You went to the training grounds first?" Shadow asked in surprise.

Carson shrugged. "I was told that's where you usually are most of the day."

Brisa sat on her throne beside her husband who quietly watched everything. "Why did you not tell us you are reaching an age when you are willing to settle down? I'll arrange for some suitable women to make your acquaintance."

"Maybe I didn't make myself clear enough in my letter, Mother. I've already chosen a woman for my future bride," Carson said firmly.

"But she is a tavern keeper's daughter," Brisa wailed.

"And what's wrong with that?" Gil bellowed. "He's the one not good enough for my daughter."

"Have you forgotten, Mother?" Thornton interrupted. "Carson always said he wouldn't marry unless he could find a woman with as much backbone as one of his men."

"Excuse me! My decision, remember?" Shadow said.

Carson turned to smile at her. "And what's your decision?"

"That I've still got far too much to do before I can settle down," Shadow said loftily.

Carson's smile turned into a grin. "In the army?"

"And why not? I'm getting better all the time," Shadow said.

"No captain would tolerate a female in their company," Nickel said. "Dore barely tolerates you and only because he doesn't believe you'll find a place in any squad."

"I would," Carson said.

"Really?" Shadow asked.

"Well my squads are in need of more soldiers."

"I think I could recommend a few people. They aren't fully trained yet, but they're trustworthy."

"Are they capable of following orders?" Carson asked.

"They are. I still have moments where I seem unable to." Shadow smiled. "Is that going to be a problem?"

"I guess you'll have to marry me so my men know I have a good reason not to be as hard on you," Carson said.

"Maybe. One day," Shadow said.

Carson grabbed Shadow round the waist and spun her around with a jubilant shout.

"Never! I won't allow it," Brisa said.

"You know, Mother," Thornton said, "Elf sight runs in families. Might be handy to have it in the royal line."

"Not many people have elf sight," Nickel said.

"No. Most people make it their mission to kill them," Gil grumbled.

"Sounds like being part of the royal family," Thornton said.

"How wonderful. Any kids they'll have will have twice the amount of people wanting to kill them off," Gil complained. "And I don't like the thought of my daughter following around after the army."

"I won't be following. I plan to join," Shadow said.

"Thought you didn't like it," Irlan said.

"Let's just say I surprised even myself," Shadow said.

Carson smiled down at her. "It's an amazing feeling knowing you've completed a mission successfully, isn't it?"

"Good god, girl!" Gil exclaimed. "You'll be disillusioned soon enough."

"I know what to expect. I know it's hard. Next time I hope to have enough experience to know how to cope with it," Shadow said.

"I'll be there to watch out for her. And the men miss her too," Carson said.

Gil turned to Irlan. "And what about you, boy? You running off to the army too?"

Irlan shook his head. "Being captured turned me off any notions in that direction. I've been talking to a merchant wanting to get out of the shipping business. I'm only waiting for the General to pay what he owes me."

Gil glared at Farnell. "He'll be doing that today or I'll want to know why."

Farnell nodded in agreement. "It'll be arranged."

"I hope you realise, Shadow, that you're putting us in a very difficult position," Nickel said.

"In what way?" Shadow asked.

"How many other young women are going to think they can join the army?" Nickel asked.

Shadow laughed. "Good on them if they want to. Better than filling tankards for drunks any day." She grinned as she leaned against Carson's side, an arm around his waist, his heavy across her shoulders. "Way better."

Free Ebook

Subscribe to Avril's newsletter to receive a free ebook. This ebook is exclusive to those on her mailing list. To find out more about this offer visit: http://www.avrilsabine.com/free-ebook/

*

Acknowledgements

Special thanks to all my beta readers and editors, including Mum, Cat, Storm, Rhys, Molly, Carol, Chris and Sam. Your suggestions were invaluable.

To The Reader

If you enjoyed this book, why not consider leaving a review to help other readers discover it too? Reader engagement is one of the few ways that lets an author know readers want more books in a particular series or genre. So leave a review and tell friends, not only about this book but also about other ones you've enjoyed, so you can continue to enjoy books by your favourite authors for years to come.

Dreams are meant to be lived,

Avril.

About The Author

Avril is an Australian author who lives with her family on acreage in South East Queensland. She writes mostly young adult speculative fiction, but has been known to dabble in other genres. You can find more information about her at her website www.avrilsabine.com where you can also subscribe to her newsletter to be kept informed about new releases, current projects, blog posts and exclusive news.

Titles by Avril Sabine

Stories about strong characters and characters who discover their strengths.

SERIES

Assassins Of The Dead- Young Adult Fantasy/Paranormal

Book 1: Dark Blade

Book 2: Dragon Touched

Book 3: Society Against Vampires

Book 4: King's Request

Dragon Blood*- *Young Adult Urban Fantasy (with elements of romance)

(5 book series)

Book 1: Pliethin

Book 2: Wyvern

Book 3: Surety

Book 4: Knight

Book 5: Mage

Dragon Mage*- *Young Adult Urban Fantasy (with elements of romance)

(Series two of Dragon Blood series)

Book 1: Promise

Dragon Blood Chronicles*- *Young Adult Urban Fantasy (with elements of romance)

(Companion stand alone series to Dragon Blood)

Book 1: Oath

Book 2: Betrayed

Guardians Of The Round Table- Young Adult Fantasy LitRPG

(Co-written with Storm and Rhys Petersen)

Book 1: Dexterity Fail

Book 2: Goblin Boots

Book 3: Singed Feathers

Book 4: Frog Mage

Book 5: Crystal Mine

Book 6: Cursed Harp

Rosie's Rangers- Young Adult Western Steampunk

(6 book series)

Book 1: Justice

Book 2: Vengeance

Book 3: Treachery

Book 4: Accused

Book 5: Wanted

Book 6: Corruption

Mark Of Kings- Children's Fantasy

(Upper middle grade/preteen)

(4 book series)

Book 1: The Arena

Book 2: The Island

Book 3: The Assassin

Book 4: The King

STAND ALONE SERIES

Demon Hunters- Young Adult Urban Fantasy/ Horror (with elements of romance)

Book 1: Blood Sacrifice

Book 2: Retribution

Book 3: Tainted

Book 4: Premonition

Book 5: Cursed

Book 6: Feud

Book 7: Extrication

***Plea Of The Damned- Young Adult Urban
Fantasy/Paranormal***

(6 book series)

Book 1: Forgive Me Lucy

Book 2: Forgive Me Aiden

Book 3: Forgive Me Jena

Book 4: Forgive Me Kobe

Book 5: Forgive Me Marti

Book 6: Forgive Me Dawson

***Realms Of The Fae- Young Adult Urban Fantasy
(with elements of romance)***

The Sword (short story in Like A Girl Anthology)

Heart Of Stone

Book 1: A Debt Owed

Book 2: Marked By The Hunt

Book 3: The Magic Collector

Book 4: An Unexpected Betrayal

Book 5: Imprisoned By Iron

Fairytales Retold (Short Stories)

Snow-White And Rose-Red

The Twelve Brothers

The Light Princess

Beauty And The Beast

Sleeping Beauty

Aschenputtel

The Golden Bird

The Frog Prince

The Death Of Koshchei The Deathless

Myths And Legends Retold (Short Stories)

Ion, Son Of Apollo

Sir Gawain And The Maid With The Narrow Sleeves

Princess Ilse, The Giant's Daughter

YOUNG ADULT NOVELS

Young Adult Fantasy (with elements of romance)

Elf Sight

Earth Bound

Young Adult Urban Fantasy

Stone Warrior (with elements of romance)

The Jungle Inside

Young Adult Contemporary (with elements of romance)

Through Your Eyes

The Ugly Stepsister

Perfect Little Princess

Young Adult Contemporary/Paranormal

Whispers In The Dark (with elements of romance and same sex relationships)

Over Too Soon (with elements of romance)

Young Adult Sci-Fi

Experiment X-One-Six (Urban Sci-Fi/Superheroes)

An Endless Dawn (Post Apocalyptic Sci-Fi)

CHILDREN'S BOOKS

Dragon Lord (Preteen/early teens) (Fantasy)

The Irish Wizard (Upper middle grade) (Urban Fantasy)

SHORT STORIES

Urban Fantasy

Eternally Late

Dealings With Joe

Glimpses (short story in That Moment When Anthology)

Contemporary

The Brat Next Door

Fantasy LitRPG

(Set in the same world as Guardians Of The Round Table Series)

Tales Of Inadon 1: The Disc (Co-written with Storm and Rhys Petersen) (short story in Game On! Anthology)

Post Apocalyptic Sci-Fi

Compulsive Directive

NONFICTION

A Year Of Weekly Writing Exercises (Creative Writing)

Cooking For Families With Allergies (Cooking) (Co-written with Storm Petersen)

Tell Me A Story, Grandma (Memoir)

For the most up to date details on available titles visit:

www.avrilsabine.com/books/bibliography

Disclaimer

This is a work of fiction. Names, characters, businesses, places, events and incidents are either the products of the author's imagination or used in a fictitious manner. Any resemblance to actual persons, living or dead, or actual events is purely coincidental. The opinions expressed or beliefs held are those of the characters and should not be assumed to be the opinions or beliefs of the author.